PRAISE FOR LAURA CA

THE CHARLOTTE ....

"Laura has an amazing grasp of what New Orleans is. I could smell it! And that's a good thing!"
- John Schneider

"I love Laura's books. They evoke the true ineffable charm and mystery that is the heart and soul of New Orleans."
- Bryan Batt

"Whether you've been there or not, Laura Cayouette brings New Orleans to life. Her Charlotte Reade character isn't just great at unraveling mysteries, she's a terrific guide through the music, food and culture of the city."
- Allison Leotta

"This book is a trip to New Orleans--not a tourist trip, but an intimate journey to the heart of the city and its colorful, exuberant people. If you love NOLA, this is the book for you. If you don't know NOLA, this book will make it come alive for you, and you will fall in love. The setting is vivid and wondrously wrought, and it's just the beginning. The novel brims with interesting characters and an engaging mystery to boot. I highly recommend this book."
- Jennifer Kincheloe

LEMONADE FARM

"I've read Laura's novel *Lemonade Farm* and can attest to its power. It evokes the 1970s in a painfully accurate way, and is beautifully written. She manages a wide cast of characters and somehow paints adults, teenagers and children with equal skill without ever condescending to any of them. Her skill at characterization and turns of phrase, coupled with a great sense of place, makes this a heck of a novel."
-Tom Franklin

KNOW SMALL PARTS:
AN ACTOR'S GUIDE TO TURNING MINUTES INTO MOMENTS AND MOMENTS INTO A CAREER

"Laura's outward beauty could have guaranteed her much more in this business perhaps even worldwide fame. She could have taken an easier route for her professional pursuits but instead chose to make it about the work and only the work. She is a role model in that regard and a true leading lady. Enjoy what she has to say and see if you can see yourself in her journey. She still has some big important parts to play."
-Kevin Costner

"She's nailed the daily life of an actor in L.A. about as perfectly detailed as it gets... You can say that Laura is amazingly correct in everything she says and sees, but she makes you hunt for the urgent need to do it which is at the bottom of all."
-Richard Dreyfuss

"Laura Cayouette is a working actress that also has a happy, well-balanced life. Figuring out how she manages this feat is certainly worth a read."
-Reginald Hudlin

"Anyone who has met Laura knows that she is unforgettable. Perhaps even more impressive is that she has found a way to translate this personal charisma and life-force into her appearances on screen, making the most of every second of camera time given to her. She has literally figured out a way to bottle lightning. I'm sure that her observations and guidance will be invaluable to the actor who is looking to make his or her mark in the film world and to build a career, moment by moment."
-Lou Diamond Phillips

ALSO BY LAURA CAYOUETTE

FICTION

The Hidden Hunstman: A Charlotte Reade Mystery

The Secret of the Other Mother: A Charlotte Reade Mystery

Lemonade Farm

NON-FICTION

Know Small Parts:
An Actor's Guide to Turning Minutes into Moments and
Moments into a Career

How To Be A Widow: A Journey From Grief to Growth
(editor only)

Airplane Reading
Contributor

LAtoNOLA
blog - latonola.com

PREFACE

In an effort to capture the unique culture of New Orleans, many of the people and places mentioned in this fictional novel exist in reality. As such, you can trace Charlotte Reade's steps and enjoy many of her experiences for yourself. In an effort to entertain, I've sometimes bent these real people and places to my fictional will so "real life" experiences may differ.

I have included an Appendix listing many of the restaurants, tours, people and events mentioned in this novel along with links to their sites. For more information and photos on anything mentioned in this book, use the search tool in LAtoNOLA (latonola.com), the blog upon which many of the book's recollections are based.

I've also built a playlist of music videos and videos of parades and other events, places and people included in this story on my YouTube channel:
https://www.youtube.com/user/latonolawordpress

You can link directly to the playlist at:
https://www.youtube.com/playlist?list=PL-T9AQ-VvsW1_CC-X6ICOCmpb8ZIjz599

And I've created a clipboard of photos on Pinterest:
https://www.pinterest.com/latonola/

Enjoy!

FAMILY TREES

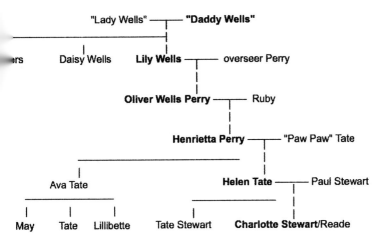

"Lady Wells" —— **"Daddy Wells"**

...ers   Daisy Wells   **Lily Wells** —— overseer Perry

Oliver Wells Perry —— Ruby

Henrietta Perry —— "Paw Paw" Tate

Ava Tate

Helen Tate —— Paul Stewart

May   Tate   Lillibette

Tate Stewart   **Charlotte Stewart**/Reade

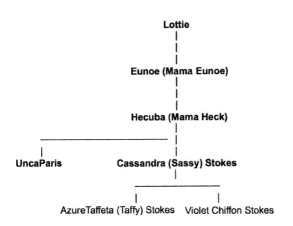

Lottie

Eunoe (Mama Eunoe)

Hecuba (Mama Heck)

UncaParis   **Cassandra (Sassy) Stokes**

AzureTaffeta (Taffy) Stokes   Violet Chiffon Stokes

Special Thanks
to
Kat Ford
Danielle Tanguis
Eliza Brierre
and
New Orleans' pink army of parade dancers –
The Pussyfooters

For "The Three Wise Men."
Quentin who told me to write it,
Ted who read every page as I wrote it
and Andy who supported me all along the way.
Thank you.

LA to NOLA Press

© 2017 Laura Cayouette

ISBN-13: 978-1978355590
ISBN-10: 1978355599

First Edition: November 2017

Back cover photo by Robert Larriviere

Many of the people and places mentioned in this fictional novel exist in
"real life." At times, the author has bent these real people and places to
her fictional will. Although the author has made every effort to ensure
the accuracy and completeness of much of the information contained in
this book, we assume no responsibility for errors, inaccuracies,
omissions, or any inconsistency herein. Any slights of people, places,
or organizations are unintentional.

Jayne –
Hope You Enjoy THIS
PEEK BEHIND THE CURTAIN!

THE MISSING INGREDIENT
A Charlotte Reade Mystery

Laura Cayouette

Chapter 1

"And action!"

I smiled, took a deep breath and found the determined housewife within me. Closing the refrigerator door, I took three steps toward the tiny piece of green tape on the floor behind the kitchen counter, grabbed the "hero bottle" of spray cleaner, spun it like a gun, then squirted once toward the camera.

"Cut!"

Everyone seemed pretty happy. The director yelled, "Play that back."

The clients crowded around the monitor along with department heads and waited to watch the take.

I reviewed the take in my head. I'd forgotten to put my weight on my left foot when I was at the refrigerator door. That was a note from two takes ago. I'd always thought directors would talk to me about character choices, motivations, accents, that sort of thing. Mostly they made camera-related adjustments and addressed practical stuff, especially on commercials.

This was my sixty-first commercial – almost all "Nationals," usually the best money. In Los Angeles, commercials had been about half of my income. Since moving to my family home in New Orleans a year and a half ago, I'd only auditioned for two commercials – and one was a "Regional" for cable-only. Not great money. Luckily, my expenses were far lower living in one of my family's rental units in a city where most entertainment was free and gas was a dollar cheaper per gallon. And my film and TV career was going fairly well.

The group in video village smiled and nodded at each other. The director yelled out, "Great. Moving on."

People started bustling, changing lighting set-ups and laying tracks for the camera cart. I found a door and went outside to craft services for a snack. The hardest shot was behind me and I felt the relief of knowing I'd nailed it. They'd hired me for that gun-slinging spray bottle spin. I'd done alright with the trick at the audition, but afterward I practiced in my kitchen. Sure, it bothered me sometimes to keep prepping for a part I hadn't gotten yet knowing my chances were slim, but I'd built my career on going the extra mile to be ready for anything.

Besides, it was the only job available to me. No telling when I'd work again. Lots of actors were convinced they'd never work again after every single job. I couldn't imagine feeling that doomed after each gig. I usually felt more certain than ever that I'd keep working. I was of the "work begets work" school of thought. That said, I was a woman in a man's industry. I was a woman in her forties in an industry that spits women out at a record pace after thirty. And I'd moved from the center of the entertainment universe to a burgeoning "secondary market." But as my best-friend-since-forever, Sofia, was fond of reminding me, I was a bigger fish in a smaller pond

2

here. I'd been so ready to leave Los Angeles that I was willing to risk having to get a "day job," but so far so good.

Anyway, I spun that spray bottle in my kitchen for two days waiting for the phone to ring. When it finally did, I taped the raw parts of my fingers and spun for another day waiting for my callback appointment. I was a regular Billy the Kid by the time the director, clients and ad agency people saw me.

As an actor, a commercial was an opportunity to introduce a fully-formed character and tell an entire story in fifteen-to-sixty seconds. I liked the challenge. I'd built a career on small parts in big movies. And being in my underwear. My career had a lot more underwear in it than I'd imagined when I was performing Shakespeare in New York over twenty years ago. Clarence Pool, my longtime friend and the defining auteur of our generation, called me the "Joe Louis of the under-five in her underwear." It was good to have a niche, even if it was only nailing five lines or less in panties. And I couldn't help but be concerned my underwear days might soon be behind me.

I'd been trying all day to keep Clarence out of my mind. Leaving the house for work, I'd found a big envelope from him on my doorstep. I knew it was his latest script. He'd been giving them to me for notes since the first week we met. Always on the first day they were printed. Sometimes, there'd be a bunch of us coming by to pick up a copy. A small party might even break out. I had to admit I'd been afraid those days were behind us now that I couldn't just drive over. I had left the envelope on the mantle and spent the day trying not to wish I were home reading it.

The towel-snap scene was next. I wasn't too worried. I'd spent three days in the kitchen on that as well. I was always looking for ways to reduce the amount of things I'd have to recollect. Between remembering lines and blocking, hitting marks and cues with perfect timing, eye-lines, director's notes and putting your weight on your dang left foot at the fridge door, it was always a LOT to keep in mind. And if you did it well, when they yelled, "Action," you had to forget everything so it looked like it was all organically happening for the first time. After practicing all the household super-heroics at home, I didn't have to remember much about gunslinging or towel-snapping. It was all in my muscle memory. I was ready for the shot where I'd slide the bottle down the counter like it's a beer mug too.

A slight woman peeked out the door and covered a mouthpiece. "They're ready for you."

I liked the days that went like this – days where I felt confident, days when I felt like a pro. Maybe I prepared because I was good at my job, but I definitely prepared out of a fear of feeling insecure on set. That could kill a performance.

I told myself we'd have to wrap when the sun went down around eight no matter what. I'd be reading that script soon enough. We finished just after seven and I was so anxious to leave, I didn't hear the announcement and almost exited while they were trying to get "room tone." A boom operator posed in the middle of the kitchen holding a mic as we all stood silently for sixty seconds. That might've been the longest part of the day for me. Everyone kept their eyes down or fixed on a wall or some object to avoid laughing. We all silently hoped no one would cough and no planes would fly over so we wouldn't have to wait even longer, standing like statues far too aware of time passing.

I started to wonder if the rumors were true about Clarence's next movie being a period piece set in the 70's. I wondered if it was his best script yet. They seemed to get better each time and he was due for another opus. Though the only part I'd ever had in any of his movies was one of my killer under-five-in-her-underwear scenes, I considered Clarence the Shakespeare of our time and was grateful to have played any part in his legacy. I let my mind wonder for one second if there was a part for me in the new script, then shoved the thought away.

"Thanks folks. That's a wrap!"

I was glad I had my car. I hardly ever drove anymore. Everything in New Orleans was pretty close to everything else so it was often easier to walk. With the historic, varied architecture and fragrant gardens, it was certainly more beautiful. Anything over three miles was easy enough with the streetcars and buses criss crossing the city for a buck twenty-five a ride. But I was glad to have my car to zip home in minutes and finally open that envelope.

It was still sitting on the mantle. My neighbor, Jason, had left a stack of mail on top. I could tell two of the letters held residual checks from movies and shows I'd done years ago, but all I could focus on was Clarence's script. I'd barely hit the couch before ripping open the large envelope and letting the script slide into my waiting hand. I dropped the envelope onto the floor and ran my palm over the cover page. "7 Sisters" was emblazoned across in funky, black type. I loved it already. I smiled at his signature, a graffiti-like rendering of "C. Pool" done in Sharpie. The style always reminded me of that "Keep on Truckin'" comic.

I settled into a plush pillow and used my legs like an easel. I could tell right away that this script was special. It wasn't just that it had more women than men in it, or that the women were all pretty cool – not just victims, girlfriends or hookers. It was more that Clarence seemed to have indulged all his favorite things about movies. There were car chases, martial arts fights and scenes driven by award-worthy dialogue. The rumors were true, the story was set in the funk and cool of the 70's. The soundtrack was going to be amazing. I couldn't wait to hear what music Clarence had in mind.

The seven sisters had three different mothers. Three girls grew up together in Harlem. I liked Kimani best. A "street queen with an ego as puffed as her afro," she had most of the funny lines and was a quick draw artist. Though it clearly wasn't a part I'd be cast in, I couldn't help but picture myself putting my newly acquired spray-bottle-spinning skills to work. Tanisha was the explosives expert with a love interest, and Ladonna was the one who always had a plan and poison in her ring for emergencies. Her part was the smallest, the one I would've had my eye on if I had a different look.

One sister grew up in Chinatown. Ji was a master ice sculptor with a gift for wielding a chainsaw. The last three sisters lived in a grand manor in New Orleans. I stopped and read the sentence again. New Orleans? Honey-haired Ashley lived in "a wedding-cake-like white house built in the 1800's, before people had to pay for labor." Though these New Orleans sisters appeared last, Ashley seemed to be another plum role fit for a movie star. She was a sharp-tongued equestrian with a gift for engineering and archery.

Younger sister Jenna was a former gymnast and master fencer. And last to enter the story was older sister Charlie. "A fortyish, tall, strawberry-blonde, cool glass of southern sweet tea. Charlie's a martial artist who studied with masters in three countries without ever losing her southern charms." Wait. I stopped and read the description again. "A fortyish, tall, strawberry-blonde, cool glass of southern sweet tea." I was afraid to hope he'd written it for me. "A fortyish, tall, strawberry-blonde, cool glass of southern sweet tea." And Charlie could be short for Charlotte. Maybe it wasn't my part, but it seemed clear I'd helped inspire it.

I looked up at the ceiling. When I was a kid, I'd always thought it would feel amazing to have inspired someone to write a song. I wanted to be the girl from Ipanema or Brandy, the fine girl who'd make a good wife, or lovely Rita, the meter maid. If I'd really inspired something in Clarence's imagination – that was even cooler than some pretty ditty.

Because we'd known each other so long, I sometimes forgot who Clarence was to the world. Most of the time he was just Clarence, my super-smart, beyond-belief-talented friend with a gift for storytelling and making me laugh. Then, I'd see one of his old movies on the TV, or hear other directors discussing his work and remember that he was also a celebrity and living legend best known for his multi-award winning films that all but revolutionized cinema. I was afraid to keep reading.

The sisters all came together for the first time at the funeral of their father, who'd been murdered. It seemed clear this would be an avenging-the-father's-death movie. The funeral scene had me laughing aloud as the very different women figured out they were all related. I tried to resist the urge, but I couldn't help but read Charlie's lines like they were my own. Especially when I realized it was the smallest of those three sisters' parts and might not need a star name.

The script was long so I didn't finish reading it until after three in the morning. I closed the last page, flipped the script over and stared at the cover again. Though he was two hours behind me, it seemed late to call and tell Clarence he was a genius.

I brought the script with me to the bedroom. Patrick was sleeping at his place for the last time. Tomorrow, he'd move his clothes into the closet and his toiletries into the bathroom. He was still sorting out his furniture situation with his ex, which was fine by me since I didn't have much room for two couches and two beds. Heck, I didn't really have room for two soup pots. I wanted Patrick to feel this was his place too, but we had some planning to do before we hauled anything bulky up the giant staircase.

The chandelier was behaving itself. The sporadic bursts of jostling and swaying still freaked me out, but I was getting used to being startled. Sometimes it even made me laugh. It helped that the chandelier made me think of Sassy, an other-mother to three generations of my family down to my mother. Sassy was like an other-grandmother to me. Her mother, Mama Heck, had raised even more generations of Mom's family. Taffy and Chiffon, Sassy's twins, believed it was Mama Heck moving the chandelier, making her presence known. I tried to take comfort in that.

Patrick still hadn't seen it move on its own. I was pretty sure he thought I was making the whole thing up. He said he wasn't much for "woo woo stuff" so the idea of a dead woman protecting a chandelier and moving it around was beyond the pale. I hoped he didn't freak out when he inevitably saw it doing its thing.

I got under the blanket and looked at the script cover one last time. Then I flipped around until I found my favorite line, "A fortyish, tall, strawberry-blonde, cool glass of southern sweet tea." I let myself imagine getting the part for three minutes then turned out the light.

Chapter 2

Patrick used his key to let himself in. I was going to have to get used to that. It'd been a long time since I'd lived with any kind of roommate and I wasn't sure I'd be great at having a live-in boyfriend. I'd fallen for Patrick so quickly that I worried he was a player. I'd been single most of my eighteen years in L.A. and had been pursued by men with black belts in seduction. Movie stars, powerful producers, agents, directors, professional athletes, rock stars and more took their shot. And many of them had the kind of charm that makes people gravitate toward them, adore them, worship them.

Now that I was pretty sure I'd found the best man I ever met, I could admit that it had been kind of fun dating extraordinary people with extraordinary lives, even if most of them weren't boyfriend material. Heck, most of them didn't rate a second date or even a kiss goodnight. It was no way to be happy, but now I could admit it had sometimes been a rare and unforgettable kind of fun.

Patrick stacked two cardboard boxes on the bedroom floor and brushed his hands on his shorts before placing them on either side of my head to lower himself for a kiss. "Morning my love. I've got more in the car. I'm going to go ahead and guess you haven't eaten. Get yourself fed so you can help me put all this away." He kissed me again. "Best day ever."

I had to admit I was still scared this whole thing was too good to be true. Patrick had courted me like a gentleman, then romanced me like a man on a mission. He wanted to do all kinds of things together and seemed to have no fear of commitment, despite his recently-ended bad marriage. He'd become my best friend and my strongest supporter. The better it got, the more I had to fight the fear that I might be missing a clue to some dark truth about him. I reminded myself of my forever-friend Sofia's advice to wait until there's an actual problem before getting worried.

I comforted myself by picturing Stella the fortune teller saying I'd returned to my soulmate. She'd said he was a workaholic, but that I wouldn't mind because it was for a cause I believed in. It was true Patrick could be a workaholic, but he worked to preserve the French Quarter and its history. I couldn't help but love him more when he was tirelessly battling encroachers and profiteers. Stella had said my soul mate would be a great communicator, that I had a need to figure things out and he'd talk stuff out with me. She thought that would mean he was older, more mature. I tried not to let the fact that Patrick was a decade younger scare me. He was a great communicator and after spending my adulthood in Los Angeles, I wasn't sure I was the most mature partner. There were plenty of times I felt Patrick was more emotionally evolved than I was. I tried not to let it make me insecure, especially since I was the one supporting myself by portraying emotions.

I wasn't sure why men said dating younger women made them feel young again. I was more aware of my age with Patrick by my side. I'd been terrified his parents wouldn't want me dating their young, no-doubt fertile son with such low prospects of eventually getting a grandchild out of it. Maybe they were disappointed but they never let me see it. Everyone around Patrick mentioned how good it was to see him happy. And I think they were all pleased at how patient I'd been about his house taking longer to sell than expected, delaying his ability to leave his former marriage behind him.

I was spreading almond butter on toast when Patrick came in to wash his hands in the sink. He gave me a hug from behind. "I've got to make another run. Do you want anything while I'm out?"

"I haven't really had time to think about shopping for two. When you settle in, we should write a list of stuff you like to have in the fridge."

He complied but I was pretty sure he didn't much care and that his list would consist of "anything's fine." Sometimes agreeable felt non-compliant. I knew a fair bit about the ways he could annoy me. None of them scared me. There were no "actual problems."

"I got a script from Clarence yesterday. It's pretty freaking amazing. And part of it shoots here."

He smiled. "Is there a part for you?"

"I've been trying not to ask myself that. I want to just be happy he still wants to include me in the feedback loop and not worry if there's anything I could get out of it."

"So it's a pretty good part."

I laughed. "It's seven sisters. That's the title. There are lots of great parts."

"Which sister are you?"

"Stop! You're going to jinx me or something."

He laughed and ripped a box top open. "I thought you didn't believe in all that thespian luck stuff."

"I don't." I took a bite of my toast

"No, you just believe in chandelier ghosts."

I held my finger up while I finished chewing. "Scoff all you want. Eventually I'm going to win this argument. I warned you I already have a roommate here. It's only a matter of time before the chandelier shows off for you, and that will be that."

"Seriously though, do you have a part in the movie?'

I finished chewing. "Honestly? I have to assume I don't. There's only two sisters I'm sorta right for and one is clearly a star's part. But even the smaller sister part is good enough for a star. Heck, I know plenty of names that would fight to get any part to be in a Clarence Pool movie. But it does seem like maybe he wrote it with me in mind, like I inspired it."

"Charlotte! That's amazing. Why? What makes you think that?"

"He describes her as, "A fortyish, tall, strawberry-blonde, cool glass of southern sweet tea."

"Come on. That's for you. He wrote it for you. Did he say anything?"

"Clarence? I haven't called him yet. It's two hours earlier there."

"I don't know how you take all that waiting and playing it cool. I'd be calling him by now. Resist vagueness!" He stole a bite of my toast and headed

13

out the door. "Be back soon."

I finished my breakfast and looked inside the box Patrick had ripped open. Shoes. Where were those going to go? And they were giant.

Back in the day, houses in New Orleans were taxed by the room. A closet was counted as a bedroom for the purposes of assessing taxes, so many houses had none. We were lucky because cousin May had converted a stairwell into a long, thin corridor of a closet when she renovated the family home after The Storm. The other two rental units in the house were even luckier as May had built floor-to-ceiling closets in both during the remodel. Since I'd lived in the place for free for the first few months, I never complained. I just packed up half of my shoes and a quarter of my clothes and gave them to a local non-profit. I wasn't going to need all those fashionable teetering heels that I couldn't walk in anymore. L.A. was a car town. You could afford to have shoes that were just for show. New Orleans was a walking town and I quickly learned how few of my shoes were actually meant for pedestrian transportation. One of Patrick's shoes took up the same amount of space as four of my sandals. We were doomed.

I pulled a pair of precarious heels from the shoe rack behind the closet door and slipped them onto my feet. They were the ones I'd worn to the premiere of the last movie I'd done in L.A., the one I'd produced with Clarence. I'd planned on waiting until noon to call him but the suspense was getting harder to ignore. My heels clacked on the hardwood floor as I crossed to pick up the landline. The phone rang as I reached for it.

"Charlotte?"

"Clarence? I was just going to call you. I didn't want to wake you though."

"I'm awake. It's nearly lunch here."

"Here where?" I could tell he was in a car.

"We're in New Orleans. We're location scouting today but can you meet for lunch tomorrow? Did you get the script?"

My heart raced. "I did. It's amazing. I can't wait to give you my notes. Wait, you're here?"

"Great. Can you do one o'clock at Galla-something? What is it? Hey, anyone know the name of the place tomorrow?"

I took a shot. "Is it Galatoire's?"

"What is it?"

"Galatoire's?"

He yelled out to the car. "Galatoire's?" Someone agreed. "Yeah. One o'clock. See you there."

I was still walking around in heels, trying to cut deeper into my shoe reserve, when Patrick returned with another carload of boxes.

He smiled. "Hey babe! I found a dollar on the sidewalk. Karmically, I feel I'm owed more, but..." He lowered a box to the kitchen floor then handed me a menu. "Found it stuck in the gate. Wasn't sure if it was for you, but it's got pho so I took it." He looked at my shoes. "Fancy."

"I'm tryin' to decide if they hurt too much to wear in real life."

"If they hurt at all, that's probably too much. But they are pretty shoes. You look great in them." He gave my pajamas-and-heels ensemble an appreciative look. "Really great. Come here." He grabbed me and gave me a kiss then looked right into me. "Best day ever." Another kiss.

"How many more boxes are in the car?"

"Not many. We'll figure something out. We still have until the end of the month to find something to do with the furniture. It makes sense to get a bigger place but I know you don't want to leave your family home."

I smiled a little. "Maybe soon. Let me get used to this first. And the unit downstairs is big enough. She's been checking out houses in the area. I think she's lookin' to buy something. We could get a storage unit if she's planning to move. It's a beautiful place and it's the size of both these units upstairs. It's got like six floor-to-ceiling closets. In a house with twenty-foot ceilings. And it's a two-bedroom so we could put your bed in there and there's a dining room, living room and great room – big enough for a breakfast nook, a den and an office. I know 'cause that's how she has it laid out. We'd end up having to actually buy furniture to make the most of it."

He smiled. "And you could stay in this house."

"Is that selfish?"

"Probably. But I get it. You get to feel at home here." His moss green eyes stared warmly at me.

"And I went without that for a really long time so it probably means more to me than it should."

He startled. "Hey, did you get the part? Are you a sister?"

"Aw man, it sounds so cool, doesn't it? I'm not sure. I talked to Clarence, but we didn't really talk about it."

"So, maximum vagueness."

I laughed. "Yes. But I couldn't really do anything about it. He was in a car. He's here."

"Here, New Orleans here?"

I nodded. "They're location scouting. He didn't seem that anxious to hear my notes but he invited me to lunch tomorrow at Galatoire's."

"On a Friday? Does he know what he's in for? There's no reservations. How did he get a table? Is it just the two of you or a group?"

"Honestly? I have no idea."

Patrick laughed. "You really gave in to the vagueness."

"I gave in to the vagueness. But he was in a car with a bunch of people and he was working. It didn't seem like a good idea to clarify things just then."

"Maybe you were a work call. You said he was working. Maybe you were a work-related call."

"Okay, I couldn't stop the giving in to the vagueness, but I can at least not take us down the spiral of tryin' to figure this out when I did such a terrible job of collecting any kind of useful information. Finish getting the boxes. I'll get dressed."

He smiled. "This isn't your unpacking outfit? I feel like I'm gettin' some false advertising. Oh, have you been online?"

"Not yet. Why? What? Did something happen?"

He chuckled. "So, that hipster place in the Marigny that just opened this year?"

That didn't narrow it down much. They were becoming a trend. "Which one?"

"The one with the King Cake thing that you can buy year-round."

17

I made an "ew" face. "What King Cake thing? Who sells King Cake year-round? Why? Who buys it?"

"It's not a King Cake. It's some kind of beignet crossed with a King Cake. I don't know, something ridiculous."

I put my hand up pointedly. "Oh! I saw it on Facebook. On your page. Oh, that hipster place. We hate that place. And we haven't even been there."

He nodded. "That place. It got robbed."

"Seriously? I didn't hate it that much. Is everyone okay?"

"They were closed. No one was there."

I needed more. "Is the place okay? What'd they take?"

"Here's where it gets extra-hipster. Only the recipes were stolen. They're saying it was to get the beignet-thing recipe. Sounds like a publicity stunt if you ask me."

I often challenged him when he sounded too cynical. "Who's saying that?"

"Who's saying what?"

I chuckled. "Who's sayin' the robber wanted that particular recipe?"

"The owner."

That didn't make sense. "How would he know?"

"He doesn't. He's just trying to create a hashtag or something. Free advertising. He's basically saying everyone wanted those beignets."

"I heard there's a line sometimes."

He shook his head. "Well that's just ridiculous."

"Probably. But maybe it's good. Maybe we're missin' out. Maybe it's the best thing ever and we'll never know because we're too snooty."

"It's a King Cake beignet. It's like me moving to Philadelphia and opening a restaurant that serves cheese-steak... I actually have no idea what people in Philly eat."

I laughed. "Me neither, but I get your point."

"I just don't like it when people co-opt our culture and sell it like it's a commodity."

"I know."

Patrick sighed. "King Cake is a tradition, not a flavor."

"I know."

"I'm just sayin'."

"I hear you."

"Okay." He smiled. "I'll be right back."

He headed down the hall and it occurred to me that this was all exactly what I wanted, what I'd always wanted. I was finally doing what I loved in the place I loved with the man I loved. It was a lot to be happy about. Randy Newman had it right, dreams do come true in New Orleans. I hoped I'd learn to quit being suspicious and just enjoy it all.

We unpacked boxes, ate delivery pho and laughed at how little spare space I had for him. It was a long but fun day.

Patrick had to get up early so I tucked him into my... our bed and returned to the couch to read Clarence's script again. I tried hard not to think about getting the part of Charlie. Then I got to my favorite page. "A fortyish, tall, strawberry-blonde, cool glass of southern sweet tea." It was me, right? But I'd been doing this long enough to know that you don't really have the part until you're on set and someone yells,

"Rolling!" Even then, you could still get fired. Ask Eric Stoltz, the original star of *Back to the Future*.

Still, it was hard not to want it, hard not to picture myself as cool Charlie quipping with sisters and avenging her father.

Chapter 3

I would've preferred to walk or take the streetcar across town to Galatoire's but I had an audition after lunch. I always felt petty when I wasn't excited for an audition but it was a drag to have to pick out an outfit that would work for both a fine-dining lunch with Clarence and a "mom on the go." I settled on throwing khaki capri pants in the trunk to change out for the pretty floral skirt I had paired with a lavender knit top. The capri pants were "character" clothes, things I bought for work and wouldn't personally choose for my own wardrobe. I owned Keds in three colors, a baby blue button-down shirt, a navy power suit, a black suit with a pencil skirt and several other outfits for women I would only pretend to be. I'd thought about trying to dress like a groovy fighter in *7 Sisters* for lunch, but Galatoire's was no place for hiphuggers and platform shoes. I decided to go with Charlie's roots, a Garden District girl out to lunch. I hoped Clarence got it, or at least forgave it.

The historic restaurant was tucked between Larry Flynt's Hustler Club and the Mango Mango daiquiri and pizza shop on debaucherous Bourbon Street. The sound of people talking and laughing spilled out the front door as I pulled it open. The dining room's interior was simply elegant with forest green wallpaper patterned with gold fleur de lis. Bentwood sweetheart parlor chairs surrounded tables covered in white cloth. Well-lit mirrors lined the room at table height so that the crowd looked as multiplied as the cacophony of conversation filling the room. I couldn't help but notice how many diners were standing and visiting or milling around the room.

A jolly-faced man came down the wooden staircase behind the hosting station. "Sorry for the delay. Welcome to Galatoire's. Did you spot your party?"

I shook my head. "I don't see them."

"Name?"

I wasn't really sure. "Pool?"

He put readers on and looked at his ledger. A young woman in black slacks and a tank top walked in carrying a clipboard. She took in the seersucker suits and festive dresses and pulled at a sweater tied around her waist.

"I don't see a Pool, darlin'. Could it be under another name?"

I laughed. "Yeah. I just can't think what it might be."

"Hey, I'm the one that called earlier." The young woman put the clipboard down on the hosting stand to put her sweater on and button it.

"Yes, of course. I'll be right with you."

An envelope was clipped on top of a stack of printed papers on the clipboard. The letter was addressed to Hudson Williams. I knew a Hudson Williams back in L.A., but he wasn't friends with Clarence as far as I knew. That said, the young woman's casual dress was exactly the kind of thing someone in our industry would wear if they'd been told, "No jeans." It was worth a shot. "Excuse me. I couldn't help but notice, is this 'Hudson Williams' Hud Williams from L.A.?"

"Yeah, are you Charlotte?"

Thank goodness. I was so glad I wasn't going to have to guess at pseudonyms or try to figure out who might be joining us. It was also not bad for me that I might have another friend at this lunch. I extended my hand. "Yes, hi."

"Seven, hi. They're running a little behind from the last location. There's construction everywhere in this town."

I laughed. "Yeah, you kinda caught us with our slip showin'. Finally got that Katrina money so they're doin' everything from potholes to handicap ramps for the sidewalks."

"I gotta take this." Seven put her phone to her ear and I smiled weakly at the host. Though the rules were more relaxed for lunch, most people here treated phones they way you would treat smoking in L.A. – you could do it in your home or the street, but certainly not at a restaurant. I hoped no one used their phones at the table. Seven seemed so loud. "Okay... Got it... No, she's here. Yeah... Cool." She looked at me. "They got confused by the one-ways. They're walking up now."

I still had no idea how many people were joining us. I was trying not to be bummed that it wasn't just a relaxed lunch with an old friend, especially since I might see Hud again. He was one of those all-around great-catch guys you almost never found in L.A. – kind, educated, fun, talented and even fairly handsome. He was a great family man to boot. A prince among the frogs. I hadn't seen him in a couple of years and was grateful Facebook had kept us in touch.

The door opened and four people in black slacks walked into the air conditioning. Clarence smiled and it warmed me. "Charlotte!" His familiar arms wrapped around me. I was making new friends here and I'd found my man, but there was something irreplaceable about old friends. They held your history.

Hud moved closer and I hugged him next. His short-shorn hair was like stubble on my cheek. I smiled. "I can't believe you're here! This is so fun. What a surprise! I saw your name on Seven's clipboard and--"

"Ha! Told you." Clarence pointed at Hud.

"What?" I felt left out of the joke.

Hud adjusted his glasses post-hug. "You're right. He said it's impossible to surprise you, that you'd know I was here somehow."

Clarence laughed. "Voodoo. I'm telling you. She's like the amazing Kreskin – knows all, sees all."

I laughed. "And don't you forget it." But I was bluffing. I didn't even know if this was a lunch or a meeting.

I was introduced to the other black-slacked people but everything was happening too fast for me to remember their names. We settled around a circular table and I noticed the corner table next to us was still empty. "I can't believe they held this for you. There's usually a big thing about the line to get in this place."

"Yes. The Friday lines are as long as our history."

The tall, greying man put his hand on the back of Hud's chair as someone younger handed us menus. "Cocktails?"

I tried to find the perfect dish quickly so I could focus on the conversation at the table. A debate between crab and shrimp started in my head and I shut it down. I would go with the Crabmeat Sardou and be done with it.

At the center of the room full of linen and seersucker-suited southern gents and their floral-dressed dates sat a table of women in form-fitting, white cocktail dresses wearing colorful Mardi Gras masks and waving white kerchiefs with bling covered hands. The grande dame of the table was a pretty brunette standing in an enchanting gold crown and white feather boa. It seemed to be her birthday or bachelorette party. The crowned woman laughed and raised her champagne flute. Her group followed suit.

Vying for most interesting thing happening in the room, a silver-haired, pinstripe-suited man entered with a decades younger blonde holding his hand. The noise hushed for a millisecond, then got louder than before.

"Oh my gosh. Do you know who that is?" I hit Hud's arm then dropped to a whisper. "That's Edwin Edwards. I saw it on the news. He just got released."

Hud took in the distinguished gentleman. "That guy? Seems a bit privileged for that sort of thing."

"He was the Governor. Four terms. Beloved. Did ten years in prison and six months in a halfway house."

Clarence was intrigued. "Ten years in prison? What'd he do?"

I put a piece of buttery garlic bread onto my plate. "Racketeering."

"He did the whole ten years for a white collar crime?" Hud seemed amazed.

"Ten and a half, all told."

Clarence watched the blonde bombshell settle into a chair as Edwards opened his suit jacket to sit. "That's pretty gangsta to show up fresh off the block."

I smiled. "He's beloved. And he's used to being talked about. I don't know much about the whole thing but the rule around here is as long as your dirty work was to benefit the state, it's cool. If you're just lining your pockets and that's it, you're persona non grata. Edwards wasn't always a good man, but he was a can-do leader who did a lot of good for the state. Look." I nodded my head toward the corner table as people crowded toward the former Governor. Ladies extended ring-adorned fingers for dainty handshakes accompanied by warm smiles. Men made small talk while patting his shoulder like they were all at a school reunion. Edwards stayed in his chair holding court as more diners popped up from their tables and made their way across the room.

The jolly-faced man escorted two more men to Edwards' table through milling patrons, bustling servers and chummy waiters.

I overheard diners standing behind me. "That's Sheridan, the liquor baron and that major jeweler, the one with the shop on Royal. Looks like someone's planning an engagement party."

A petite spitfire laughed. "Well, he'd certainly like everyone to think so."

The room was a hive of activity as we ate

delicious dishes and discussed the locations the *7 Sisters* group had toured so far. The Galatoire Goute, a trio of shrimp, crab and crawfish preparations separated by fresh, sliced tomatoes, was outstanding and the conversation was easy.

The white-dressed grande dame had traded her crown for a dainty, white boa halo and basked in the glow of good friends, good food and plenty of cocktails. She grabbed a few white kerchiefs from her table and looked around the room. I locked eyes with her for a moment as she took in our table. I wasn't sure what to expect as she approached.

She waved the kerchiefs as she landed next to Clarence. "It's my birthday!"

Only Clarence and I responded right away. Hud wiped his mouth with a napkin as the other two producers and Seven turned to find the birthday girl. She passed out the white kerchiefs printed with her occasion's details. Her name was Suzy Bergner and she was hosting her annual "Gals at Gal's Birthday Fete." As she spoke, she had a way of making her eyes exude and her lashes flutter that should have had an accompanying ultra-feminine magic fairy dust sound effect. Clarence, Hud and the two guys whose names I couldn't remember were mesmerized. A resident of Houston, Suzy explained she was born in Louisiana. As if on cue, I heard the unmistakable sound of a brass band and realized why we all had white kerchiefs. Three horn players paraded through the dining room blowing out *Go to the Mardi Gras* as the white-dress-wearing women encouraged everyone to join them in a second line.

There were many moments since I'd moved to

New Orleans when I was so filled to bursting with the joy of this place, that tears welled up in my eyes. Watching grown people dancing through a restaurant in fine clothing waving their kerchiefs behind a brass band was one of those moments. I wondered what everyone else at the table was making of the whole affair.

A portly man in a chef's coat joined the back of the second line parade as it made its way past the kitchen door. He jumped off of the parade at our table. "I hear y'all are visiting our fair city."

Clarence pointed at me. "We're visiting. She lives here."

The portly chef smiled at me. "I hope you told them to get the Cafe Brulot after the meal."

I was too embarrassed to admit that I loved almost every taste, but I hated coffee. Couldn't even bear coffee ice cream or coffee chocolates. "No, I didn't. Thank you for pointing it out."

Clarence laughed. "Is that coffee? She hates coffee."

The chef's eyes widened. "I'm gonna have to insist that you try it. I won't have it any other way."

As much as I already knew I'd hate it, I was even more certain that no good could ever come from insulting a chef. "I will."

Clarence nearly dropped his fork. "You will? No you won't."

I laughed. He knew me too well. "I will. I promise."

He looked at the chef. "If you can get her to try a coffee, you're a better man than I. Hey, settle a bet for us."

"Sure."

"Charlotte says gumbo is different at every restaurant. Bruce says it's always the same spicy, brown seafood soup on rice, like how marinara is always marinara."

Bruce! The guy with the sunburnt nose was Bruce. One down, one to go.

The chef smiled at me. "Your local friend is right. Firstly, there are several types or categories of gumbo. The roux can be anywhere from blonde to dark chocolate colored. There's okra gumbo and filé gumbo. There's even green gumbo. There's seafood gumbo, traditional gumbo with chicken and andouille and exotic gumbos with game like boar or gator. And that's 'fore we get into spice choices."

I jumped in. "And some people put it over potato salad. I once saw best friends almost come to blows when one of them tried to add pickles to his gumbo."

The chef laughed. "I could see that." He leaned in. "You know, chefs can be fairly particular about recipes. If it's passed down, you're literally messin' with their mama and if its original, that's when things can get downright litigious."

Bruce looked confused. "Litigious? On what grounds?"

"We sign non-disclosures."

Hud laughed. "Really? We've got those too. What do yours cover?"

"The restaurant's recipes and techniques mainly. We also sign away creative rights. We aren't allowed to claim a restaurant's recipe as our own even if we've added our own flair. Say we create a recipe while we're working at a restaurant, that recipe becomes the restaurant's property in perpetuity. I learned that phrase. In perpetuity. All the way to forever and back. I got lucky though. I was at L'assiette since I was just startin' out as a sous chef. Mister Fred taught me everything he knew. I learned all his dishes perfectly. No one could tell which of us'd prepared his signature dishes." The chef puffed with pride. "He was gonna cut the Coq au Vin when it fell out of favor in the late 80's. I asked could I work on it and he said surely. That'd be fine. So I did and the dish became a bestseller again. After that, he let me bring in new things for him to try, dishes I'd come up with on my own. A few of 'em ended up on the permanent menu. Mister Fred retired in the early two-thousands and left me in charge of the kitchen."

Clarence interrupted. "So you had to leave all those recipes when you came here?"

Hud added, "Seems like those dishes should be your intellectual property."

The chef smiled. "I told y'all I got lucky. The owners retired after The Storm and the kids decided they wanted to update the place. Specializes in creole fusion food now. So, I got to keep my recipes."

I swallowed a bite of crab. "Are any of them on this menu?"

"Yeah, I've got one but I'm keepin' the rest in reserve in case I ever open my own place or if my kids want them."

"Wow." I smiled. "It's your legacy."

"Exactly. In my will and everything, just like all my other valuables."

Valuables. Like in a theft. "Did you hear about the break-in over at 504Ever?"

He looked confused. "Was it a break-in? I heard nothin' was broken."

"Like someone had a key?"

"Or was hidin' in the water closet. We had someone try that here once."

I laughed. "They were tryin' to steal y'all's recipes?"

"No, never heard of that before. No, I think they were after the cash. All I can say is if those thieves were after that establishment's recipes, they certainly aimed low."

Everyone laughed. The chef had peaked and he knew it. He smiled and walked away with an arm flourish. "Enjoy."

Hud looked at me. "What's a water closet?"

"A bathroom. For either men or women. That's how they used to be here."

Clarence clarified. "So someone stole recipes from a restaurant?"

The one whose name I still couldn't remember piped up. "Sounds like a lot of work for not a lot of payoff."

I thought about that. Maybe they were family recipes, but then the recipes would be most valuable to the owner's family, not a stranger looking for something to cook. Maybe those beignets were really amazing. Maybe they were the kind of thing you could build a franchise around, like Krispy Kreme. But then wouldn't the owner just turn around and sue the thief for the value when stores started popping up? What would a thief do with stolen recipes to turn them into money?

A steady stream of people passed by Edwards'

table, joined in the celebration at Suzy's fete or visited friends throughout the room. Our meal was over and I still wasn't sure if I was part of the movie or a local that two of the people at the table were visiting.

The Cafe Brulot arrived and we all stopped our chattering to watch the show. A combination of coffee, orange, lemon, clove, cinnamon, sugar, Grand Marnier and brandy was prepared at the table in a large silver bowl. The waiter set the bowl on fire then used a ladle to trace a curly line of blue-flamed booze around the entire tablecloth – twice.

Clarence clicked his cup against mine. "You said you'd do it. You promised."

I grabbed a bite of Hud's Bananas Foster as a chaser and gave my cup a sip. It was the least coffee-tasting coffee I'd come across and was overwhelmed with magical boozy, fruity flavor. Not bad. I wasn't surprised everyone at the table thought it was amazing.

As our flame extinguished, singing waiters led patrons in *Happy Birthday* to Suzy. Confetti bombs went off while she executed her apparently annual tradition of standing on a table or chair.

Hud laughed. "You guys really take lunch to another level."

"We never miss an excuse to celebrate."

"Us either." Clarence lifted his cup. "We found our locations and we're locked to shoot here. One less thing to worry about."

Everyone joined. "One less thing to worry about!"

I looked at my phone and gasped. "Dang it! I gotta go. I've got an audition across town."

Everything in me wanted to stay until I knew for sure if I was involved in the movie or if my friends were just including me in their day. Both were wonderful but one meant I'd have plenty more to celebrate.

I gathered my hugs and waved goodbye to Suzy as I exited onto the calamity of Bourbon Street. Around the corner, I stopped to dial my agent Claudia and let her know I was going to be fighting construction and might run behind. A guy in a suit was fussing at a guy in a Galatoire's chef's jacket behind a flower delivery van. The suit guy seemed very angry.

The chef-jacket guy seemed defensive. "That's crazy. Who would I sell them to?"

"Chefs!"

Claudia's machine picked up. Her gargled-with-gravel voice bid me to leave a message as the chef-jacket guy yelled, "That's absurd!"

"I know about the black market. I'm no fool."

The machine beeped. "It's Charlotte. On my way but a little behind."

The chef-jacket guy hit the side of the van with his fist. "You're being ridiculous. What chef would buy them?"

What was I watching?

"An ambitious one! A greedy one! An out of town one! A desperate one."

The chef-jacket guy gathered himself. "Look, I signed that thing and that's the end of it. Sue me if you think you've got somethin' to prove. Otherwise, leave my name outta your mouth. I'm done." He took the jacket off dramatically and threw it at the suit guy than stormed off. The suit guy spotted me so I looked down at my phone like I was reading a text, then dropped the phone into my purse and casually headed for my car. My hand was shaking by the time I slipped the key into the ignition. I took a deep breath and centered myself.

The waiting room was pretty empty. I signed in and ran into the bathroom to pull my capri pants on under my skirt. I tried to focus on my lines but my brain kept returning to the argument I'd witnessed. Was there a recipe black market? How would that work? Did that chef-jacket guy steal recipes from Galatoire's? Was he a recipe thief? Did he steal from 504Ever? Was he trying to start his own restaurant?"

"Charlotte? You're up."

I followed the casting director into his office and tried to focus.

"For the slate, I'll need name, height and city."

I hated when they asked for height. It usually meant the lead actor was under-tall which usually meant I wouldn't get the part no matter how spectacular I was. Tall women with average-height men seemed to be the final frontier in diversity for some reason. A bridge too far. I was more likely to be cast as the love interest of a woman than a shorter man.

In real life, I'd endeavored to remain open in matters of height. I figured at least seventy percent of men were average or shorter which seemed far too many men to cut out before we'd even spoken. I saw Patrick's nearly six-and-a-half foot frame as my karmic reward for not caring all those years. And he was handsome to boot. So handsome, I'd never forgotten his face after seeing him just once at the back of a streetcar while I was busy meeting the actor, Bryan Batt, in the front. That was the day that started me down the path of discovering the identity of the stalker Bryan had been plagued by, and even solving the mystery of the missing drowned kid. What had that chef-jacket guy stolen? It had to be recipes, right?

I looked down to my sides and took a deep breath to clear my head. I asked myself the magic questions. Who am I? Who am I talking to? What do I want from them? "Ready."

We did it twice. It was probably pretty good but I was always tough on myself. And the odds of getting the job were always bad.

Patrick came home with Cane's fried chicken so I wouldn't have to cook. He seemed to understand I was adjusting to sharing my space and was eating my free time finding places for his clothes and toiletries. "You heard about the recipe-theft thing?"

I was intrigued. "Somethin' new? I heard about the window in the door being broken. Guess that's how they got in."

"They're saying there was security footage and the guy was wearing a Mardi Gras costume."

I laughed. "What?"

He handed me a warm styrofoam container and we quickly blessed our meal. "Yeah, so the guy wore a Mardi Gras costume. There's a video of it. The restaurant has a post on their page asking people to come up with a name. The winner gets those stupid beignets."

I was fairly shocked. "Are you serious? That

seems... I don't know, but wrong somehow. Is the video online? I thought the camera was broken."

"The one at the door where the window was busted out was broken, but they had another one in the register area. They haven't released it yet but I guess the owners already saw it."

I stopped eating. "And decided to turn it into a naming contest? I mean, I know we tend to turn anything into an excuse for a party but it seems strange."

"It's stupid. King-Yaygler is winning."

My face went sour. "Jeeze."

"I wrote 'Trash Collector.'"

I laughed. "You did not."

"No I didn't. But honestly, they can't be good."

"Agreed. Hey, have you ever heard of a recipe black market?"

"A recipe black market? What is that?"

I dipped a fry in ketchup. "I don't know. Like a network where you buy recipes from restaurants?"

"No, I don't think so. Sounds made up."

"Yeah, maybe. I'm just tryin' to figure out why anyone would steal a recipe from a restaurant. Did you know that some chefs have to sign non-disclosure agreements? And some of them sign their rights away. Like if they invent a recipe, it becomes the property of the restaurant."

"That makes sense from the owner's standpoint. Can you imagine if you were a restaurant with a signature dish and then the chef wants to take it with them when they go? Doesn't a science lab own the things scientists come up with on their dime?"

I dipped another fry. "I guess. Probably depends.

They probably gotta sign things too."

He took a bite of Texas Toast. "You think someone wanted to sell the 504Ever recipes on a black market?"

"I don't know. Maybe. Why would anyone bother to break laws and put themselves in harm's way of going to jail for recipes."

"Maybe they're playing the odds. The police don't have time for a crime with no victims. The guy had copies of all the recipes on his computer. Only the press cares and they only care for today."

"Yeah, but if the press keeps caring, the cops might feel pressured to care."

Patrick chuckled. "No victim, no crime. Someone's probably being shot as we speak."

"Yeah, you're probably right." I raised a fry to my mouth then stopped. "But still, somebody stole somethin'. And we don't know who or why. Doesn't it bug you?"

"I'll live with it."

I laughed. "Yeah, me too. But still."

Patrick laughed. "Did you get the part? Are you a sister?"

I exhaled.

"No? Seriously?"

I stopped him. "No, I don't know."

He closed his styrofoam container and shoved it into the plastic Raising Cane's bag. "Still?"

"There were all these people at our table. Oh, Hud's one of the producers. The perfectly sane friend of mine I always wanted to work with?"

"Come on, Charlotte. They have to be hiring you. Why didn't you work your magic and trick them into telling you?"

"It was lunacy in there."

He looked unconvinced.

"Seriously! Edwin Edwards was at the table next to ours. It was a total scene."

"Seriously?"

"Yes, and there was this big birthday bash and at some point an actual brass band led a second line. I'm tellin' you, it was a lot to compete with."

He laughed. "A second line?"

"Yes! There was a freakin' parade and then they set our table on fire. You can't know."

Patrick laughed again and added my styrofoam to the bag. "Okay. I get it. What're you gonna do?"

"I'm gonna read the script again and do some deep stretching in case I'm playing an expert martial artist in an amazing Clarence Pool movie."

He kissed me and headed for the trash can under the sink. "Let's watch *SVU* then I'll leave you to it."

"Deal."

Chapter 4

I was glad Patrick was coming with me to the family reunion. I didn't really know most of my dad's side of the family and outside of blood, I wasn't sure how much we'd have in common. Turned out, all it took to get Patrick onboard was the promise of crawfish.

It was a mercy that the family tradition included name tags. There were dozens and dozens of people spread through the sprawling yard, many with my father's wide-bridged, rounded nose. Pigtailed girls and boys in rompers played with giant soap bubbles blown by someone's dad or uncle as an older group of boys and girls in swimsuits ran through squirting each other with neon plastic water guns. Men carried giant coolers of crawfish from the driveway to the picnic tables near the river. Through the glass doors, I spotted my aunt Carol stacking brownies on a crystal cake pedestal. I tugged Patrick's hand and led him toward the kitchen. "Come on. I found someone I know."

Aunt Carol was older than my dad by a few years and lived on the northernmost edge of the state. That had to be a long drive. I hadn't seen her since Dad's sixtieth birthday party but she'd always taken an interest in me and my career, and I was used to being her family. Most everyone else here felt like strangers sprinkled with a few vaguely familiar faces I'd maybe seen in old photos.

Carol squared a brownie on top of the stack then spotted me. Her arms flew wide. "Charlotte! Oh my goodness." She hugged me. "Oh, I'm so glad you made it. I was so hoping you'd come."

I felt loved.

It turned out that several people there had memories of me as a child. Most of their descriptions included words like "doll" and "perfect." I could only go downhill from there. I couldn't help but wonder why I hadn't known these people growing up. Sure, my parents were divorced and my mother raised me, but it still seemed odd to think I could've met them on the street and never known we were family.

Sitting at a picnic table, I twisted the head off a crawfish and pinched the tail to get at the spicy meat. "Carol, do you remember Dad's pipe, the carved one?"

"He still has that?"

"You know it?" My heart pounded. Maybe I would finally find out where it had come from, why it was carved with the same symbol as Sassy's chandelier and the silver flask in the old brothel.

"He's had that thing for decades. And it's forever old. Can't be sanitary."

"Do you know where he got it?" I shot Patrick a hopeful glance.

A relative of some sort passed our table and said, "Don't forget to leave room for sweets! Have you seen that spread inside? Diet starts tomorrow, right?" She laughed at her own joke and walked toward her table carrying a plate of potato salad and homemade sweet pickles.

I looked back to Carol. "You were sayin'? About where Dad got the pipe?"

"Oh, right. Yes. He was maybe sixteen? He caught Mother throwin' it out and he pitched a fit. She said it was owned by trash and belonged in the trash. That just made him angrier. They were fighting a lot by then, but this one stood out. Your dad was so passionate, but Mother was adamant."

"About throwin' it out?"

Carol nodded. "Said it was bad luck or cursed or something. Paul said she was being ridiculous, superstitious. It went on. Finally, Mother took the trash out and dumped it by the curb. I didn't find out he had it until I saw him smoking it at a restaurant when he was in college. I guess he went out there and dug that pipe out of the trash. Mother would've had a field day with that. I don't think she ever found out."

It seemed like a lot of work for a pipe. "Why was he so passionate about it? Whose was it? Your dad's?"

"No, it came down on Mother's side."

"It was her father's? Your grandfather's?"

"Yes." She took a sip of her Abita Strawberry and dabbed beer foam from her lip with the back of her thumb.

"He got it from his father?"

"I'm not sure. Maybe I don't remember or maybe I never knew. Old stories."

I scanned my own memory then looked to Patrick. "Didn't Dad say his great-grandfather was a wealthy plantation owner?"

He shrugged and finished working on a corn cob. "Sounds familiar, but don't hold me to that."

Carol smiled. "Maybe. We never met our grandparents. I don't even know their names. Except that Mother said she was named for her father. But she hated the name. Birdie? Hated it."

"Do you know why?"

Carol giggled. "Well, it's not exactly a popular name."

"But did she have a reason?"

"She said it lacked dignity." Carol wiped her hands with a wad of paper towels. "Your grandmother wasn't always the happiest person. She could have a way of lookin' at things that put her in a certain kind of light. As controlling as she could be, she liked to think a lot of things just happened to her. Like she was at the whims of the wind, not responsible for her life." She wiped her mouth with the spice-stained paper towel wad. "But she came by it honestly I guess. Her father died when she was just a tot and she felt abandoned right off the bat."

"Fair enough. I mean, in that case, she really is just a victim. It's not like a toddler created that scenario."

"She carried that on her. Like a burden. Like he didn't want her enough to stick around I guess."

I knew the feeling. "You think that was it?"

Carol paused. "I never really knew. She wasn't known for her clarity of purpose. The only thing I really remember is she was angry at her dad, or maybe ashamed. Never even wanted to talk about him."

"And you don't know your own grandparents' names? I mean, I get not meeting them maybe, but to not even know their names?"

She leaned back a little on the bench. "Like I said, our grandfather passed when Mother was a tot and seems like she left home soon as she was old enough. Never looked back I guess."

"Seems cold."

Carol smiled. "We all have our ways of gettin' through whatever we have to get through. Your grandmother didn't have the easiest life. She did her best, I guess."

I smiled. "Sure. Of course." I pushed my last few crawfish into Patrick's pile. "What could it be though? The name. She was named for her dad, right? Maybe he was Finch."

Patrick swallowed. "Robin. Wren."

Carol tried some. "Sparrow, hawk, pigeon."

Patrick swigged his beer. "Jay."

"Jay." I smiled. "That's a good one. But why didn't she just change her name if she hated it so much?"

Carol pushed windblown auburn hair out of her face. "I asked once. Her mother made her swear, said she'd haunt her for life. Mother wasn't particularly obedient but she could be pretty superstitious. Said it wasn't worth foolin' with. I think she just didn't like the constant reminder of her father every time someone said her name or she wrote a check. But at the same time, it was her father's name and really all she had left of him."

"I get that. My nose bridge is wide because I have Dad's nose. This modeling agent in New York sent me to a plastic surgeon once who could 'fix it,' give me a thinner, more elegant nose."

Patrick looked shocked. "That's terrible."

"Showbiz. So he wants to fix this thing that's always bothered me and I was like, 'But that's my father's nose!' After Dad left, the only way I'd see him around the house was in my own face. Tate favors Mom. Mad as I could get about the whole situation, he was still my dad. Always my dad." Carol smiled and I could see Dad in her face too. "I'm really glad we came today."

Patrick finished a garlic bulb. "Yeah, this has been amazing. Really nice."

Carol hugged me and I kept my orange, spicy hands fanned away from her. "Ready for dessert?"

The kitchen was crowded with people eating home-baked goodies from paper plates. We joined the line around the wooden kitchen island. A variety of cookies, brownies and Rice Krispie cereal treats were stacked on platters. I spooned some English Trifle onto my plate along with a lemon bar.

Patrick nudged me. "You know what this reminds me of?"

I smiled. "Meeting me at the funeral?"

He kissed me then cut an oozing slice of chocolate Bundt cake drizzled with ganache.

A stranger who was probably related to me interjected. "Y'all met at a funeral?"

I laughed. "Yeah. After. At the dessert table at the repass."

The young man smiled and I could see my dad's face in his. It was an unusual sensation to look into a stranger's face and see family. But it felt good to know these were my people. I'd known my mom's side all my life but maybe there was still time to get to know this side of my roots and heritage. I put my hand out. "I'm Charlotte, Paul's daughter. Birdie's granddaughter. And this is my boyfriend, Patrick."

He clasped my hand and shook. "Phil. Hey. I'm Stephen's son. Brick's grandson."

I laughed. "I don't know any of those people."

Phil and Patrick laughed too. Phil pointed to his chest. "That's the genius of the name tags."

Maybe it was unusual to need Sharpie-written tags stuck to our chests, but it didn't take away from the fact that blood meant something. After so many years of feeling foreign in L.A., I kept finding new ways I felt at home in Louisiana.

After our longish drive back into town, Patrick said he was fine with me going alone to meet Clarence. I still felt a little odd about meeting him in a bar while Patrick watched TV at home, but I was glad to finally have an opportunity to remove the vagueness. It was like a plague in L.A. I could spend hours trying to figure out things like, "What did they mean by that?" or "Was I supposed to call first?" It was ridiculous how much energy I'd put into figuring out where I stood with people.

Most great bars in New Orleans were dives. Many had live music or pool tables. There was usually some indicator that the Saints had won the Super Bowl. I checked the address twice before parking. With its glass-sculpture lighting and chrome liquor display, this bar seemed right off the Sunset Strip. Clarence was sitting in a secluded booth and jumped up when he spotted me. "Hey!"

We hugged and settled into the half-circle beige leather high-backed bench.

He smiled and waved at a waitress. "You want a

Diet Coke?"

"That'd be great."

"Diet Coke for her and I'll take another of these." He sat back and beamed at me. "I wanted to tell you yesterday, you look great."

"Thanks. You look great too."

"No, but I mean you seem really happy."

I smiled wide. "I am. Like, the happiest. It's pretty great."

"So, you really live here now, huh?"

I laughed. "Yep. Really do."

Clarence shook his head. "You're really not coming back?"

I laughed again. "Why do people keep asking me that? No. God willing, I'll die on this dirt."

"What have you seen that's good?"

I knew he meant movies. It was one of our favorite things to talk about. We could go on for hours. Except I hadn't been to the theatre in a while. In L.A., I caught at least one movie a week. Since moving to New Orleans, I was down to about once every month or two. "Something strange has happened. I mean, I've seen *Bridesmaids* and that was great, but I really haven't been going to movies that much."

He looked disappointed. "What do you mean?"

"There's just a lot more to do here. I'm always at a parade or a free concert or a festival or somethin'. These are all like, you-had-to-be-there, bucket-list kind of things. Every weekend, heck, every day, there are so many things to do that you couldn't possibly experience them all and you wish for a clone but all your clone would do is make more clones. There's that much amazing stuff to do. And no velvet ropes, no lists, no snooty self-important doorman givin' you side-eye and most of it's free. And a lot of it gives back to the community. Movies always helped me escape, but now, I'm fully in my life. I don't wanna be anywhere else."

The waitress placed our drinks on black paper napkins and smiled at Clarence. "I put it on your tab." She snapped up his empty and headed back to the bar.

"But you still watch TV." He looked to me for reassurance that we still had common interests.

"Of course. Patrick and I watch a ton of TV. Probably too much. And he gets us all the movies as soon as they come out. He's got a big flatscreen I'm tryin' to figure out where to put."

He spun his straw around his glass. "So you're fine with missing things on the big screen?"

"I don't mean to freak you out but I'm fine with missing things altogether. I mean, really Clarence, it's like Hollywood's not even trying anymore. Everything's a remake or it's got a number after the all-too-familiar name. I'm not sure I'm missing' anything by skipping *Transformers Six*, or whatever they're on. Some CGI monster fighting a CGI robot or whatever. Great dialogue like, 'Run!' or 'Look out!' Some old dude with a young airhead. It's tired. The longer I'm away..." I took a breath. "It just seems irrelevant. Like, who cares? The studios don't seem to care enough to pay attention to what I want, why should I pay attention to their latest paint-by-number billion dollar star vehicle for some dude?"

He laughed. "Whoa! You need to do a two snaps up or something after a speech like that. That was straight outta the Julia Sugarbaker *Designing Women* school of speeches. Preach!" He threw his hands up.

I laughed and felt relieved I hadn't divided us. "You know I'll always love movies more than I hate the things in them, but I don't feel like I'm abandoning movies, I feel like they're abandoning me. And the more I live with people whose lives don't revolve around movies, the more time I spend with regular work-a-day folks talking about food and weather and local stuff that directly affects us, like the BP oil spill, the more I feel like studios have lost their way. The Gulf is full of like a zillion gallons of oil and Corexit. You think I'm scared of robots? You know what I'm scared of? Shrimp. And getting mugged. And finding work in an industry that doesn't create work for interesting, experienced women like me. You wanna know why the latest Owen Wilson or Vince Vaughn should-I-settle-down movie wasn't the blockbuster their names should've guaranteed?"

He grinned. "Definitely."

"Because they're forty! Only in L.A. are men just gettin' around to the idea of settling down at forty. Heck, they're wrestling with it like they've got their whole lives ahead of them. Like it's a death to their youth. But in the rest of the world, forties is middle-aged. People are parents by forty. I know grandparents in their forties. Those movies seem totally irrelevant to the things forty year olds are wrestling with in the world. They're not deciding whether to date the twenty-two year old, they have their own twenty-two year old they sent to college or whatever."

"Except that gangsta guy at the restaurant

yesterday."

I laughed. "Edwin Edwards. Yeah, the exception that proves the rule. But usually, if you show up with a twenty-somethin' on your arm here, people are going to assume that's your daughter." Clarence looked concerned. I shook my head. "When my dad visited me in L.A., people automatically assumed he was my boyfriend – and we look alike. I'm just sayin' that from this distance, it's really clear which one is the norm. I don't know, movies just seem to care about things people aren't really thinking about. Even if it's an escape, it's supposed to be something you connect to, right?" I touched his arm for emphasis. "Why do you think people get so excited when you're gettin' ready to make another movie? Because they know it's gonna be cool and different and fun and entertaining. They're going to see people like people they know or wish they knew or wish they were. People know you genuinely care about movies but even more, you genuinely care about your audience. You want to take them on a ride, show them something familiar they've never seen and leave them breathless. But that's just you."

Clarence laughed. "I'd argue, but I like thinking you're right."

"This is funny."

"What is?" He stirred his glass absently.

"I'm the one doing all the talking." We laughed. "Tell me about you. What's the best thing that happened to you today?"

"Ah, I'm onto you now. I'm not gonna let you use your Voodoo-magic question on me."

I laughed. "Why not? Afraid you'll reveal your

inner secrets?"

"I know it for a fact. You confessed it was your magic question. You told me it was how you knew I 'derived supreme joy' from my work and that I didn't need other people to be happy and entertained, that I was one of the rare sane people who was comfortable being alone. And you got all that from me saying that the best thing that day was that I'd figured out the ending to a script I'd been working on for ages. But that's not why I'm not telling you. I'm not telling you the best thing because it hasn't happened yet."

I laughed again. "Big night for Mr. Clarence, eh? Got a hot date with a southern sweetie later?" He grinned. I changed gears. "I'm really glad we met that day. Honestly, you restore my faith in movies and the potential of our industry. Plus, you're awesome."

"Said the super-cool chick."

I smiled. "I know you're here to work, but I hope you get to see some music and eat our good food, maybe go to a parade. There's a second line every Sunday with a brass band and dancing. It's like a block party that parades through the city. You'd love it."

"I will." He finished his drink. "I'll try. You know how I get when I'm working. I will try, but you know there's something about movies that none of that live stuff has. Film is forever. It's cool to be part of something for an afternoon, but when you spend an afternoon on set, you immortalize that day. It lives forever. You live forever."

I smiled. "I love that. I do. You and I don't have children so movies are like our legacy, our offspring, our creation. I can't even imagine what it must feel like to be you, to know that people study your movies in college now. You didn't even get to go to college. Talk about providing a better life for your progeny. I just have a well-documented body that appeared fleetingly in dozens of movies and TV shows."

He looked at me quietly then, "You never really did get that break you should've had. It always broke the wrong way for you."

"And yet, I got to produce a movie with THE Clarence Pool. That ain't nothin' and like you said, film is forever."

"Yeah, but even that one broke wrong for you. I've always felt like I wished people could see what you're capable of. What'd you think of Charlie?"

My heart raced. "I thought she was using her martial arts training to walk the line between her leather and lace, you know? Her sugar-sweet southern upbringing and her alpha-female core. Martial arts lets her own her grace, find power in it. I felt like each sister's weapon was the key to their struggle or their identity, their sense of self. It's really cool in a way. Reminds me of a play in that way. Charlie's lines are actually really open. They're not as inherently directed as your usual dialogue."

"I did that on purpose. Do you want to read a few lines?"

I snickered. "Here?" I looked around the dimly lit bar, took in the volume of the music we were competing with and wondered if I was supposed to have memorized all of Charlie's scenes.

"Yeah, come on." He slid out from the booth and motioned to our waitress. "We're on the front porch." He grabbed a bag from the floor.

I tried to remain calm and confident. I reminded myself that this meant he was considering me for the part, which meant he probably wanted me to do well and was on my side.

"Here." He handed me a script from the bag and we settled under the front lamp encircled by bugs banging themselves on the glass encasement. I was certain I was going to get a couple dozen mosquito bites but I hoped it'd be worth it. We read three different scenes together, me playing Charlie and Clarence playing everyone else. I loved when he did voices. Heck, I always loved acting with him. He was so committed, so shameless and free. And he always seemed like he was having the time of his life. It reminded me to be grateful that I get to do something I love for money and that plenty of people would be more than happy with my career and just the chance to do a scene with Clarence. I tried to focus on that and forget about getting the part. I tried to focus on being grateful and having fun and showing off my ideas for Charlie.

We were laughing at a flubbed line when the waitress came out. "You okay out here? Need anything?"

Clarence laughed the words. "We're good. The check, please." He closed his script. "That's plenty."

I closed my script too. "That was fun. People are gonna love this movie." Now, I couldn't stop wondering how I'd done.

"So the studio has a list they want me to see."

My stomach tightened. "Ah, the list. L.A. loves a list. That, and celebrities."

"Yeah, big names. But I wrote the part open like

that because I don't know nothin' 'bout southern belles."

"*Gone With the Wind.* Best ever. Definitely best female lead role ever."

Clarence smiled wide. "So, I wanted to hire a genuine belle to fill Charlie in, give her some mannerisms and cultural truths."

"Julia Roberts it is!" I immediately wished I could take it back. What kind of fool offered up a better name for a part like this?

"We're movin' really fast so I don't have time for a bunch of meetings with people originally from Brooklyn and Michigan. I need someone who can just be this woman, just bring it fully formed. This is not one of those do-an-accent-get-an-Oscar kind of parts. Honestly, it's not the lead. It's not even the fourth lead. It's too small for all that unnecessary celebrity weight. It's the perfect size to show the world what an actor's capable of without needing them to bring box office."

I was having trouble focusing. My mind was racing, trying to follow and skip ahead at the same time.

He took my hand. "So, the best part of my day is getting to tell my friend that she got the part."

My heart pounded, my breath quickened and my brain felt like it exploded. "I got the part?" I was so afraid he'd take it back but I needed to be sure.

"You got the part!"

"I got the part!"

Clarence yelled at a man walking past with his dog. "She got the part!"

The guy waved. "Congratulations!"

I loved my city. I hugged Clarence. "I got the part."

We separated and he smiled at me. "You got the part."

"Holy cow." I was breathless. "Thanks. That's amazing. Thank you. I got the part."

He laughed. "You got the part. You'll be getting a call about your fitting in L.A. We're having a cast dinner and a table read so you'll be there a few days."

I couldn't wait to tell Patrick but I couldn't help but worry about having to work out of town. Patrick was the first man to make it through a whole movie with me without breaking up, but my jobs had all been a day or two of work, a week or two when I got lucky. This gig could go on for months.

Patrick was still awake when I got home so we got to celebrate by reliving the night together on the couch. I told him about our discussions and acted out Clarence acting out the different voices when I auditioned on the porch. Patrick seemed genuinely happy for me. It felt so good to have someone care that I'd done well, someone to share my joy and excitement.

Patrick turned in and I sat at my laptop to write my blog about the family reunion crawfish boil. I quickly checked Facebook and found a bunch of posts about the restaurant robbery. The owner, Travis Bend, was quoted as saying the thief was definitely after the King-Yay! recipe and that he was looking into his options.

I clicked on a black-and-white still from the surveillance video. The thief's face was obscured by a wide-brimmed hat decorated with plastic food and a stuffed bunny. It was hard to make out the jacket's theme, but the black-and-white wide-striped pants seemed like something a clown would wear. The still photo had caught the thief dramatically scaling the tall counter rather than just walking around it. The shoe looked like it was encrusted with glitter. There was a lighter splotch of glitter on the toe. A lemon? An apple? It was hard to tell, but it looked more like a pear shape. What else was pear-shaped? Maybe it was a teardrop. No, it was definitely more of a pear than a droplet. Pretty big shoe. Probably a guy.

It wasn't a very good costume. It didn't seem to have any cohesive theme or clever commentary on society or any historical or cultural ties. Other than the food hat, maybe. But why a bunny? Wait! What if the hat was an Easter bonnet? Then it would make perfect sense. It might even mean something – like maybe it was worn by a chef.

But everything else was so random. Maybe that was the point. Maybe they were all pieces from different costumes. Stuff he was done with and wouldn't mind tossing. I wished there were some way to look up people's past costumes. If I knew who it was, I could give Facebook a shot. But I didn't.

I opened another window and started to relive the beginning of my long and amazing day. But my mind kept returning to the thrill of knowing – I got the part!

Chapter 5

I arrived in L.A. in time for Nia's fifth birthday. Sofia and Nia had decorated the yard with the Mardi Gras beads and throws I'd sent as well as helium balloons. Nia wore a baby blue princess dress and the plastic tiara I'd mailed the year before. It seemed impossible that I'd missed so much of her life and growing. She was chatty and adorable, leading her little friends around the yard as parents sipped wine and snacked on Trader Joe's pita chips and cheeses.

I didn't really know anyone and I felt a little left out. It was a feeling I'd grown accustomed to as a kid so I had a high tolerance for making brief and tenuous connections with strangers.

A woman arrived with three parrots and put on a small show, then let the kids pet the feathered acrobats. There was singing and a cake with a parrot topper. Apparently, I was stumbling into Nia's parrot phase. I'd altogether missed her love affair with hippos. It felt like I'd just been holding her tiny baby body in the crook of my arm yesterday. Here she was holding court and expressing her own personality.

As the sun set over the hill, I helped clean up while parents said their goodbyes holding sleepy children on their hips. I was looking forward to having the house to ourselves. Mark was on the road with another sculpture exhibit. Since being featured on *Sex in the City*, he was suddenly the hottest artist on two legs. It didn't hurt that he looked like a tousled movie star or the lead singer in some band cast by *GQ*.

Sofia let me tuck Nia into bed while she finished up in the kitchen. I sang the songs I used to sing to Nia before she knew words. She smiled, laughed even, but didn't seem to remember any of it. I held onto the joy of her remembering me and let that be enough.

Sofia was quick-mopping the floor when I returned. I leaned against the counter. "She's out."

"I think she had fun."

I smiled. "Everyone did."

"Right? It was a good party, right? People are doing these crazy things now where they rent a hotel ballroom or bring in Cirque de Soleil or something."

"Ugh. Like the kid's even gonna remember all that. You know what I remember from my fifth birthday? The cake had a Barbie in it. That's what I remember. The cake dress was yellow. That's it."

Sofia laughed as she put the quick-mop away. "We could've just stuck a Barbie in the cake and called it a day."

I laughed too. "I'm just sayin'. That's all I remember so who are they doing all that ballroom stuff for? What's the point?"

"It's the new Prada purse. It's how people show off."

I followed her out to the porch in the backyard. "I'm so glad I don't live here anymore."

She propped her feet on the stone wall around the Koi pond. "Do you miss anything?"

"Besides you and Nia? Yeah, I guess. I miss lunches at Mel's. I don't even have people to go to lunch with anymore. People in the world have regular jobs with regular hours. They can't blow half a day over salad and herbal tea talking about movies. I kinda miss that sometimes. People hardly ever talk about movies and when they do, it's not usually some deep discussion that goes on for hours. It's like, 'That was pretty good' or 'I love Vin Diesel' or whatever. Then they talk about other stuff. I don't tell my Hollywood stories anymore. Most people in New Orleans don't even know what I do for money. They know me as the lady with the blog, always at events taking photos and jotting notes."

Sofia leaned back and looked at the stars through the eucalyptus leaves. "That's kinda nice though. No one trying to get to you to get to your fancy friends. No one using you to get their projects made or get into a premiere or whatever. You could even pretend you were a teacher or a bullfighter."

I laughed. "Yes, a bullfighter. Totally believable."

She started laughing harder. "An astrophysicist, a pearl diver."

I loved when Sofia got like this. If I kept it going, I knew we'd get to the part where she was cry-laughing and barely forming words. "The inventor of glow sticks, a lion tamer."

She laughed harder. "I don't think they have those anymore."

I laughed harder too. "We're so old."

Tears rolled down her cheeks. "I know, right?"

I gasped. "You know what I miss? And I really do miss this. Closets. Jeeze. My kingdom for a freakin' closet. And hot and cold water coming out of the same spigot. I mean, this is madness!" She laughed as I acted out having to mix the hot and cold water in my palms. "And always do the cold first so you don't burn your hands. Learned that the hard way."

She wiped her cheeks with the back of her hand. "Roughing it old school."

"Seriously though, we don't even have an electrical outlet in the bathroom. It's like a museum of how people used to live."

She doubled over in laughter again.

"But I love it, and Patrick's cool with it so it's fine."

Sofia got more serious. "How's that going?"

"Amazing. I have no idea where we're gonna put his furniture and I feel like a brat for insisting that we stay in my place for a while at least but, yeah, amazing."

"Has he seen the ghost?"

"You mean the chandelier? Not yet. He thinks I'm making it up, or mistaken or whatever, but it's a matter of time."

She shivered. "Uck. I couldn't stand that, sleeping every night under a chandelier that may or may not move at any given moment. No thank you."

"It's not that bad. Honestly? I feel a little guilty that I'm supposed to understand it better or something. That fortune teller lady, Stella, said I was the Protector. And my neighbor told Tom--"

"Aw, green gloves guy. I liked him."

I nodded. Tom had been a fun first boyfriend to have in New Orleans. He liked teaching me about the city's history and enjoyed taking me to new things.

"He said my neighbor heard there was a ghost in the house that protects a family secret. If I'm supposed to be protecting some family secret, shouldn't I know what it is? What if the family secret is our magical dancing chandelier and I'm telling you and Mom and Lillibette and Patrick and whoever?"

Sofia was laughing again. "You should put it on Facebook and see what happens." She shivered again. "Ah! I can't even joke about it. I'm not going to be able to sleep tonight if I keep thinking about it."

I laughed. "The chandelier's pretty far away. But, I think it's about the symbol somehow. Or maybe the initials that were scratched into the top of the chandelier where it attaches to the ceiling. I'm thinking that hanging the chandelier is the way I'm supposed to protect the secret. It was even in Sassy's will so it's logical that the symbol or the initials have something to do with the secret."

"And the symbol is?"

"A water pump. A well. I'm almost certain it's the symbol for the name of our family plantation, Wells. It's on a silver flask at May Baily's Place, this bar that used to be a brothel back in the Storyville days. And it's also carved into a pipe my dad got passed down sorta from his grandfather. Then we found it on an envelope when I was doing that movie with Bryan Batt and Mom and Julia came to visit." I let my voice go up like a question to make sure Sofia was following.

"Right."

"And inside was a bill of sale from Wells plantation for a slave named Lottie."

Sofia recoiled. "Ew. That's awful."

"I know, right? That fortune teller also said to be careful what I wished for and not to ask questions I didn't want the answers to. But I have to know the secret, right?"

Sofia played with a Mardi Gras bead strand like it was a rosary. "Maybe you don't. Maybe you just need to keep it hung and keep wondering." We laughed together. She twirled the bead strand on her finger then went back to fidgeting with it. "Okay, so the woman who raised your mother--"

"Sassy."

"Sassy. She brought the chandelier to New Orleans from Texas?"

I ran my fingers on her fake bug-free lawn. "Her mother did. Mama Heck. She raised my Maw Maw. Or maybe it was Mama Eunoe, who I think raised my great-grandfather. It depends on when they made the trip. And I'm pretty sure it's the same chandelier from my family story where the girl who ran away with the overseer took a chandelier."

"So your family gave it to one of those women that worked for them? That's a pretty big tip."

"I haven't really thought about the why a lot yet. But you're right, why does a plantation runaway bride or her son or whoever end up giving the family's other-mother a crystal chandelier? It's not just super-expensive and hard to come by, it's a totally inconvenient gift. It's nearly an imposition."

Sofia laughed. "Right? Like don't buy me a chandelier for my birthday, okay? I have eight foot ceilings and the totally wrong furniture for that."

"Done. No birthday chandelier for you." I laughed.

"So what are the initials?"

"LW or SW first, then DW or OW. I figure W is for Wells."

"Do you know any Wells in your family?"

"Aunt Ava ran through the names and I'm guessing the first set is for Lily Wells, the one that ran away with the overseer."

She nodded again. "That makes sense."

"I'm just hoping it's not circular logic where each thing is the only thing that proves the other things. I'm kinda persnickety about facts."

She twirled the bead strand. "You don't believe in facts?"

"I do but I always try to remember that it was a 'fact' that the Earth was flat. Plus, I had this experience once that was like a before-and-after moment for me. My brother and I were playing this game, Mastermind. One person creates a sequence of four pegs behind a little cover. There's like six or eight colors to pick from and you put them in any order and the other person tries to guess your sequence. It was a board that had like ten or a dozen chances to match the sequence. You'd make a guess then get feedback. A white peg meant you'd guessed a color right but not in the right place and a black peg meant you'd gotten both the color and position right. But, you couldn't know which of the pegs went with which peg in your guess. It was a deductive reasoning game."

Sofia laughed. "I thought Checkers was hard. How old were you?"

"I don't know, nine maybe? And Tate was seven, I guess. Sometimes it could get pretty frustrating for him. Anyway, listen. So this one time, we're playing that game and I keep making guesses and Tate keeps putting the reaction pegs out and we get to the very end, which I was usually able to avoid, and Tate says I still didn't guess right. I checked all my logic and found that hard to believe. He lifted the cover and revealed that, in fact, I hadn't guessed right. I went over the board again and again, checking his black and white reaction pegs against my guesses. Perfect results. So, at nine years old or whatever, I figured out that you could look at data and draw perfectly logical conclusions that weren't right. So, now when people say 'it's a fact,' I think about that game and the evidence for a flat Earth and try to keep my mind open to the possibility that the 'fact' may be wrong. And I try to watch my assumption that I know what I'm talking about. I was really certain Tate had cheated or gotten it wrong. I wasn't that patient about it either."

"You were nine." She picked up a bottle of bubbles one of the kids had left on the lawn and blew a few soapy orbs. "It's not going in the water, is it? I don't want to kill the fish."

I shook my head. "Naw, you're fine. But case in point, I assumed my brother was lying or mistaken. I based that on my history with him. He was a kid, he lied sometimes. He was almost adorably bad at it so we knew he did it. That was a fact. Also, he was young and Mastermind wasn't the easiest game in the world. More facts. Felt safe to assume he could've made a mistake. All of that said, I actually had no evidence he was wrong. I just assumed he was wrong, based mostly on my fairly egotistical assumption that I was right despite all evidence to the contrary. I'd never made a mistake in reading his feedback, I had to be right, right?"

"Right." She blew another cloud of soap bubbles.

"Except assumption is not evidence. We assumed the game was inherently perfect in its design and wouldn't have allowed for the possibility that both people could use perfect logic and not reveal the correct answer within ten tries. It had to be super-rare, for sure, but not impossible. Neither one of us allowed for a flaw in our basic assumption of how the whole game worked in the first place."

"You think a lot." She laughed and closed the bubbles bottle. "You sound like a lawyer. But I see what you mean. I'm sure I've done it."

"Like, right now in New Orleans, there's this restaurant that got robbed. Except all they took was recipes. The owner says they wanted the recipe for these King Cake beignet things and now he's getting all this free advertising. Patrick immediately jumped to the conclusion it's a publicity stunt. And maybe it is. Maybe that's exactly what happened. But I can't let it go at that like he can, just assume I'm right and move on. I have to assume I don't have enough information to know what happened yet. And if it is a publicity stunt, why? Seems like a lot of work to go through to sell donuts. Why not just give away free samples like everyone else?"

"I could go for a donut."

I laughed. "Right?"

She sat up. "There's still cake. Want some? I'm getting a piece."

"Yeah." I followed her inside and we cut pieces of

parrot cake then quietly headed out.

I settled back onto my large fuchsia cushion "I should be doing sit-ups and stretching and reading the script again."

"Stretch here."

I looked around the yard. "Okay."

"After you eat your cake."

"It's so good."

"I know, right? Why is store-bought sheet cake so good?" She ate another forkful. "What kind of name is Eunoe?"

I licked frosting off my lip. "Greek."

"Greek?"

"It's from *The Iliad*. She was the mother of Hecuba so I think that's Mama Heck's name."

"Another Greek name?"

"Yeah, and Sassy is Cassandra who was Hecuba's daughter."

"Why *The Iliad*?"

Yellow buttercream melted on my tongue. "Not sure. I mean, I think the reason they're all named that way is so they had a through line, breadcrumbs leading them back to their heritage and roots. But I'm not sure what started the whole thing. Eunoe was born a slave so I'm assuming--" I wagged my finger. "There's that word again. Anyway, I assume Eunoe's mother didn't read which leads me to the assumption that she was named by her master. I looked it up. It wasn't uncommon. Then maybe the daughter who ran away from the plantation kept the tradition? Or she told Eunoe where her name was from? Or maybe Eunoe was raised with that story? I don't know. And it's not like there's a lot of records of that kind of stuff. And Sassy changed the tradition with her kids and named them for clues to their birth mother. Which I still think is pretty cool. Azure Taffeta and Violet Chiffon."

"But the one goes by Taffy, right?"

"Yeah, Taffy and Chiffon."

She pressed crumbs against the bottom of her fork. "That whole story was amazing. Laundry basket babies? But you helped them find out who the birth mother was. You might be able to figure this out somehow."

"The other big clue I don't want to over-assume about is Eunoe's mother. Her name was Lottie and the slave on the bill of sale from the Wells Plantation that I found at Bryan Batt's store was for a slave woman named Lottie. Totally possible that they're the same person, but I have no actual evidence of that. But that would definitely mean my family owned Sassy's family. Not awesome."

"And I'm assuming Lottie's not in *The Iliad*?"

"You assume correctly. No Carlotta, no Charlotte."

"That would've been weird."

I laughed. "Right? The haunted chandelier I'm supposed to protect is enough. Anyway, yeah, not in *The Iliad*." I put my plate down and started to stretch my legs.

Sofia licked her fork and smiled. "This is fun. I'm glad you're here."

"Me too. So far, I'm lovin' being in this movie."

She held her fork up. "To *Seven Sisters*."

I lifted my fork to hers. "To Clarence, from whom all good things come."

Chapter 6

Sofia had given me the keys to her car and she took Mark's. The winding canyon road was very familiar, but it was strange being in the hills after so long on the flat basin of New Orleans. The "highest point" in New Orleans was a dirt mound called Monkey Hill that was built in the 1930's so children would know what mountains looked like. Children still rolled down the stubby mound in Audubon Zoo.

I definitely didn't miss L.A. traffic and aggressive, impatient drivers. New Orleans was a live-and-let-live town but aggression was generally frowned upon there.

I drove up to the studio gate and gave the man my name as I dug for my I.D. He made a call on the landline. "Charlotte Reade is here... Okay." He hung up, checked my license and filled in a parking slip. "You're gonna go to Lot J. Do you know that one?" He handed me the slip and I slid it onto the dash.

I looked up and smiled. "It's been a while."

He smiled back. "You know the one to the left of the giant mural?"

"Where the water tank used to be? The fake ocean?"

"Yes. There's another one past that, right before New York street." He smiled. "It's closer to the building."

I smiled wide. "Thanks."

A receptionist directed me to a long hallway lined with photos of movie stars in familiar costumes from favorite movies. A mannequin wearing animal pelts and a bear hat stood near a water fountain. A young woman in silky overalls popped out of a door ahead of me. "Got it. Do we glue gun it or sew it on?"

A voice answered, "Sew it."

"Yeah, it's gotta survive a lot. See ya later." Then she took off down the hall.

I peeked into the office as I passed the open door. An older woman pinned metallic piping onto leggings. Her office was crammed with racks and shoe boxes.

The hallway was long enough to give me time to wonder if I'd missed room 176. I pushed the insecurity away along with the fear that I'd be late. A bright pink piece of paper was printed with big block letters, "7 Sisters."

The room was truly huge. Four women sewed near a row of windows. One area was staged entirely with desks and office equipment. Another featured dressing booths and mirrors. The rest of the cavernous space was row after row of rolling racks of clothes. I got excited in a new way. I was a "Sister" in the next Clarence Pool movie. This was real.

A delicate blonde man in his seventies made an entrance. "Charlotte?" He lifted his diamond-ringed hand as he crossed toward me.

I lifted my hand to meet his. "Mack?"

"Charmed. Follow me."

I joined the other two people following him as we wound our way to the dressing stalls. I assumed I'd be popping behind one of those curtained booths, but they kept walking and I followed them through a door. The large room inside was carpeted. A couch and coffee table sat off to the side. A rack held my options. The center attraction was a carpeted pedestal surrounded by three well-lit mirrors.

Mack put his hand on the rack possessively. "Let's just get an idea of where we're at. We have a few different ideas for the funeral scene and we're still landing on her fighter look."

"I can't wait to see everything!" I pulled a flip book from my bag. "I have a few ideas if you're interested. Just thoughts I had based on the different styles people wear in the Garden District and the French Quarter."

He smiled. He was certainly my elder in this industry. He probably had Oscars. Maybe I shouldn't have mentioned my own ideas yet. But I was a dare-to-fail kinda girl and I loved collaborating on a character's look. During my years as a runway model, I'd learned that wardrobe, make-up and hair could affect everything from my posture to the way I moved. Most importantly, it could affect my attitude and whether I projected fun, sophistication or flirtation on the catwalk.

Mack slowly lifted his hand from the rack and took the book. "Clarence speaks very highly of you. We all loved you in *Make It Straight*. Did you really do those splits?"

"For about forty minutes, over and over. But that was years ago."

He put the book down and held up two different black dresses. He alternated holding them up to me like I was a paper doll. "Can you still do them?"

"The splits? Yeah, but not like back then. Used to be able to invert. Could put my front foot up on a chair and still sit flat on the floor."

He held the bell-sleeved black dress out to me. "Try this first. Be right back." He picked up the book on his way out and I got hopeful he might actually look at it.

I tried on eight funeral dresses, got photographed in each and shared opinions with Mack and the other two wardrobe people. Then Mack picked up my book, flipped through it and pointed at a black linen party dress.

I laughed. "Oh yeah, that's my answer to 'What if she just wore a garden party dress, but in black?'"

"With a black, wide-brimmed straw hat. Bev, grab the navy dress we pulled for the flashback scene."

Bev hurried out of the room as Mack unzipped the Chanel dress I was wearing. Bev returned carrying a flouncy-skirted navy linen garden dress. When I presented myself, we all agreed it was the one. Mack clapped his hands like my mom always did when she was delighted. I felt beautiful and feminine with my waist pulled tight over the fullness of the knee-length skirt.

Mack started tugging on the shoulders. "Alfie, pins." Mack tacked the shoulders higher, then took me in while running his hands under my chest. "Now look, the quicker picker-upper." He smiled at me. "You look like southern Barbie. Wait until I get your hat. I want a brim you could live under. Alfie, ask Cindy if she thinks we can get this to true black or should it stay navy? Maybe we could just go super-dark navy. That might be better. She'll know. Go ask."

They photographed me in wrap dresses in wild prints, flowing maxi-dresses and sexy nighties with furry kitten heels. We tried mini-skirts with go-go boots and flared hip-huggers with platform shoes, clogs and wedges. As I was leaving, Mack handed me the look book. "The crochet bell bottoms, are those yours? You're wearing them in the photo."

I felt proud. "Yeah, I crocheted those."

"I assume you don't have them here?" He shook his head for me. "So, you'll bring them once we land in NOLA." He nodded for me. "Can I copy this photograph?"

"You can have it. I have the original on my computer."

I left feeling so excited that I couldn't knock the silly grin off my face. I was beginning to fall in love with the character of Charlie. She was buoyantly lethal, a terrific hostess and an even better killer.

Sofia and I had no time to go over my amazing fitting. I rushed into cocktail attire and tried to put some order in my curls. Darker eyeliner, richer lipstick, another coat of mascara and out the door.

The cast dinner was at a restaurant with no sign at the entrance. Either you knew it existed or you didn't. The paparazzi clearly knew. I was almost always glad they didn't have much use for me outside of premieres. But tonight, I wouldn't have minded a record of how I felt walking in and joining the cast for the first time.

Clarence stood as I found the group at a private table in the back courtyard. You could almost always eat outside in L.A. I missed that. Clarence's arms

71

flew wide and I went in for a hug. "Guys, this is Charlotte Reade – Charlie, the cool glass of southern sweet tea. Charlotte, I think you know Ra."

I turned and screamed. "Ra!" I ran and hugged my longtime friend, one of the many lost in the move south.

Ra let out a low-voiced chuckle. "Keep a little in reserve. It's gonna be a long shoot."

I laughed and clenched him again then pulled away. "I'm just so glad you're in this. Who are you?"

"Easy, the retired fighter slash pool hall owner."

I gasped. "Wait, don't we have a scene together?"

He laughed his familiar low laugh again. "We'll talk about it later. Meet everyone."

"Right! Of course." I turned to the table and took in all the celebrity faces. Most needed no introduction. Some I'd been watching all my life. It was often like this for me. I'd spent most of my career surrounded by household names and award winners. I should've probably felt intimidated, but I was always too busy feeling privileged to work with such talented pros and get the opportunity to learn from the best. "Wait! before I meet everyone, I have to announce that Clarence has just done the impossible." I smiled at him and gave Ra a presentational arm flourish. "You totally surprised me." I turned back to the table. "Sorry, but that was a long time coming. I'm Charlotte." I already felt liked I'd talked too much, made too big a deal of myself.

"Street Queen" Kimani would be played by Oscar nominee and rap artist, Layla. Explosives expert Tanisha was Brooklyn Sutter, the Golden Globe winning star of some hit shows I'd never seen. Seated next to her was Aliyah Thomas who would be playing planner and poisoner, Ladonna. I'd have to look her up later.

Ji was cast older than I'd thought. I was glad not to be the only woman over forty at the table. Clarence explained that Kicho was huge in Japan. Apparently she was a beloved actor and a chainsaw juggler. Suddenly my splits didn't seem so special.

Engineering archer and equestrian, Ashley, was perfectly cast with multi-award-winner and indie-comedy favorite, Madison Frye. Jenna the gymnast-fencer would be up-and-coming it-girl, Astrid Fuller. Many of my scenes would be with them.

Mega-star Graham Paisley would play the murderer we hunt down along with his son, aging heartthrob Aaron Roberts. Grown-child-actor Jamal Harper would be Tanisha's Love interest and Ra would be Easy, the only man we could trust.

I couldn't believe Ra and I would finally get to work on the same project. We'd started out together back in the early 90's. We'd watched each other move up the ladder, get knocked down, then move up again. We believed in each other.

A steady flow of sushi arrived at the table as Clarence dropped fun factoids about many of us. He kept the conversation light, fast and illuminating. There was a big discussion about paparazzi and how cell phone cameras were changing everything. Many people at the table felt a new level of fear now that any random moment could be memorialized. That said, it was apparent that some of the people at the table envied the fame of others. Nothing was ever enough in this town. Not all of us hungered for the adoration of tabloid fans but even the coolest of us wanted to be relevant. Clarence could give us that. It made him special. It meant he could have almost any actor he wanted in almost any part in any of his movies. This time, we were those actors. It was fairly mind blowing.

The chef came to the table and we showered him with compliments. When the chattering lulled, I decided to take a shot. "Chef, have you ever heard of a recipe black market?"

Our table looked at me quizzically. The chef thought for a moment. "Like a criminal thing?"

"I guess." I was beginning to feel self conscious about stealing focus for something small and personal again.

"I know of people stealing recipes, if that's what you mean. Knew a guy in Chicago, his whole concept was jacked by some guy. Took the recipes and ideas to a joint he went with less than a mile away. My friend's still suing the guy."

Clarence laughed. "That's not black market, that's just plain old copycatting."

Everyone laughed. The chef nodded. "Yeah, I don't know about a black market. I did sell a recipe once when I was starting out. I'd won a contest in Jersey and sold the recipe to this swank joint where I'd dreamed of being even a busboy. Didn't really think it through about the recipe being worth money, you know, ongoingly. Got 300 bucks for it and felt lucky at the time. Should've probably hung onto it for my first menu offering."

I smiled. "Did they end up hiring you?"

The chef shook his head. "It was a legacy place.

Had to wait for someone to retire or die. I'd already moved to L.A. long before they had an opening."

Clarence lifted his saki cup. "Their loss." The table agreed and toasted along with him.

Maybe there was no recipe black market. I couldn't imagine how it would work, where the profits would come from. If you could just outright buy a recipe for a few hundred bucks, it hardly seemed worth it for there to be a criminal element involved.

Maybe there was no black market but that chef-jacket guy in the street sold recipes directly to a restaurant. Chef-jacket guy made it sound like that was absurd, called it "ridiculous." But, clearly there were circumstances where chefs sold recipes and there were places that would buy them. Maybe the chef-jacket guy had been caught selling recipes. Maybe the thief of the beignet recipe stole it to sell it. Maybe the same guy was involved. New Orleans was a pretty-small big city. It was more likely that one guy did two similar crimes than that there would be two different recipe thieves among our citizenry. Maybe chef-jacket guy was a mass recipe thief.

Ra and Clarence laughed, shaking me from my puzzling. Clarence pointed my way. "Remember that, Charlotte? You were dating that disappointing guy?"

Though I wasn't quite sure what topic we were on, I joined the laughter. "You're gonna have to narrow it down for me, Clarence." Ra laughed. He'd sat up with me several times over the years, helping me sift through confusing and offensive behavior from guys I assumed had wanted to impress me.

Clarence ramped up. "The one who had a girl

waiting in the car the whole time he was hanging out at your house once?"

"Oh Lordy. I forgot all about that guy."

Graham clarified. "He had a girl waiting in the car while he was at your house?"

Layla laughed. "Tha's messed up. He showed his side piece where you live? Tha's messed up."

I was glad to finally be interesting. "Honestly, I don't think she even knew. He had to have lied to her. At some point, he said he had candies for me and went out to his car for a while. Like a longish while. Then he came back with nothing but excuses over misplaced candy. After he left, it was my neighbor who asked why there was a woman sitting in front of the house or I wouldn't have known either."

Kicho looked confused. "So he left her in the car like a dog?"

Aaron laughed. "Did he at least crack a window?"

Then everyone laughed. It used to quietly hurt inside when I'd use my ridiculous dating life to entertain others. Now, I quietly smiled inside thinking of my wonderful boyfriend missing me. I'd never survived shooting a movie without it breaking up whatever attempt at a relationship I was involved in at the time – even if I only worked a day. This would be my longest shoot ever but I was doing a pretty good job of not being worried, of waiting for an actual problem to show up before I freaked out.

Kicho folded her napkin and placed it on the table. "What is New Orleans like? You live there, yes?"

My new favorite topic. "Yes. It's amazing. Incredible food and music and my favorite people in the world."

Clarence shot me a look. "Um..."

I smiled at him. "Top ten, Clarence. You'll always be one of my favorite people. But, I hope y'all get time to experience some of it. There's music everywhere and a lot of it's free. There's festivals all the time and every Sunday, there's a parade with brass bands and dancing in the streets."

Aaron waved his hand dismissively. "That's too much parading. If it's all the time, it's not special anymore."

I looked him in the eye and smiled. "Then only go once." I turned to Ra for reassurance. "It builds community, brings people together. It's like a rolling block party."

Aaron laughed to himself. "Doesn't seem to have helped the crime rate."

I didn't like having to defend the indefensible. "Yeah, it's a city. Cities have crime."

Ra came to my rescue. "Do you have recommendations for where to eat?"

"Sure. I have a blog with all my favorite stuff listed. Everything from best gumbo to my favorite smell."

"Smell?" Astrid laughed. "What is it?"

"Sweet olive. It's a tree that blooms a bunch of times throughout the year and it fills the air with this thick perfume of like a honeysuckle smell mixed with something citrus."

No one asked the name of my blog as Clarence rose prompting our goodbyes. L.A. had a way of bringing back high school memories of cool-kid tables. Unlike back in school I often had a seat at the cool table in L.A., but I rarely felt like my position was secure.

People waited for their cars inside, avoiding the paparazzi – or perhaps building the anticipation.

Ra walked me to the metered spot I'd found down the street. "Is it hard to be back?"

I hugged him. "It's a good reminder."

Chapter 7

Patrick called while I was shoving my script into a purse. He wanted to know how the dinner had gone. I still felt insecure about some of the evening but Patrick reminded me Clarence had written Charlie with me in mind and that most of the other actors were cast after the script was written. Patrick had a way of making me own my confidence and accomplishments. "Did that other thing call? The audition you went to after Galatoire's."

I laughed. "They don't usually call if you don't get the part. It's like after bad date. But it's only been a few days. If it were TV, I'd say it's over, but it's a movie so it could take months to hear from them if I got it."

"Today's the table read?"

"Yeah. I'm nervous."

He chuckled. "You're gonna be fine. You're gonna be amazing."

"I'm being serious. I don't usually get to do table reads so I don't know if I'm any good at them. I'm not even entirely sure what that means, to be 'good at table reads.' Usually if the movie has a big enough budget to have a table read, my part is so small that they let someone else read it. Either someone already there or they have someone who just reads all the small parts." I took a breath but my nerves didn't settle. "A couple of the smaller budget movies had table reads, but then I was usually one of the most experienced actors at the table so it wasn't like I was gonna learn a lot there. Ugh. I just wish I worked more consistently so I could be more in shape when I get work. It's like I have to shake the rust off and remember how I do this each time. If I worked all the time, I would have better work habits and a better understanding of what's expected at the dang table read."

Patrick's voice got low and calm. "You are a pro. And your worst is better than a lot of people's best. You came by your seat at that table honestly."

I thought about that, then sighed. "Thank you." I felt supported. Then I felt a wave of missing him crash through me. I was still settling into the idea of letting myself need someone, but it was beautiful and terrifying to realize how important I'd let Patrick become.

Sofia and I drove separately to Mel's on Sunset. So "L.A." My regular valet wasn't there so I hoped the place hadn't changed too much. My table on the patio was empty, thank goodness. It was a larger, round table and there were plenty of two-seaters available but I felt like I deserved the table anyway, for old time's sake. Janet spotted us through the glass wall, jolted, smiled and waved vigorously. We chose the chairs against the stone wall so we could both face the car show rolling by on Sunset Plaza – Ferraris, McLarens and my preference – old muscle cars made cherry.

Janet came out holding glasses of Diet Coke and iced tea for us. "Hey! Oh hey! You're back!"

I got up and hugged her, careful not to knock her 50's-style paper hat. "Just for a minute. But you know we had to come here."

Janet yelled at the busboy as he came out carrying a grey plastic tub for dishes. "José, look!"

José smiled and joined us. "Good to see you. Welcome back."

I smiled. "Thanks. You look good. Are you good?"

He nodded. "Very good." He walked away as Janet caught up with us a little then took our order, or rather, confirmed our usual order. I was looking forward to the warm, comforting tuna melt.

Sofia smiled. "Is it really different being back or do you feel like you're just back in it again?"

"With you, I always feel like we just pick up wherever we left off, you know? It's been that way since high school, and we've gone years without even being in touch. But yeah, it's different being back. I brought my mom here to Mel's once. We'd gone to the gas station where everyone says hi to me and the Trader Joe's where they know me and she said it was amazing how I'd made this giant city into a small town for myself. But in New Orleans, people just say hi to each other. It's not special and it doesn't take some monumental effort on my part. People just seem to agree on making eye contact and greeting each other."

"Sounds like Italy." Sofia had lived in Italy for years and still visited family there annually.

"You'd love it. It's a lot like Italy. And the food is insane."

Sofia's face changed. "Don't look, but look to

your right."

Two guys in their late twenties headed our way on the sidewalk. The tall, lanky one was dressed entirely in black. His skinny pants were tucked into spiked Goth boots. His deliberately messy hair was dyed black and stuck out in pieces around the giant holes in his ears plugged with black rings. Tattoos ran up his neck under his studded dog collar. He completed the high-maintenance attempt at appearing to not care with smudged guyliner. The shorter guy next to him was wearing almost the exact same ensemble, right down to the giant ear holes and neck tattoos. After they passed, we both laughed quietly.

Sofia shook her head. "So much effort to look different and then they look exactly the same kind of odd. They wanted to be different in exactly the same way."

"That's one thing that's really different there. In New Orleans, people value community, not conformity. But it ends up leading to everyone dressing exactly how they want to. I mean, people want to look good, but you don't get extra points for the latest, most expensive stuff. I don't think most people there would know a Prada bag if Ruth Buzzi was hitting them over the head with it. There's this one store, Trashy Diva, that sells dresses that make every woman look amazing so maybe three women will show up to an event in the same dress and they'll end up bonding over it. And maybe the dress is from four years ago and no one cares."

She laughed. "That was something I decided not to adjust to when I moved here. I know people judge me but I'm not going to spend all my money on clothes. And I don't want Nia growing up thinking it matters if she can afford Jimmy Choos or whatever. It's too expensive here to spend all your money on stuff that's just going to be considered out of style next year."

I laughed. "Next season. In New Orleans, you can assume you'll run into people everywhere you go, just like it was for me here, but you can also assume they're not judging you for throwing your hair in a chip clip or getting groceries with paint on your clothes or whatever."

"But like, who cares? Right?"

"Exactly."

Janet brought our food and we enjoyed some of the few things I missed about L.A. – Sofia, Mel's comfort food, eating outside without bugs or weather and spending a couple hours at lunch. Then I headed into the Valley to face the table read.

Graham and Aliyah were smoking outside and greeted me as I headed into the office building. "On the left. Follow the signs."

Brooklyn and Aaron were laughing near the restrooms. I suddenly remembered they'd both been in *To Name A Few* when she was just starting out. I was glad Ra would be at the table today. My loyal friend Clarence would be there as well, but now he was my boss.

A stack of scripts sat at one end of the long conference table. I couldn't imagine coming here without a prepared script, but producers might be here as well. Most of the cast was already inside but no one had taken a seat. I wasn't sure what to do with my purse. That's how I knew I was feeling insecure, which almost always meant I felt underprepared. In this line of work I should've probably been more vain and insecure about my looks, but I liked the genetic hand I'd been dealt. The height and strawberry hair were a rough ride as a kid and worse as a teen, but they'd also given me the modeling work that helped pay for my degrees. That security in my looks left me free to panic over my work.

I hugged Clarence. "I'm so excited to be doing this together. Thank you so much for including me."

He smiled warmly and pulled me into his chest again. "This is exactly what I wanted." Then he pushed me to arms length. "You got the part!"

I laughed. "I got the part!"

Ra arrived just as we were taking our seats so we just waved to each other. I'd been hoping to ask him for pointers on doing the reading. Thwarted. I reminded myself that my character didn't show up for a little while so I'd have time to observe.

Hud rushed in and shot me a smile as he took a seat near the window. I sat between Madison and Astrid and noticed others grouped up as well. It was kind of remarkable to see more women than men at a reading. It was rare to see more than a love interest and two or three supporting females sitting between dozens of men. Three of the producers sitting in chairs near the window were women as well. I felt suddenly empowered. I felt safety in numbers. I couldn't help but wonder if this was how men in my industry felt all the time.

Clarence quieted the room. "Okay, okay, okay, let's get down to it. Welcome everyone. We're just going to go through it all. It's a long one so we're going to take a break after page 103. Turn off your phones or face my wrath."

A bunch of people fumbled for their phones. I double-checked mine.

"Ra, can you take the male small parts and uh... Aliyah, you do the women. Okay. *Seven Sisters*, a Clarence Pool flick. Interior, funeral home, day. A distinguished gentleman is laid out in a plushly-lined black casket. Hands place a wreath on an easel. A card reads, 'Your beloved daughter, Ji.' We pull back to see a cluster of seven wreaths in seven different floral selections – red roses, Gerber daisies, lilies, dahlias, spider mums, pink roses and peonies. We follow the funeral director back out to the lobby. His wife adjusts a black bow in her black beehive."

Aliyah took her cue. "Be arrivin' any minute. Check the front door lock. Don't prop it. Too hot to be air conditionin' the world today."

Clarence continued. "The funeral director shuffles to the front door and pushes it open, flooding the room with sunlight. Nearly blotted out by glow, he turns to his wife."

Ra used his own deep, strong voice. "It's open." He lowered his volume. "I've never forgotten. Not one time."

Clarence laughed a little. I loved watching his enthusiasm. It always reminded me how much I loved making movies. "He turns back as classic blonde beauty Ashley emerges from the light, black netting obscuring her well-bred face."

Madison had notes all over her script. I noticed a few of the actors had the scripts from the stack including Aliyah, Graham, Aaron and Jamal. It didn't seem to affect their performances. Everyone was great. Layla was downright riveting. It was way too early to think these thoughts and she was at a demographic disadvantage, but maybe Layla would finally get her richly deserved Oscar.

During the break, I invited Ra to Sofia's open house and we made lunch plans before he peeled off to visit with Clarence. I thought of joining the loud, laughing group of stars and producers but got pulled instead to Kicho standing off to the side. "This is your first time in New Orleans?"

She smiled and pushed her bangs out of the way. "Yes, but Hud sent me the link to your blog and it seems to be an amazing place. Very rich culture."

"I'm gonna to take that as quite the compliment comin' from someone who's from Japan."

She laughed a shy laugh. "Yes. I think so. I liked it very much, your blog. I want to have grits at Camellia Grill."

I laughed. "Yes. Do that. Japan's not exactly known for its corn cuisine."

Kicho laughed then nodded toward the group dispersing. "Looks like we work again."

"Let me know if you need any recommendations or anything." I grabbed a card from my purse and handed it to her then took my seat. I had a lot more to do in the second half of the reading. Some people were fading. Graham was nodding-off, bored, for about half an hour. The perils of playing the corpse.

By the end, I felt like we'd all accomplished something together, done something rare together. We were a group now. This movie would connect us forever. But that didn't mean any of us would stay in touch. I'd learned that long ago – no matter how many times someone proclaimed, "I'll call you."

I was glad to be ending my lengthy day surrounded by longtime friends at Sofia's. She was dumping different snacks into colorful bowls to set out on the bar separating the kitchen from the dining area. "Oh hey! How'd it go?"

"It was good." I grabbed a cracker. "Kicho seemed nice., the one from Japan. And Layla was freakin' amazing. I felt like I shoulda paid to watch her."

"You know who I want to know about. How was Graham?"

I laughed. "Bored. I don't think he's used to havin' to be quiet for so long at a reading. He's been as star since we were born."

She pointed to the fridge with a roll of crackers. "Your accent's back. The cheeses are in there if you want to get them out."

"Yeah, the accent comes and goes. Both the southern and the newscaster-D.C. accents are mine but it's kinda weird how often I sound like my mother now." I stacked a brie, a sharp cheddar, a Gouda and a Stilton with dried apricots and brought them over to the counter to arrange on a platter. The first wrapper was hard to pull open. "It's beginning to hit me that I'm in this movie."

Sofia smiled. "It's pretty amazing, right? But I'm glad. It seems right. It means he meant all those nice things he said about your work over the years."

"I always took him at his word, but you're right. He put his money where his mouth is."

The door opened and Sherry walked in blowing a

ash-blonde curl from her lip. "Yoo hoo! The door was open. Oh hey! Hey!" She hurried across the living area for hugs.

Someone knocked and I ran to answer it. "Sofia, we should put a sign up in case we're all in the back."

Sherry looked around. "Where's paper? I'll do it."

The Dude had his arm around a woman about my age. I gave him a big hug and led him out to the backyard as Sherry helped Sofia finish with the snacks.

I motioned to the chairs around the fire pit. "We're gonna end up out here so y'all can have first choice of seats if you want."

The Dude got down on his knees and ran his hand over the grass. "Is this fake?"

"Pretty neat, huh? And no bugs. I'm not usually a fan but this ain't your daddy's Astroturf."

He rolled over onto his back and looked up at the sky. His mop of grey curls tangled into the lawn. "This is amazing. I'm just going to sit on this all night."

And he did. When the cold air rolled into the canyon, Sofia wrapped him in Nia's pink Disney Princess sleeping bag. The Dude never seemed to care whether anyone thought he was ridiculous – which made him unpredictable in the best possible way. It was easy to see why the Coen Brothers had been inspired to write a movie character based on him.

About a dozen more people joined us including my old manager, Marilyn, and eventually Ra. It was the perfect sized group to be able to visit with everyone at some point. A few of my friends weren't very good at long distance relationships. I could feel the distance they were keeping between us even as they spent the evening reconnecting.

Finally The Dude asked the question many of them wanted to know, "So who's this Patrick guy? How'd you meet?"

Sofia laughed. "At a funeral. She finally found the guy you couldn't scare off with death talk."

I laughed at our private joke. "It's true." I realized it might take too long to explain why we were both at the funeral for a street character so I skipped that part. "We went out for coffee a bunch of times, for a few weeks. Then he took me on a proper date and courted me old school, just like I always wanted and couldn't find here. I even had people here tell me I was ridiculous for thinkin' anyone did that anymore."

Sherry giggled. "You have to tell us one thing that tells us who he is as a person."

The Dude patted her leg from his prone position on the grass. "Good one."

"Okay, one thing. I can tell you something that told me who I was dealing with. We'd just had our first date and it was magical. I mean, like even when things went wrong, they went wrong in that perfect, fun, memorable way. So, it's the end of this amazing night and we're standin' on the sidewalk under this giant live oak on St. Charles. Very romantic. And he's been patiently waiting to kiss me for like a month. He puts his arm around my waist and finally goes for the kiss and it's perfect. Like perfect perfect. And a streetcar rolls past and I guess it caught his attention 'cause the next thing I know he's looking at me with this sort of desperate expression and says, 'I'm so sorry but I have to do this.' So he runs across the street and I see this man, really drunk, tryin' to get into his car. He's dropping the keys, pickin' 'em up, dropping them again, a complete mess. Patrick goes and talks to him, takes his keys and sits with him on the curb. Then I see him take the guy's phone and call someone. So I finally go and join them and Patrick feels terrible. He's sure he's blown it with me, abandoning the perfect kiss for some drunk guy. But all I could see was a guy who was willing to put a stranger's needs above his own. It'd been a long time since I'd met a guy who thought like that. He's a giver, a protector. He protects the French Quarter for a living."

The Dude raised his beer. "Amen! I'm all for that. I love the Quarter. Lots of memories there. But nothing could've made me stop kissing you. I'd've let that guy go and hoped for the best."

I laughed. "No you wouldn't. You might've let it go on longer but that guy was death on wheels."

He adjusted his puffy pink shawl/sleeping bag. "I don't know."

Sherry smiled. "He sounds great."

Surrounded by the people who'd gotten me through my time in L.A., I suddenly missed Patrick. "He is."

Chapter 8

Though it was hard saying goodbye to Sofia, I was excited to get back home and go apartment hunting with Patrick. Not only could we find a solution to our storage issue, we might get to live out a fantasy we discovered we had in common. It was Patrick who suggested that we look for a weekend place in the French Quarter. Both of us had always wanted to live in the Quarter but neither of us was a kid anymore, willing to deal with parking issues in a tourist trap every day or music and noisy drunks until the wee hours every night. I crossed my fingers we could find a place we liked that was cheap enough to allow a sometimes-working actor and a non-profit worker to pull off an uptown-downtown life. There was something very romantic about carrying on a lifestyle as old as the Garden District.

Patrick had spent my time in L.A. searching for potential spots and securing appointments to see them. He'd scheduled four. The first place was down a long narrow pathway, up a rickety flight of stairs then down a long wooden balcony, slanted to keep rain from collecting. A kind, older woman opened the door and it was clear the space was too tiny before we even walked inside. We politely followed her through the unit then to the courtyard. Shaded by giant tropical fronds, the patio was idyllic, but uncollared, unkempt cats wandered lazily on tables and sunned themselves on chaises. Patrick bristled. The kind woman explained that the cats belonged to everyone and that everyone fed them. Patrick was the best man I'd ever met but he didn't share my love for cats. That said, neither of us wanted a yard full of alley cats. We thanked the woman and walked around the corner before Patrick took out the list. He crossed the top address off with no discussion.

A man in ivory linen pants gave us a once-over then took us up another long flight of stairs to an attic unit. He put key after key into the lock to no avail. I noticed the other door on the landing and wondered if we were at the right one, but waited quietly. The door finally opened from the inside and an irritated tenant asked us what we wanted. I tried to see past him into his place but he shut the door after a round of apologies.

The landlord tried the other door and, once again, we knew before we even walked in that the sharply slanting ceilings weren't going to work. I stepped inside the shower and wasn't able to straighten my neck without hitting my head. Patrick didn't stand a chance.

The next place was at a VooDoo shop and museum. John, the big man behind the desk, welcomed us then warned, "The building has snakes."

I'd been around too long to bite right away. John elaborated that there were a couple of snakes around and he hoped we weren't afraid of snakes.

Patrick smiled. "I gotta tell you, your sales pitch could use some refining."

John pulled a crease-worn paper bag from a shelf and took out some photos. The first few were of John with a giant yellow snake laying across his shoulders like a boa (ah, so that's where those feathery confections got their name). He pulled out more photos of himself with a big, brown boa while I tried to remember aloud the name of the snake the yellow boa resembled from *From Dusk 'Til Dawn*. Bananas? Lemon? "It looks like that snake in the movie--"

John beamed. "*Dusk 'Til Dawn*. That's my baby. Danced with Salma Hayek."

I decided to believe him. As he and Patrick chatted about the snakes' acting careers, I took in the small cloth dolls, colorful hand poured candles and images of Marie Laveau, the Voodoo Queen who passed in 1881 but whose face adorned many local walls. Four tourists payed the five dollar fee to enter a curtained door that I'd originally thought led to a small photo booth.

A petite woman entered carrying two cold beverages. "I'm back."

There must've been an alley entrance to the apartment but John led us through the curtain and into the fairly roomy museum hidden behind it. Dimly lit in green and blue, the walls and cabinets were packed with gris gris, paintings and bones – both human and animal.

The apartment was at the end of a beautiful courtyard with bicycles parked beneath a balcony. The door opened to a large living area with high ceilings and a giant window facing the courtyard. Though it filled the room with light, I immediately thought about privacy and having to be aware of what

I wore around the house. As someone who worked out of my home, I could be fairly careless about my house clothes. The floors were visibly wonky. I wasn't sure how furniture was supposed to work with all the bumps and waves in the linoleum tiles. I was excited to see the private patio but it was filled with cinder blocks, a wheelbarrow and other construction materials. John shut the door. "Should be done workin' on that in a month or so."

The bedroom was impractically laid out, but it had charm. No closets, but charm.

John led us back out to the sidewalk and we thanked him then headed toward Royal Street. I waited until we were out of earshot. "That place had its charms."

Patrick chuckled. "Stories would abound. It wasn't bad but did you notice the floor?"

I laughed. "I think it'd be impossible not to."

"We could ride our couch like a seesaw."

I laughed. "I still have too much PTSD from the '94 quake to handle furniture that jiggles, but it was a lot of space and the whole VooDoo museum, snake-guy situation is definitely an only-in-New-Orleans thing."

He took my hand. "I saved the best for last. This is gonna be the one. You'll see."

The last place was on the "velvet line," the street that marked the gay section of town. We were early so we wandered into a bar where absolutely no one cared to hit on me. Unlike the perfectly manicured, plucked and buff gay men I was used to in L.A., this bar was full of guys that reminded me of Homer Simpson and Joe the Plumber.

At the end of the street was the rust-stained white metal archway of Armstrong Park. Before the Civil War, most masters gave their slaves Sunday off and many would go to barter goods and play drums in Congo Square. The drummers' traditions came from all over Africa and various island cultures. Those Sunday drum circles, where people improvised and blended their various cultures without losing their individual flavors, were the beginnings of jazz. Armstrong Park was built around Congo Square to preserve "The Birthplace of Jazz." Sadly, the gates were chained shut after Nagin's botched revitalization project.

Wearing a Saints cap, the property manager sat on the stoop. I loved the idea of sitting on a stoop watching the colorful world of the French Quarter going by. As soon as the door opened, I felt like Goldilocks nestling into the perfect-sized bed. The ceilings in the shotgun house were high, the floors were beautiful, dark wood and the shower was tall enough for Kareem Abdul-Jabbar.

Back on the sidewalk, Patrick shook hands with the property manager who handed him a card. "I'll be honest with you, this is the best place on the market at this price so I've got a lot of people interested." We couldn't argue his point. "I'm asking anyone who's serious to email me a short essay about why you want to live in the Quarter. I hope you understand, I'm in a position to do right by our neighbors and find the right tenants for this place."

Patrick nodded. "Yes sir. I'll get that to you by tomorrow morning."

A tour group walked past. A few people stopped

to snap a photo of a mule-drawn carriage giving another tour. As they moved on, I spotted Christine Miller guiding the group. I'd been on her *Brothels, Bordellos and Ladies of the Night* tour when I discovered the silver flask with the Wells Plantation symbol stamped into the bottom. She turned before I could wave.

Patrick and I walked away quietly until we rounded the corner. Patrick stopped and looked at me. "I told you it was the one. I'll write the essay tonight."

"I loved it. It's perfect. No closets, but perfect. Do you want help with the essay?"

"I'm good."

Of course he was. He made a living making sure people understood the value of this neighborhood. He took my hand. "You wanna grab a bite before we head uptown?"

"Sure. Oh my gosh, guess where Ra and I are eating tomorrow. No don't. You'll never get it. 504Ever, the recipe robbery place."

He pulled away. "Whoa. How'd that happen?"

"That's what he picked. Someone told him it was great. He's all excited to try a King-Yay!"

"Good, now I don't have to go to satisfy your curiosity. You can have a bite of his."

I laughed. "I can bring one home for you."

"King Cake in August? I'll pass."

I laughed some more. "You love sweets."

"There's nothing someone who makes out-of-season King Cake whatevers can offer me."

"Purist."

He tapped the brim of his fine straw fedora. "At your service."

"Do you think it was an inside job? The robbery?"

"I honestly can't imagine anyone else wanting their recipes enough to steal them. It's a stupid crime. Not worth the trouble. Don't get me wrong, I've seen people here steal everything from shoes at the gym to potted plants off a front porch. But those are useful things. I get why they were stolen. What's the point of stealing recipes for anything, much less some donut no local chef would touch?"

"What if the owner wanted the recipes stolen?"

Patrick checked the time on his phone. "That's what I've been saying. Publicity stunt. What time's the premiere?"

"Seven, but we have to do the red carpet."

He stopped suddenly. "I told you before, Charlotte, if you love me at all, you won't ask me to be in pictures."

I was still getting used to being with a guy who didn't want anything to do with the spotlight. I kissed him. "That's fine. I'm used to doin' it alone. Honestly, it's easier." I wasn't lying.

Patrick led me past a brass band playing on a sidewalk. I raised my voice over *When the Saints Go Marching In*. "So, you think the owner broke in himself?"

"Or got someone else to do it."

"I heard this guy say he knew about the black market and the guy he was arguing with was like, 'What chef would buy them?' and the accuser guy listed some ideas like a greedy one, an ambitious one, an out-of-town one or a desperate one. He seemed very certain people stole recipes and chefs bought them somehow. Maybe it's a thing and we just don't know about it, a subculture like the candy cars."

"The candy cars are cool." He opened the door to Palace Cafe.

"I know, right? But what if someone really did steal all the recipes, because it kinda reminds me of when an agent leaves their agency and takes clients with them. There's even been times when an agent will hijack a roster and open their own agency. What if the chef took them so he could open his own place?"

"Why don't you ask him tomorrow?"

I turned my chin up. "Maybe I will."

We laughed, ate and headed home to change into fancier clothes. I'd shot a bunch of movies since moving south but this was the first one that would have its premiere in town. I didn't bother buying anything new to wear. One of the advantages of moving was that all of my once-worn photo-ready dresses had never been seen here.

Bryan Batt was smiling for the five cameras as we walked up to the theatre. I shot Patrick a smile. "Are you sure you don't wanna try it? It's a super short carpet. Five minutes at the most. I've done forty-five minute ones. This is a piece of cake."

"It looks horrifying."

I looked at the five locals, one with a phone for a camera, and laughed. "Try this little one and if you hate it, I'll never ask again."

Trevor, Bryan's stunt double, walked up and gave me a big hug. "Long time, no see. You look beautiful as always." He extended his hand to Patrick. "Trevor."

I left them talking as Wendy from the wardrobe

department arrived. "Hey!"

We hugged and chatted about getting together for lunch someday as Ethan and Todd, the producer and director, walked up. Ethan's arms flew wide. "It's my happy ending girl. Come on. Photos."

Wendy stepped aside as we formed a group shot around Ethan and Todd. After we'd shot a few, Ethan waved to Wendy and Trevor. "Come on, get in one."

I saw Trevor trying to get Patrick onto the carpet. Ethan called out as they delayed the next pose, "Who's that? Get in the shot."

Trevor smiled. "Charlotte's guy, Patrick."

Ethan waved his arm at them. "Get in, Patrick. Group shot."

Patrick pushed his hands into his pockets. "That's okay." I gave him a pleading smile and he headed to my side of the group and put his arms around me and Wendy.

The whole thing took about two minutes and I was happy Patrick had finally gotten a chance to see it wasn't that big of a deal. He took my hand as we walked into the theatre and whispered into my ear. "Please don't ever ask me to do that again."

I checked his expression and he was definitely not kidding. I'd heard of being camera shy, but my handsome hunk of a man seemed genuinely rattled by the experience. I don't think I really understood how serious he'd been all day until that moment. Then I felt terrible that I'd pushed him so far out of his comfort zone when he knew himself better than I'd realized. I was so grateful he wasn't the kind of person who was just using me to go on the Hollywood-ride that it hadn't occurred to me that he might genuinely want nothing to do with showbiz – that it wasn't a perk but a liability he had to see past. "I won't. I promise."

Ethan and Todd got up and gave speeches then prompted Bryan and a few of the other stars to stand for applause. As I stood, I looked down at Patrick's face and saw that he was perfectly content applauding me.

Dancing Man 504 led the Treme Brass Band into the theatre. Uncle Lionel bumped-and-grinded through a bass drum solo that got us all on our feet. Though he had Don Knotts' slight build and around eighty years of character written into his face, Uncle Lionel was sexy-as-heck in his black suit and cap. He basically turned his giant drum into an extension of his manhood and taunted us all with it's thrusts.

In L.A., nobody danced at premieres. If there was live music, it was at the after party. I loved that New Orleans took a more life-is-uncertain-eat-dessert-first approach to living.

My small part was edited to even smaller, but both Mom and my niece, Julia, made the cut as background actors so I took it all in stride. I might still have to do red carpets alone but the man sitting next to me loved me and didn't choose me because of my fancy friends, party invites and photo ops. The premiere was more fun with him there and the bummer of having scenes cut from the film bounced right off my ego. Maybe it was good I'd had so many bad dating experiences. It gave me a rare appreciation for how good life could be when shared with someone wonderful.

Chapter 9

I didn't usually have to get an insurance physical before working but they weren't much of an inconvenience. Lots of forms, then a short interview along with blood pressure, weight, that sort of thing. Ra had scheduled his appointment near mine so that we could carpool across town to 504Ever.

When we arrived at the restaurant, the shattered window in the door had been replaced and an "Open" sign hung behind new frosted glass. The place was fairly packed with t-shirt-wearing tourists and a youngish crowd clothed in a hodge-podge of styles I'd worn in their original decades.

A frame on the hostess stand displayed the restaurant's recent nomination in *Gambit Weekly*'s "Best of New Orleans" contest. An arrow urged us to "Vote!" Another frame held a printout of their website, Facebook and Twitter addresses with the command, "Follow us!"

The hostess was clearly a fan of Ra. She couldn't stop touching her smoothed brown locks. Ra's body-like-Arnold-with-a-Denzel-face looks always got a lot of attention.

The menu was a list of twists on local favorites. The Deconstructed Jambalaya looked particularly egregious. I went with the Bourbon Shrimp & Grits and hoped for the best.

Ra handed the waitress our menus and smiled at me. "You seem really happy."

I smiled back. "I am. Like, I'm almost scared to be this happy. I'm not used to havin' this much to lose. I was already dealing with the reality that there could always be another Katrina around the corner. Nothing's changed. The levees could definitely breach again and wash away everything I care about. Then I met Patrick and it's like there's this person out in the big, bad world that's so critical to my life and it scares me to think of anything ever happening to him."

"I hear ya. Trust me, I got kids."

"Right. Of course."

He chuckled a little. "It's good. Having it so good that you're afraid to lose it is good. Remember all those times you were sad because you never knew if you'd find a guy who could out-man you? Done."

I smiled wide.

His voice went even deeper. "I'm just glad that town didn't break you. Got worried about you those last few years. Seemed like you got a new kind of unhappy."

"I think it was the same kind but with the added relentlessness of it not changing for too many years in a row. I'm not happy Sassy died, but I'm glad her funeral brought me here. I'd always planned to retire here but after spending the holidays with my family and the Saints winning the Super Bowl during Mardi Gras, I just--"

"What do they say?" He slapped the table. "Who Dat!"

Someone inside the kitchen yelled, "Who Dat!" I

turned to look through the window separating their grills from our dining area. Three guys in aprons hustled over chopping blocks and boiling pots. One had a mass of ratty blonde dreads piled high under a shower cap and another disposable shower cap strung from ear to ear over his beard. Seemed like an awful lot of hair for a chef.

Ra took a sip of ice water. "I'm just glad you got out before the place got to you."

"But you're good?"

He chuckled. "Learnin' who my friends are. Maybe things are different on the way down but on the way up – turns out anyone'll kick it with you when you've got nothin' goin' on, but it gets weird once your name's on the poster."

"Yeah, but it's a good problem to have so it's hard to find anyone who'll throw you a pity party." I threw him a warm smile. "Hey, I didn't know Hud knew Clarence. Did you?"

"They knew each other back when they were starting out, like us, but only like acquaintances. Hud said that at some party, they'd dreamed up this movie idea about deadly sisters who were raised by different mothers."

"Seriously?"

"Years go by. One day, Clarence is watching a Hong Kong movie about sisters and he remembers the idea they came up with." He tilted his head and looked up for a moment. "I wanna say Kicho's in that movie. Anyway, he calls Hud and that's it. We're makin' a movie."

"So Hud's producing this movie because of a conversation at a party years ago? Is Clarence the most loyal guy in Hollywood or what?"

Ra laughed. "Doin' alright by us, that's for sure."

The waitress placed a bowl in front of me and a plate of baked chicken with sweet potatoes and some fried balls of something in front of Ra. It all looked pretty good. We blessed the meal then dug in. My dish wasn't authentic to the area and I wasn't sure why'd they'd made the glaze so sweet, but it was tasty.

Ra swallowed a mouthful of chicken. "I always knew we'd do okay, even back when you first got to L.A. You're a sexy beauty, but I knew because you worked hard. Everybody else's sittin' around cafes complaining about their agents or not getting an agent or whatever roadblock they're hiding behind. You're out there skippin' past the whole agent thing, goin' directly to the producers and directors and creating your own work."

Ra had a gift for making me feel appreciated. But I had no illusions about why doors opened for me. "That was the one benefit to being a woman out there. I wasn't a threat and I looked good so I could get a few minutes of most men's attention."

"Yeah, but let's face it. All the pretty girls get attention. It's what you did with those few minutes. Most of the other women would leave with a date, you'd leave with a connection."

"You know what it was? My magic secret? I almost never talked about work. Clarence didn't know what I did for a living until someone else told him. We were talking to this random actor who I'd loved in this little indie and he starts freakin' out, hitting Clarence on the arm, 'Do you know who this is? Do you know who this is?' And I'm sorta dreading what's next thinkin' he's got me confused with Laura Dern or Kelly Preston or somethin' and he says, 'Did you see *Gang of One?*'"

"Which you're actually in."

I laughed. "Exactly, but for like two scenes. So now I'm realizing this actor might actually like my work. But Clarence hadn't seen it. Then the actor hits Clarence again and says, 'Dude, did you see *Flag on the Play?* I wrote a freakin' sequel in my head for her character.'"

Ra smacked his thigh. "Well alright then."

"Yeah, it was pretty much the most perfect way Clarence could've found out what I do for money – an indie actor we recognized who turns out to be a superfan of my bit parts. I wanted to hug him." Ra laughed. "Seriously. I felt like I owed him money or something. But the point is, Clarence and I had been hangin' out for hours by this point and I'd never talked about work. He saw me as a person first."

"A person who gets invited to the same parties he does."

"It was actually my friend's party."

"Of course it was." He pointed to his plate with his fork. "Try some of all this. You know I'm not gonna eat all the fried things."

"I'll have a bite." I ignored the chicken and went straight for the sides. The sweet potatoes had cinnamon or something in them that made them a little too pumpkin-pie to be a side dish. I was beginning to assume the chicken would be sweet as well. I liked sugared meats as much as the next guy but preferred to balance things like ribs slathered in barbecue sauce with more savory fare like greens with onions and pork.

The balls were fried dressing – a mushy mix of bread, shrimp, onions and other flavors and textures that might've been chopped golden raisins, pecans and apples among other less identifiable ingredients. As odd as the combination was, I was certain I'd had it before. "That's weird."

Ra chuckled. "Yeah, but it tastes pretty good."

"No, I mean it tastes almost exactly like a dish I had somewhere else."

"Is this a traditional local stuffing?"

I laughed. "No. It's more like two or three local recipes with some random hipster stuff thrown in. But it's good."

"Good is good."

"At least it's not too sweet. We haven't even seen a King-Yay! and I already feel like I had dessert."

Ra laughed. "I thought it was me." He took a bite of my grits covered in bourbon sauce. "Pretty much the same sauce on my chicken. Good though."

"Good is good. You can't really sell bad food here, though. I mean there's some fried-seafood-platter type places for tourists but locals can afford to be choosy – at any price point. That's so weird though." I took another bite of the dressing and closed my eyes while I chewed the odd texture. Was that baked pear? Squash? Eggplant? "I know I've tasted this before. But I don't really eat at hipster places. I don't love it and Patrick is very anti."

"Maybe it's that recipe black market you were talking about at the sushi place. Anyway, beats the heck outta the old days of Ramen and canned tuna."

I chuckled. "Definitely."

The waitress took our dishes and brought a plate with the theft-inspiring King-Yay! It was basically a beignet covered in white icing encrusted with three stripes of purple, green and gold sugar crystals. Ra cut the treat in half and took a bite. I took a bite as well. It should've been good and I guess it was, but the texture was wrong and it was too sweet even for me – and I had a very enthusiastic sweet tooth.

Ra took a swig of water. "Is that authentic?"

"To what? There's definitely a beignet in there but those are usually topped with a mound of powdered sugar. The donuts come hot out of the fryer with the outside still browning as they put the sugar on so it's a lot lighter than this and the edges of the beignet are a crispy golden brown. I think they have to let these cool to put the icing on. Beignets don't age well. They're like french fries." I tapped on the beignet with my fork. "These are kinda rubbery. Patrick will be so happy he's not missin' anything."

He was. And he was happy to hear he might be onto something with the publicity angle, that the restaurant seemed very into their web presence and creating a fan base. And he was happy to turn in early so I could work on my part. I loved that we could share everything but still have our separate worlds. He'd sent in the essay he wrote and was waiting to hear back on the French Quarter place. Before saying goodnight, I made him promise to send me a copy. I already knew it would make me proud. I liked that I could trust him to handle things for us.

Law and Order reruns played as I Googled images and stories from 1970's New Orleans. There were photos from Pontchartrain Beach, the amusement park Bryan Batt's family owned. The Superdome was under construction. Mahalia Jackson sang at the first Jazz Fest, held at Congo Square. Superfloats were introduced by the Krewe of Endymion in the '76 Mardi Gras parades.

Men wore straw fedoras, newsboy caps, bucket hats and ivy caps. Some sported long sideburns and push-broom mustaches. Some guys had shoulder-length or longer hair. Lapels were wide and prints were plentiful. Some women still fought the humidity to tease up-do's into submission. Others wore wild waves or lush afros. Most women still wore dresses ranging from Jackie Kennedy-inspired boxy pastel suits to braless halter-topped sundresses. Heels ruled the day for men and women. Stacked heels, boot heels, clogs, wedges, spool heels and block heels.

But what was most striking was what remained the same. I found videos of people dancing on Bourbon Street and mule-drawn carriages riding past the artists selling their wares on the fence line of Jackson Square. Chris Owens' burlesque club was the same except that she was younger in the posters. Steamboats rolled past, their paddle wheels spinning as calliopes played.

I was fascinated by an old couple in one of the videos. The husband or brother stood, rhythmically batting a tambourine. The bonnet-topped woman sat with books on her lap. The book on top was open and the woman appeared to be singing the words as she was reading them – something about "higher ground." But it seemed unlikely a book or Bible would have a chorus about "higher ground." Maybe she was reading silently while singing something totally different, but that was probably beyond the scope of even the best of multi-taskers. Both performers seemed very old, probably born before the turn of the century. It'd been a while since I'd heard anyone sing spirituals in the Quarter. It made me sad whenever I saw a part of the city's culture fade away. But it was still common to find families performing together.

I created files, downloaded images and made lists of links to videos along with descriptions of their contents. Then I opened a spiral notebook with a peace sign on the cover and moved on to Charlie's family tree. I started with what I knew. My sisters were Kimani, Tanisha, Ladonna, Ji, Ashley and Jenna. I guessed I was the oldest, though it could be Ji or even Kimani. I'd have to ask Clarence if he cared since we'd grown up in our own smaller families. I was clearly the oldest of my family. Madison Frye, who would play Ashley, and I were the same age, but I couldn't imagine anyone wanting the word "oldest" anywhere near her character.

My mother was a southern belle, Sarah Covington. She'd passed and we stayed on at the family manor in the Garden District. That would be easy enough to imagine. My father was Jake Covington, a ne'er do well who we worshipped. I figured life was a party when he was around, but he often wasn't around.

Dad was also the murderer as it turned out. He'd elaborately faked his own death to avoid prosecution for money laundering. He'd been aided by his son, JayJ, who it turned out was our brother. That was going to make those flirtation scenes with Ashley and Tanisha kinda tricky.

But all Charlie would've known growing up was her mother, father and two sisters. That was her family. She probably wouldn't have had much access to her dad's parents so she probably wouldn't know that side of her family. Easy for me to relate. I'd have to assume my mother's father was a charismatic bon vivant, able to keep women loyal while only giving them sporadic attention and piles of lies. That would explain my mother's attraction to a man like Jake. She could've also been reacting to coming from a boring dad, but that seemed less likely given the entire extended family's alpha-approach to life.

I filled in the rest of the blanks with details from my own family and figured I'd fix them later. I found a new page and drew a tree chart starting with Charlie Covington at the bottom along with her sisters and brother. I filled in the next layer with Jake and Sarah Covington and gave her my mother's maiden name, Tate. I filled in the rest of the tree with my own family names. Her parents were Henrietta Perry and Edward Tate. Then came Ruby and Oliver Perry. The last one I knew was Lily Wells, my great-great grandmother. The brave woman who left her plantation behind for the love of the overseer was just the sort of woman who might make a great-great-granddaughter who traveled all over the world learning about martial arts. And bringing the chandelier when they made a break for it was just the sort of southern-belle detail that could lead to offspring who were as comfortable at a cotillion as at a dojo. That would do for now. Charlie was beginning to take shape.

How did Sassy's family end up with the chandelier? Wouldn't Lily have passed it to her son Oliver? Maybe she did and he gave it to Mama Eunoe or Mama Heck. Taffy and Chiffon said their family legend was that Sassy's family was given the chandelier after slavery ended. But why not give money or property? Why would they have given the Wells' family chandelier to Sassy's family? If Sassy's family had sold it to buy the house in Treme, maybe it would make sense, but just to have it hanging around as a gift seemed odd.

I'd have to figure it out later. I still needed to find songs for my inspiration soundtrack and download them into my iShuffle. And I still wanted to find photos of all the women playing my sisters as well as the rest of the relevant actors so I could print them and fill in my character journal and family tree. I was hoping to find photos that could pass for 70's era looks. I had hours of work ahead of me but I felt energized. It was rare I had an opportunity to dig this deeply into a character. I felt inspired to fill in every detail of Charlie and her story. I'd have to put off looking into every detail of my own backstory.

Chapter 10

I was glad Ted, the guy with the gentle face, was working when I popped into the Garden District Book Shop. He'd been the one who pointed me in the direction of the secondhand shop owner who led me to the burlesque expert who sent me to the man who finally settled the identity of the twins' birth mother.

"I've got another strange request."

He smiled. "My favorite kind."

"I'm looking for specifics about living in New Orleans in the 70's. Photos? What people were eating, who the musicians were, what people were wearing. Stuff like that."

"Hmm." He looked around the shop, scanning shelves he knew by rote. "You'd be surprised how little there is about 70's New Orleans." He put his hand to his chin and rubbed twice. "There are a few titles."

I followed him past shelves full of kids books and playthings to the local-centric books. Ted scanned the spines of a lower shelf. "Ah, here." He pulled the book out and handed it to me. "*Managing Ignatius* by Jerry Strahan is probably the best. Over two decades of life in the Quarter as experienced by Lucky Dog vendors. There's also *The Last Madam*, but that covers a lot of decades. Same with *Mr. New Orleans*." He pointed to a book sitting on the shelf near me.

"I just realized I came to a bookstore knowing how little time I have to read." I hoped I wasn't wasting his time. I followed him past the "employee favorites" shelves and got distracted trying to spot Ted's picks.

He explained as I caught up to him. "In our out-of-print books, we have a pictorial Mardi Gras history by Mitchel Osborne and Errol Laborde published in 1981. Again, many decades, but some great 70s photos."

"Great!"

He located the title and pulled the book out, handing it to me as he excused himself and assisted another customer. I scanned the photos and fell in love with our city all over again.

I left with the Lucky Dog book and thought about what it would've been like to grow up here in my family home like Charlie had. My hips bopped to *Superstitious* playing in my earbuds. I thought about being a kid at Mardi Gras, about whether I would've played an instrument or marched in the parades with my schoolmates. Then I thought about going to school dances in a city where you can't escape your exes. Forever. Maybe that made people treat each other better.

The chandelier was swaying when I got home. Patrick still hadn't seen it do anything other than provide light and beauty. I was glad I finally knew the symbol was the Wells Plantation property mark, but I hated wondering if it could've been found on people. I could accept that the flask in the May Bailey's Place brothel collection may have been left by any number of men either related to me or who'd somehow come into possession of the flask as barter or a gift. It could've been left behind accidentally after a visit to Storyville's brothels or given or bartered to a "lady of the night." I accepted that I'd probably never know the flask's story, but that it obviously traced back to our Antebellum home. The only real evidence I had of anyone traveling from there to New Orleans was the bill of sale for Lottie signed by Leonard somebody of the Wells Plantation. But there was no way of knowing if it was Leonard whoever's flask.

But the thread I couldn't stop pulling was Dad's pipe. Why would Dad have a pipe from my mother's side's family farm? More to the point, why did his mother's father have it? Could he be Leonard? No, Leonard's last name was Percy or something. Whatever it was, it wasn't Stewart. But, Dad's mom only used her married name. Maybe her maiden name was Percy or whatever.

I dialed the phone and hoped my busy brother had a minute.

"Hey! Good timing. I just finished a report and lunch is in seven minutes."

I cradled the phone on my shoulder. "Oh good. I'll get to the point so you can get to your food. Are you still doin' the ancestry thing on the internet?"

"Not really. I got to the point where I'd have to pay a bunch and got frustrated. I would've done it but I never even found Dad's mom's maiden name so I don't know how to get past that without checking into marriage registries or something."

"Aunt Carol didn't know it either. So weird to not

know your own mother's maiden name."

Tate's voice got authoritative. "Not really. Now, sure. But historically, lots of women only used their married names. Can't find their maiden name in a census, death records, nothing. I already tried looking online for some of those documents, but I think I'd have to go to the actual church or county where she was married and I have no idea."

"I'm guessin' Carol won't either but I can ask if you want. She did say Birdie was named for her father and that she hated the name."

"I'm gonna go ahead and say that's not going to help the search much unless you know his full name."

"Nope." I switched ears. "Did Birdie ever tell you her mother was a wealthy plantation owner's daughter?"

He paused. "She said her mother was trash."

"Seriously?

"She'd had a few and was saying she'd had a hard life and then she said, 'But what do you expect from trash?'"

"Wow." Maybe it was good that we didn't know her very well. "Carol told me a similar story but I guess I assumed Birdie was talking about her dad being trash since she hated her name so much."

"Maybe it was both. I dunno. She liked sympathy. Maybe she made all of it up – the rich plantation daughter and the trash thing."

"Or maybe it's all true but we don't understand it. But if she did lie, it was probably about the things that reflected well on her. It's far less likely that someone would lie about havin' a worse life than they had."

"Makes sense. Alright, I'm heading down to the sandwich shop. I'll call you later."

"Okay. If you figure out a way to find the maiden name, I'd love to have it."

"I'll see what I can do."

I still had one more thread to pull. It wasn't a very promising one but I knocked on my neighbor's door anyway.

Jason was yanking a t-shirt over his wiry frame when he pulled the door open. "Hey! Sorry, just got out of the shower."

"I can come back."

He opened the door wide. "No, come in, come in. What's up."

His tabby got up from the couch to make way for me then rubbed against my legs as I sat. I could feel her purring. Though Jason was my neighbor, I'd actually met him through Tom, my only New Orleans ex-boyfriend. "I have a weird question. Tom told me you said we had a ghost in our house. Did you say that?"

He chuckled and sat in the nearby armchair. "Yeah."

"You said it was the protector of a family secret?"

"Yeah, I went on that ghost tour that goes through our neighborhood and the tour guide said it. Said the ghost guards a family secret."

"Did they say what the secret was supposed to be about?"

"Naw. Talked about the horse buried in the backyard and the chandelier."

"What'd they say about the chandelier?"

Jason looked at me for a moment. "You okay over

there?"

"What? Yeah, great."

He gave me a tepid smile. "Okay, 'cause you know that place sat empty for a while. Never did find out why the woman who lived there before you left and the tour guide said the place used to have stories."

"What kind of stories?"

"About the chandelier doing stuff."

I felt revealed. "Now?"

"No, back when it hung here. Thing was long gone by the time I moved in, like a really long time ago. Gotta be honest with you. I was glad the tour wasn't about ghosts wandering around now or murders or any kind of bad juju."

I couldn't figure out if it was more rude to not answer his honesty with honesty, or to tell him about the activity and burst his bubble of ignorance. "Um, it's hangin' in our bedroom. The chandelier. Since around Mardi Gras."

Jason leaned forward, his hands on his knees, and rocked a little. "Oh, seriously? Does it do stuff? Is it haunted?"

I felt even more torn. "Has anything changed over here?"

"No, nothin'. Same old place in need of a good scrub. I hate cleaning in the summer. Too hot."

I laughed. "I know, right? Slow livin'. Did the guide say anything else?"

"Not really. I wanna say the family's son became a merchant with a shop on St. Charles. Or was it Canal? I don't remember. Only reason I remember all the other stuff is self-preservation. I like a good ghost story as much as the next guy but I'm not a big fan of the idea of livin' with somethin' going bump in the night, know what I mean?"

"Yeah. I should probably go. I've got a ton of work to do. Plus I need to get busy ignoring my housekeeping chores."

Jason laughed.

I got up and the cat jumped onto the couch to rub against my thigh. "Thanks for the info. I hate to interrogate you and run but--" There were several framed photos on the built-in shelves behind Jason. The picture in front was of a group of guys and I would've sworn one of them was the guy from the news, the owner of 504Ever. I pointed at his face. "Who's this?"

Jason's face scrunched. "Travis. You know him?"

"No, do you?"

"Used to. Back then. That's me there. He pointed to a nearby face.

I smiled at the younger Jason in a white Izod-type shirt and khaki shorts. "What's this photo from?"

"Golf club at Loyola. Crazy days. Tough to focus on college in a party town. We hadn't learned the value of pacing ourselves."

I laughed. "That's the key to the whole city   the food, the festivals and free music, Mardi Gras, all of it. Pace yourself."

"Yeah, you right."

I laughed to myself. Tom used to say that. He and Jason were friends so it was no mystery how they came to have the same colloquialisms, though they didn't grow up in the same neighborhood. Some phrases could be very specific to an area here. Locals could easily tell if someone was from Chalmette, Uptown or Metairie. "Is he from here?" I took in Travis' baby blue polo shirt and pale yellow shorts.

"Travis? No. Philly maybe? Honestly, I kept my distance."

"Really. Why?"

"He was shady, slick in the wrong way, you know what I mean?"

After eighteen years in L.A., I definitely knew what he meant.

"But it was really this guy I was avoidin'." He pointed to the face next to Travis. The friend was shorter, clean-shaven like the rest with a Joey-from-*Friends* type haircut and the requisite polo shirt with pale knee-length shorts. "He was what you call a bad influence. Don't get me wrong, Travis was a class-A jerk all on his own but Beckett really brought out the worst in him, egged him on. There was even a rumor that Travis' dad offered him a bribe to leave Loyola."

I was intrigued. "Just Loyola, or New Orleans in general?"

"Honestly, I'm just truckin' in gossip now. But I do know that the dad hated Beckett. Blamed him for everything. My brother was standin' next to him at a tournament and said the dad called Beckett a lowlife, said he was probably cheatin'. Said he went on about how his boy was a good kid and it was Beckett's fault Travis was gettin' in trouble."

"Easy to see how he might inspire rumors even if the specifics weren't true."

He slapped his belly. "Yeah, you right."

"Was he a local? Beckett?"

"Naw. I wanna say they knew each other from

home. But, like a toldya, I mostly stayed clear of the both of them. Know what I mean?"

"Yeah. No, I get it. Wise move, I'm sure." I headed for the door. "Thanks for all of this. I know it's a little weird coming over to ask your neighbor about ghost stories. It's not exactly a cup of sugar."

Jason laughed. "It's fine. Toldya, I like ghost stories, just not the idea of one walkin' around my place. Kow what I mean?"

"Yeah. Yeah I do." I put my key in the lock. "Thanks again. Have a great night." My phone rang and I raced down the hall and fumbled to answer it before it went to voicemail. Taffy. "Hey!"

"Hey! You got a minute? You sound busy."

"No, I'm good. Just got in is all." I adjusted a pillow and settled onto the loveseat. "What's up?"

"Chiffon and I been talkin' to the new real estate lady and she say there's a potential buyer. Sounded real interested."

My heart sank. "Dang. I love that house."

"Yeah, it's got me feelin' some type-a-way. Me and Chiffon both. But we tried to hang onto it. Just not cut out to be long-distance landlords, ya heard me?"

"Yeah, I know." I got over myself. "But that's great. I'm happy for y'all. Be good to get that money too."

"I know tha's right."

I laughed. "You need me to keep the chandelier?"

"Could you?"

"Yeah, of course. Don't even think about it."

Taffy opened a door and yelled. "Y'all play nice! Don't get Jojo all riled up. Supper's soon." The door clicked shut. "Thanks Charlotte. We appreciate it. Takes a load off."

"No worries. Listen, I've been puttin' some pieces together but I haven't been tellin' you about any of it 'cause I'm just guessing. It's all just circumstantial."

I heard a fridge door open and close. Taffy's voice sounded concerned. "What is it?"

"The chandelier seems to come from the Wells Plantation, our family farm from way back. There's a symbol on the top part that's a stamp the Wells' farm used on a bill of sale I found."

Metal clinked like Taffy was setting places at the table. "A bill of sale? For what?"

"For a person. A woman named Lottie."

"Lottie?"

"Yeah. But, I don't have any real reason to believe it's the same Lottie in your family. It could just be a coincidence. But if it's the same woman, that means my family owned your family."

The clinking stopped. She took a deep breath. "So that's your family chandelier?"

"No! No, of course not. I mean, it was, but no. That's definitely y'all's chandelier. It just seems to have come from our family farm. So, I'm guessing it's the chandelier Lily took with her when she ran to Texas. But that would mean my family didn't meet your family here, Lily would've brought Lottie or Eunoe with her from the plantation. Maybe even as property."

"Tha's messed up."

"I know."

"Damn."

I waited quietly as Taffy processed. Down the

hall, I could hear the chandelier rattling.

"Tha's messed up. I mean, I know Mama Eunoe was born slave, I was used to that, but yeah, that's somethin' different."

"I didn't know whether to say anything 'cause I don't really know. But everything keeps pointing to Sassy's people comin' from the Wells' place and that can only mean one thing, right? I wasn't sure if I should say anything. I mean there's nothin' we can do about it but feel feelings, but I didn't want to seem like I was hiding anything. Especially 'cause it's your family chandelier. It's y'all's story." I heard the door open behind her.

"Down Jojo. Baby, get this dog some water 'fore it passes out. Poor thing ran itself ragged."

Her son dared to talk back. "I'm thirsty too. Who you think he was chasin?"

"Now you know only one a you got hands to get your own water. Get that water for Jojo and go wash up. Tell your sister we eatin.' Lordy. Summertime. Kids all the time underfoot. They cute though. You see the photos from the fourth?"

I smiled. "Yeah, looked like fun."

"Look, we can't help what we come from or how we came to meet. But I do have one question. You say you found the plantation symbol on the chandelier?"

Busted. "Yeah, the day you and UncaParis came to hang it."

"I didn't see nothin'."

I had to tell her. "It was under a piece of old masking tape that was peeling off. I peeked when y'all were preoccupied with your arguing."

She chuckled. "Yeah, UncaParis can drive me to distraction. Tha's what family's for though, I guess."

"I'm not sure why I never told you. I guess I felt bad 'cause it was none of my business."

"Ha! Sound like it's exactly your family's business. So there was a bill of sale?"

"Yeah, but I'm only certain, well, pretty sure, that it came from our family farm. The chandelier had initials carved into it too. Both ended with W. The symbol was the same symbol that was pressed into the wax seal on the bill of sale from the Wells Plantation. That's as sure as we're likely to get. But I really have no idea how common a name Lottie was back then so we can't really know if that bill of sale has anything to do with your family."

The chandelier was getting louder. I wished Patrick would get home from the gym to witness it.

Taffy turned a faucet on. "Listen, I gotta go. Supper's ready."

"Yeah, I gotta prep an audition for tomorrow and after that, it's my first day of work on *Seven Sisters*."

"You gotta audition before work? Seems crazy to have to look for work when you just got a good job."

I laughed. "Showbiz."

She laughed too. "Let me know if you find anything else out."

"Are you sure? I mean, I feel weird about all of this."

"Yeah. All in the past. But I'm curious. Like you say, it's my heritage even if it ain't my roots. I'll let Chiffon know."

"Oh, right. Thank you. Hey Taffy, you said the chandelier never moved at the Treme house, right?"

"Naw. But look, I gotta go. Have a good one."

I hung up and started down the hall to check on the chandelier. Patrick walked in and I jumped. "Quick, look!"

"What?"

The clinking stopped. I ran into the room to find the chandelier settling. Patrick came in behind me and followed my gaze to the unimpressive swinging of a few crystals. "What?"

"The chandelier. It was just doing it."

He stared a moment as everything settled to a stop, then chuckled a little. "Scary."

Dang it.

Chapter 11

The audition was for a two-liner in a big movie. Not much to flesh out. I tried not to get bent over having to audition for an under-five when I was getting ready to play a part written with me in mind – in Clarence Pool's mind. I'd basically had to start over when I decided to stay in New Orleans. Eighteen years of relationships and a track record of almost two decades of auditions and work all but went out the window. It wasn't that my resume had lost its impressiveness, it was that most of the movies and shows that came here had already cast the parts I would've gone out for in L.A. The bigger the budget, the more likely the local parts were leftovers, a line here, a scene there. It was humbling, but not humiliating. I clung to the difference.

The set was bustling when I arrived for work. I found someone with a walkie talkie and asked where my trailer was. The young woman with a ponytail pulled through her Saints cap walked me over to my new home away from home. We passed flashy trailers with pop-outs and patio furniture under awnings. Those would be for the stars. One had a large patch of Astroturf marking their patio's space.

We passed production trailers, wardrobe and makeup, then hit a patch of plain white trailers – the kind some called "double-bangers." It meant the trailer was cut into two units. Beyond our trailers were the ones cut into four units. Those might have a toilet in the room with you or might mean sharing a public bathroom – the trailer units we called the honey wagon.

I sprung the door latch open and climbed the metal steps into my room. It was plenty spacious with a daybed, well-lit vanity, microwave and sink and a private bathroom with a standing shower. There was a TV but they were rarely useful since networks quit transmitting to antennas years ago. I put my set-bag down on the vanity's padded folding chair and headed over to makeup.

I was careful to pop the door open before mounting the steps. Crew usually announced "Stepping up" as they entered hair and makeup. Either way, it gave everyone a warning that the trailer might shake and allowed them to stop working on precise things like applying eyeliner. I could immediately see they weren't ready for me. Nearly every barber's chair was full of actors with bigger names than mine.

An older woman in a tie-dye tank dress waved to me. "Charlotte?"

I smiled. "Yes."

She pushed thick locks with a hand covered in silver rings. "Yeah, no room at the inn. Give us maybe ten? Twenty at most."

"No worries."

I headed toward the studio hoping to run into a friendly face. Someone rushed past carrying a laundry basket of throw pillows. I followed her past a guy pushing a cart full of electronics and wrapped cords, then past a trailer full of sound equipment and video monitors. I saw someone coming out of a door eating an apple and headed in that direction. The door was to a smallish room lined with tables full of snacks. Hot dogs spun on a rotisserie next to warming pots of coffee marked "Caf" and "Decaf." Small sets of plastic drawers held vitamins and supplements. There were wicker baskets of gum, protein bars and candy from the 70's like Necco, Bit-O-Honey and fireballs.

I popped back out and found another food mecca, a trailer with ice chests offering sodas, milk and juices. Above the cold drinks, a chalkboard menu listed the day's breakfast offerings between the order and pick-up windows. They'd stopped serving hours ago but the items for the make-your-own omelets and breakfast burritos looked good. I especially approved of the avocado.

A bell rang and a red light next to an industrial metal door flashed to life. I waited a few minutes for it to turn off then pulled the heavy door open. There was another metal door with a small window at eye level. A guy in a headset rushed at me and I got out of the way then went inside the giant hangar-like space. A big guy in a Saints jersey stopped as he passed. "You got any electronics? Phone or somethin'?"

"No. Left it all in the trailer."

He raised his hand for a high-five. "Atta girl." He pushed the door behind me open and whistled to himself while exiting. An empty row of director's chairs were labeled with some of the stars' names. One said "Cast." That would be mine. People hurried in and out of the front door of the Garden District home set. I'd hoped to walk around a while before I had to pretend I'd grown up there so I was glad things were running a little behind. I went around the side to where the walls had been removed and wandered through the dining room.

Clarence stood drinking bottled water next to his director's chair. Aaron had him laughing at some story. Aaron wasn't scheduled to work today so I figured I shouldn't interrupt whatever he'd come to do. But Clarence waved and came my way. "Hey!"

I opened my arms for his familiar hug. "Hey." We took each other in and smiled. "How's it goin'?"

He looked around. "So far, so good. Got most of the morning in the can. I'm sure we'll get to you after lunch."

"Lunch" was always six hours after the crew's call time which meant it could be any time of day or night, but today it would actually land around noon.

"Cool. I was hoping to walk around the set a little but maybe I'll just leave lunch early."

"Yeah. If you could."

A guy in a headset walked up listening to his earpiece. "Yeah, okay." He lifted his eyes to us. "They're ready for you Clarence."

I gave Clarence another quick hug and headed for the makeup trailer. The silver rings lady waved me over while she finished a conversation with the guy working next to her. I settled into the chair and waited for her to finish.

She turned to the mirror and we talked to each other's reflections. "Charlotte. I love that name. Regal. I'm Tulip."

My reflection smiled at hers. "That's a fun name.

You almost never hear that name."

"Done me good so far. Production sent me those photos you emailed. So we're going with a natural glow look for the training flashbacks, then more of a Breck-girl, beauty queen thing for the funeral stuff, house scenes, etc., then a more dramatic eye and pale lip for the badass fighting scenes. Good?"

"We'll have to see with the mod look. I don't always look great with a pale lip. I'm sure you'll find a pretty shade. My right eyelid is kinda lazy and my lower left lip isn't symmetrical so it usually needs a little liner help. Oh, and my brows obviously are light and the tails are super thin so, yeah, eyebrow help. Oh, and I'm so sorry but I had an audition before this so I had to wear makeup. It won't happen again though, I promise. Probably."

She smiled back and waved a hand at the mirror. "Don't worry about it." She grabbed a bottle of clear liquid and some cotton balls and went to work.

All the good set gossip came out in makeup trailers so when I wasn't getting to know Tulip, which I would have plenty of time to do, I kept my ears in other people's conversations. Madison was already working on set but my new "little sister" was a few chairs down getting her bouncy brunette waves pinned back from her forehead and fixed into place with a baby blue ribbon. Long ringlets were curled on either side of her dewy face. I remembered when looking that fresh came easy. Now it required some art.

Clarence usually liked to shoot the script in order if possible. They'd already shot the opening funeral parlour scene a couple days ago, but we wouldn't have that location again for a few days. Seemed business was booming. We were skipping ahead to the slumber party scene, where the sisters decide whether to join forces with the other sisters while dressed in sexy nighties and furry kitten heels. I only had six lines so I wasn't that nervous.

The woman with a ponytail pulled through her Saints cap brought me back to the set for a rehearsal. I'd been theatre trained at the American Academy of Dramatic Arts in New York and various other conservatories before moving to L.A. In Los Angeles, I spent the first couple of years doing more theatre training and taking scene study classes for film and TV actors. Though some of the techniques were different, all of the training was based on repetition. Heck, for the first few weeks at the Academy, we spent about an hour a day doing an exercise called "The Repetition Exercise" where two people just repeat a phrase like "You have brown hair" back and forth until the words lose their meaning. It was maddening to keep repeating the exercise for weeks before we were finally given a play to read from, but it taught us that most of our meaning, intention and expression didn't come from the lines. As Stella Adler said, "The play is not in the words, it's in you!"

The other thing repeating the repetition exercise illuminated was the ego's desire to perform. It was pretty natural for actors to think they had to make the repeated phrase somehow interesting to watch. "You have brown hair" could be twisted into an elaborate soap opera involving everything from suspicion to remorse. It taught me to move past the need to come up with ego-driven emotional tap dancing and just let the person in front of me affect me. Honestly, the hardest part of the exercise for most of us to adjust to was staring deeply into someone's eyes for long periods of time. For the first few days of class, people struggled with bad cases of the giggles. But acting was about intimacy, the revealing of the self. The job was to let people see into you. If you couldn't do it with a classmate, it wasn't likely you'd do much better in a giant theatre or in front of the lie detector of the camera lens.

It felt like we did those exercises long past their usefulness but I continued to learn. I found that if I quieted my own ego, there was room for a new ego to enter and speak from inside me. I could push all those "I would never do that" thoughts aside and find ways to justify this new ego's choices.

A lot of my training was based on repetition – rehearsal. But outside of the world of theatre, rehearsal generally meant a run-through of the lines as we walked the scene for marks. Though we were free to act things out during that walk-through, the rehearsal served more as a reference for all of the other teams. Someone would lay colored tape at our toes every time we stopped on set, marking where the stand-ins would stand for lighting, camera and sound decisions and set-ups. So we were free to act, but rehearsal in film meant literally having someone underfoot and an audience of preoccupied people.

Madison and Astrid were already there when I arrived on set. They were listening to Clarence run through the actions. He shot me a look. "There you are. So, as I was already saying, we'll start with Ashley on the bed talking to Jenna."

Madison found a pose on the bed, did a quick shimmy and found her inner-Ashley. "How do we know they're tellin' the truth? Maybe they're just lookin' for a payout."

Astrid read from her minis, the pocket-sized copy of today's scenes. "Honestly? I felt like I could see dad in Tanisha's face. Couldn't you? And they all have his smile."

Everyone flipped their script pages as Madison continued. "I didn't notice. They don't smile much"

Clarence looked at his leather-bound script. "Charlie comes in – on time." He looked to me again and I began to wonder if I was late to set. I'd come as soon as they came for me. Didn't even stop at my trailer. I checked the script. "On time" wasn't written there. I looked for the wall clock then remembered it was stopped at 11:20. Time almost always stood still on movie sets. I tried to focus as Clarence continued. "You show them the photo album."

I walked to the bed and a curly-haired guy marked my toes with orange tape as I said my first line. "I knew I wasn't crazy. When dad used to take me to Japan on those business trips? Look."

Clarence nodded. "You show them the photo, your kid-self training martial arts, and they spot Ji in the background. You guys on the bed should be sitting at attention now, so find that. And Charlie, maybe you settle in with them. In the middle? Yeah, holding the photo album."

Madison and Astrid sat up and I sat down as we went through the rest of the scene and the reveal that dad had taken each of us around our sisters when we were kids.

Everyone was already eating by the time we got to the dining hall of long tables with benches. Apparently, we'd agreed to take a meal penalty before I arrived on set. I didn't mind eating a little late in exchange for a couple hundred bucks, but it cut into my time to explore the set. I was hoping to at least go through the bedroom set before we shot there.

I always hated shooting body stuff right after lunch. Slim as I was, I always felt like it gave me a belly. Being human in front of cameras could be brutal on the ego.

A lanky guy holding a mic-pack politely introduced himself. "Emmett, hey."

"Charlotte."

His curly long lashes lowered. "I think we're gonna have to go for the thigh."

The thigh was never anyone's first choice. It meant Emmett strapping a large elastic strap around my leg and finding somewhere unobtrusive for the mic-pack's antenna to go. Then the cord would wind it's way to where Emmett would have to secure the mic between my breasts. It was no small wonder people on film sets became so intimate so quickly. We spent our days showing off our best work, eating together, problem solving, and strategically placing microphones under butt cheeks and between breasts. Emmett and I were sure to become fast friends – if only out of self-preservation.

I was glad we ran the scene again before shooting. We did the master first, getting the whole scene start-to-finish in a wide shot. I was always glad they shot the stars' close-ups first. Having the camera on the back of my head gave me take after take to rehearse and try things. I understood the value of capturing emotions when they were fresh, especially in a highly sensitive and impassioned scenes, but I always felt more confident with preparation. If I were a star, I liked to think I'd use my power to ask to go last. It kinda baffled me that anyone would give away rehearsal opportunities. But I'd seen plenty of amazing acting shot right from the hip. As Clarence was fond of saying, "You can argue with success, but you'll be wrong."

It was a very long day and I was glad we had the weekend off. I wanted to rework my journal now that I was getting to know how my "sisters" were going to play their roles. It was clear Madison had decided our relationship was competitive. Astrid seemed to be relating to me as a maternal figure. Made sense. We had a sizable age gap and our characters' mother had passed when Jenna was very young.

Patrick was asleep on the loveseat when I got home. I paused the TV and shook him awake. "Hey baby."

His moss green eyes fluttered open. "Hey. Hey baby." He sat up. "How was it? What time is it?"

"It's late. It's after two. Come on, let's get you in bed."

He patted the cushion next to him. "I wanna hear all about it. You've gotta be ridin' a high."

I smiled. I wasn't sure how he knew that I was dying to stay up and tell my best friend about my amazing first day at work, but I was grateful.

Chapter 12

I'd been training during my days off. Charlie was an expert in several disciplines of martial arts. I was just a former gymnast who'd stayed flexible in my forties. I wasn't sure why Clarence had so much confidence in me, but he seemed certain I was going to be amazing. Letting him down was not an option. The trainers had been focusing on Naginatajutsu, the Japanese art of commanding a naginata – a bladed weapon that looks like a pole. The trainers, three cousins from Japan, taught me that naginata meant "the reaping sword." I pictured Charlie as a reaper in go-go boots.

The trainers didn't speak much English. A lot of our communication was just mimicry. They'd show me what to do and I'd try to do it. It was easy when we were just doing stretches and exercises, but now we'd moved to working out the actual fights – complete with pool cues. The cousins would start by clapping their palm on their chest as they said which actor they'd be playing. I wasn't sure if I should feel bad for the cousin who had to play my female part. The cousins would show me the sequence once through then do the whole thing again in slow motion. Then they'd do it again at medium speed and again at full speed. Then whichever cousin playing Charlie would become our director of sorts as

I joined in and we ran through the routine in slow motion. We'd repeat it over and over until I had the sequence. One missed block or wrongly-timed thrust could really get someone hurt. Then we'd move to medium speed and run it until I'd gotten that worked out with no mistakes. Then we'd go at full speed.

I was amazed at how easy it was to learn this way. I was beginning to think Clarence might be right about me not needing a stunt double. I was getting so excited that, in addition to the choreography, I tried to perfect two super-cool-looking moves I hoped might make good shots.

It was all pretty thrilling but my body was angry with me. My shoulders ached. Epsom baths helped with muscle fatigue and soreness but the shoulders required ice, arnica and aspirin. I was looking forward to having a regular New Orleans weekend with music and food and no weapon wielding.

Satchmo Fest was founded to celebrate Louis Armstrong's birthday. The soupy heat of August wasn't ideal for dancing, but a few shirtless men slicked with sweat danced among women in pretty-print sundresses and kids swinging each other around.

The yard of the Old U.S. Mint was filled with booths of local tastes, cocktails and tented halls to beat the heat. Music played on stages on either side of the building. There were also seminars and discussions inside the air-conditioned Mint, but we'd be skipping those today.

We started with a delicious bowl of Creole Tomato Gazpacho with Louisiana Crab Meat from Three Muses. The pureed tomatoes were so fresh and refreshing. Strawberries and tomatoes were always so much better in Louisiana. We had a Creole Crawfish Sausage PoBoy from Vaucresson Sausage Co. and finished with a Nectar Creme Snoball from Plum Street Snoballs. Cold heaven in a cup.

As we were heading out, Treme Brass Band led a second line parade through the festival. Children carrying black-and-gold umbrellas marched around the perimeter before filtering onto the stage. Next, Shamarr Allen & the Underdawgs, then the Soul Rebels Brass Band would be kicking the festivities into high gear. It seemed strange to leave a party that was clearly getting more fun as the day wore on, but we wanted to run home and change into white clothes for White Linen Night, a celebration of downtown art galleries.

White Linen Night's dress code honored the years before air conditioning when New Orleanians wore white linen to reflect the summer sun's heat. Again, there were cocktails and two stages of live music, but the food booths were more high-end at this festival. We had the subtle Lobster Dumplings from GW Fins and Chilled Seafood Ceviche from Broussard's Restaurant. I took a bunch of photos for my blog and tried to remember details to share.

The nearly twenty galleries on Julia Street had their doors open wide, inviting everyone to come in to enjoy chilled air and purchase art. We wandered past many of the open doors, taking in the artwork's different styles and subjects. Occasionally, we'd roam inside to get a closer look. I'll be honest, sometimes I just wanted a closer look at people's clothing. White Linen featured beautiful artwork, delicious food and top notch music, but the people-watching was my favorite part. Everyone looked so sharp and fresh in their crisp, white clothes. Some women wore high-end, full-length gauzy sundresses, others wore lacy shift minidresses. There were bold white belts and dainty gold or white sandals. Men sported white ties, suspenders and hats to accent their white suits or shorts. The effect was elegant.

I pictured myself as Charlie, the woman who'd been raised in linen, sipping cocktails and sampling seafood while listening to live music. Would I be the type who bought a new dress every year for the event? Or would I just pull something white and cute from my closet and not worry if I'd worn it before? Some people even wore the same outfit every year like it was their fest uniform. No, Charlie would have at least three choices for every occasion. She fancied herself as prepared for anything – and was usually right.

Patrick headed for a food booth with a vase of white flowers next to the menu board. He waited for the guy cooking in the backward baseball cap to look up. Patrick smiled. "Hey man."

"Oh hey!" The guy wiped his hand on his apron and extended it. "Long time." He looked to me and I felt like I'd seen him before.

Patrick followed his gaze. "This is my girlfriend, Charlotte."

He reached for my hand. "Hey. Dal." He motioned to Patrick. "We knew each other back in his lifeguard days. Worked the same pool."

"Back in high school?"

Dal grabbed a wipe to sterilize his hands and

went back to dicing bell pepper. "Yeah. A regular *Bay Watch* poster boy, this one. Not only did the girls have crushes, the moms did too. Heck, I think he even had a few of the dads checkin' him out."

I laughed. "What can I say, I have exquisite taste. What're you makin'?"

"The shrimp dish."

I pointed to the peppers. "Is that for the trinity?"

Dal smiled to Patrick. "I see you got a southern girl. But darlin' can you make a roux?"

"All the way to the dark chocolate."

He laughed. "Well alright then. Keep this one."

Patrick pulled me close. "I plan to."

I smiled. "Honestly, I'm lost without my Trader Joe's, but I'm good with a recipe."

Dal scooped the peppers into a plastic tub and put it into a cooler then got to work on an onion. "Good luck with that. 'Round here, people don't much like sharin' recipes. Be very suspicious if someone just hands one over. Givin' a recipe is like a magician revealing secrets. Some are family secrets passed from the country of origin. Someone gives you a recipe like that, you can assume they left somethin' out." He laughed. "You think someone's gonna perfect a family recipe and hand it over to a stranger? Naw. What if you make it better than they do?"

We all laughed.

Dal pointed to the bins of food. "Y'all wanna try this?"

Patrick got his wallet out. "Sure."

Dal leaned forward. "Be honest with you. It's not how I'd do it. The head chef's pretty particular about his signature spices, but not every dish calls for his signature. I'm just sayin'."

I wished I could remember where I'd seen Dal's face before. "I once witnessed two friends since childhood almost come to blows over whether you could put pickles in gumbo. One of them had grown up eating gumbo over potato salad so pickles seemed fine to him. The other was used to rice so the pickles sounded like an abomination. But the fight wasn't really about the pickles. No one could get in that big a fight over pickles. It was about a purity of culture."

"Exactly." Dal scooped the shrimp and eggplant dressing into a styrofoam bowl and stuck two forks into the mound. "I just started workin' for these people or I'd slide you one."

Patrick paid him. "No worries. I'm happy to pay. So, you're not at Galatoire's anymore?"

Galatoire's? Did I see him when I had lunch there?

"Naw. Got ugly over there. Lotta pressure to be the best restaurant in a town full of the world's best restaurants."

Suddenly, I could see Dal in a chef's jacket. He was standing next to a van arguing with a man in a suit. The man was accusing him of stealing recipes. I stifled a gasp. "How long ago did you leave?"

Dal put the money in the register and cleaned his hands again. "This is my second week here. Good gig."

It had to be him. I wasn't sure what to tell Patrick.

Patrick started to walk away, still eating. "We should get outta your hair. Thanks for this. Tastes good. See you soon."

Dal waved. "Good seein' ya, man."

I waited until we were out of view and far out of earshot. "Patrick, is your friend a good guy?"

"He saved my cousin's life."

I almost laughed. "Seriously?"

He smiled. "Yeah, at the pool. She dove in, hit her head and didn't come up. Dal got her out, gave her mouth to mouth and saved her. They ended up dating for a little while."

"That's crazy." I wasn't sure if I should bring up the argument. I didn't really know what I'd seen. In L.A., they could've been actors practicing a scene for class. Maybe the whole thing was a misunderstanding. Maybe I'd misheard them. I'd certainly found no evidence of a recipe black market. But it was interesting that Dal saw recipes as equal to a magician's secrets. I knew there was a market for those.

Did I know anything else? Had I seen him inside the restaurant before the fight? I reviewed the barrage of faces, the maitre'd, the head waiter, Edwin Edwards and the Gals at Gal's birthday party.

Wait! That was where I'd tasted the dish from 504Ever. Suzy Bergner's offered bite. Was that the dish Dal had stolen? Her bite wasn't in a fried ball form but it was definitely the same dish in a pre-fried-ball state. But if he'd stolen the dish for 504Ever, shouldn't he have gotten a job there? Maybe he just sold it to them and that was their only connection. Or maybe there really was a black market and 504Ever had no idea who'd taken the recipe. In any case, wouldn't that mean 504Ever knew they were using a stolen recipe? Maybe they saw it as the same thing as making King-Yay!s, doing their own spin on a classic. But no, that was a very unusual dressing. It wasn't a classic. No, they had to have known they were hiding Galatoire's recipe inside those fried balls.

But I didn't really know anything. Only that Patrick's friend got yelled at by his boss and was working somewhere new now. Heck, if Galatoire's recipes were showing up at random restaurants, maybe the boss man in the suit was just paranoid or lashing out at everyone. I decided to wait until I knew more before mentioning the argument.

Patrick offered me the last bite. "You okay?"

"I had a dish recently that had a bunch of ingredients and there's one I can't figure out. It had bread, shrimp and onions and I think golden raisins, pecans and green apples. Except I don't think the apples were apples. It was like an apple but savory."

"Like a mirliton?"

"Mirliton! I bet that's it." The seasonal squash resembling a vegetable pear was common in local dishes. It was easy to see how I'd confused the two. Both had pale meat and green skin and neither was particularly sweet. Both got softer when cooked but retained a firm texture. But apples were rarely used in Creole cooking and mirliton was common, so odds were for the local squash. "I think you're right. Mystery solved. Thanks." I rolled up on my toes and kissed his cheek.

Chapter 13

I pulled nude sport-shorts on and tucked a white blouse into them before snapping the suede miniskirt over my hips. I left the bottom snaps open so my legs could move freely, then tugged white go-go boots over thin socks. Today's scene would be the first time we'd see Charlie in her funky fighter mode rather than her Uptown girl persona. I loved the whole look. My hair was a giant mass of curls, parted on the side and smoothed on top – just like the women at Studio 54 back in the day. It was savagely glamorous – part Veronica Lake, part lion's mane. I felt ready to take on the world.

I left my trailer before anyone came to get me and walked across the street to the pool hall. Clarence didn't seem to mind the cast observing. He sometimes even hinted that he liked it. Music was playing when I got near the set. I stopped at the sound truck and waved hi to Ishmael. "Damn, that's sexy. Who is it?"

Ishmael rubbed his bald head and smiled. "Isaac Hayes, *Do Your Thing*."

"Indeed."

"I've got a good one for you today. Well, Clarence does. You're going to like it."

I smiled. "Yay. I'm excited!"

He blew me a kiss and I went on my way. Rudy, the electronics guy, was wearing headphones and knew I didn't usually carry a phone, so we just waved as I entered the pool hall. Isaac Hayes was being piped in somehow as everyone hustled for a new setup. Aaron, Brooklyn and Madison were laughing with Clarence in a corner. They looked amazing and I suddenly remembered how average it was to look amazing on a movie set.

I waited by the door wondering if I should leave. Then everybody settled in as Clarence headed toward his chair just to my right. He smiled wide when he saw me. "That's awesome. You look perfect. Gotta love those boots. Are you staying?"

"Sure."

They were finishing up the scene where JayJ flirts with Tanisha, then Ashley. It was a longish scene full of the kind of dialogue actors long for, the kind that can inspire dreams of gold statues. JayJ was supposed to sidle up to Tanisha and do verbal battle. She would dismiss him and leave, then he would make his way to Ashley standing near the jukebox and try new lines he believed were perfectly tailored to her. The effect was that we didn't like JayJ being a player, but we had to admire his skills and moxie. Later, when everyone finds out we're all siblings, the whole thing would be gross in retrospect. Patrick told me he once ended up on a date with a second cousin. They figured it out about halfway through dinner. After that, he avoided dating anyone from the Irish Channel.

They were already on the seventh take when Brooklyn flubbed the line, "I'm sure you're all that at the neighborhood pool, but I already got a man don't need a tan and he's waitin' on the other side of that door."

The script supervisor tapped Clarence's arm. "She said, 'I'm sure you're all that neighborhood pool instead of, 'All that at the neighborhood pool.'"

"Cut." The bell rang and everyone stopped as the "scripty" gave Brooklyn the note. Brooklyn looked surprised then nodded.

The scripty looked to Judd, the First AD, who yelled, "Going again.!"

The scene started again then Brooklyn did it again, "I'm sure you're all that neighborhood pool--"

"Cut! Make sure she's got the line before we go."

The scripty ran over again. Brooklyn nodded again, said the line a few times, then smiled to Clarence. "Ready."

"Going again."

They started from the top again and the crew collectively held their breath when Brooklyn got to the line again. "I'm sure you're all that neighborhood pool."

Then again. And again. And again. It was hard not to feel bad for her. We'd all been there, stuck in some hellish loop of failure. With each repeat of the cycle, we all knew her self-esteem took another hit laying the groundwork for the next failure. Clarence tried giving her a semi-private pep talk. Aaron and Madison assured her it happened to everyone and not to worry about it. Clarence and Judd decided they had plenty of choices for the beginning of the scene and let Brooklyn cut straight to her line. Nothing helped. It would've been funny if it weren't so human and diminishing. The longer it went on, the more concerned I was she'd have any confident sass left in her performance by the time she got the words right. In the world of "film is forever," it was tragic and it became increasingly difficult to witness. Brooklyn finally got it on the twenty-third take. Of course no one clapped, though it was obviously an achievement just to have survived the whole thing without running away crying.

The scene had to go on and finally arrive at Madison's part. She'd been noticeably supportive and patient for someone who'd been forced to wait because of human error. Either Madison really was as nice as she seemed, or that was her move – to kill 'em with kindness. I'd learned long ago that almost nothing was as it seemed in Hollywood, and almost everyone had an agenda. Sofia's since-high-school friendship had been my oasis among mirages out there. I couldn't help but wish she'd move to New Orleans where I had good no-nonsense friends but no old friends. Clarence knew me longer than anyone local. Hud and Ra too.

Once Brooklyn was finished with her part, she wordlessly beelined for the door. Clarence headed over to energize Aaron and Madison and Judd wandered over to me. He looked toward the front door of the pool hall. "Why don't you go ahead and head to your trailer. We're a little behind and it's getting hot in here with all the lights. Don't want you wilting."

"Cool." I tried not to feel like I was being kicked out. I didn't usually like sitting in my trailer. I loved being on a set and hanging out with the crew. But it was August-hot and highly humid and my glorious hairdo was at stake, so I took Judd's advice. I peeled my boots off and ran the lines while stretching my shoulders and arms. I ran the fight sequences in slow motion and wished I could do them with the pool cue in my hands. Not likely in a double-banger trailer.

It felt like I was in my trailer a long time. I tried to stay relaxed and focused without over-preparing and burning myself out. My iShuffle full of 70's tunes helped. Finally Tina, who apparently always wore a ponytail pulled through a Saints cap, knocked on my door. I zipped my go-go boots up and took a deep breath.

When I arrived, everyone was already on set and running a rehearsal with the three trainers. The bad-guy actors were running through their moves. It seemed odd they would've started without me. And I wasn't the sort to spend much time indulging self-consciousness, but I could've sworn people seemed irritated with me. Was I late? Why would they bring me to set late for my own rehearsal? Did someone make a mistake? Maybe Tina wasn't good at her job. Maybe she had some sort of bad habit she was tending to when they let her leave the set to come get me.

I tried to shake it off and focus on the trainers demonstrating the fight for the cast and crew. It all looked pretty exciting playing out inside the local-dive pool hall. I wondered if we would look as cool as the trainers did. I had no doubts about Ra, he had black belts in eight different disciplines. Plus he had that whole Arnold-body Denzel-face thing going for him. And he could leap into the splits five feet in the air. He was gonna to kill this scene. I had no prayer of stealing it, even though I'd be knocking out two guys to Ra's one very big guy.

The trainers subbed me in and we ran slow motion rehearsals with the bad guys until we all felt we had it. Then we ran it at medium speed until we were confident, then at full speed. The two bad guys I'd be fighting were stunt men. They had no lines. I was glad I was fighting pros who weren't distracted by wanting camera time. And the odds for injuries were far higher with all amateurs doing stunts together. Ra would be fighting Pooch Martin, an NFL legend who'd finished his career with some shining moments in his three losing seasons with the Saints in the 80's. I was glad I didn't have to trust him flailing a pool cue around my head. He and Ra would mostly be boxing since Ra's character, Easy, was a retired fighter.

I headed to craft services for a snack while the crew finished setting up for the master shot of the entire scene, fight sequences and all. I focused on my entrance. This would be the first time the audience would see my fighter-mode makeover so I really wanted Charlie to own it, flaunt it, use it like a weapon.

Ishmael came over to the snack cart and grabbed a banana. "I played your song earlier but you weren't here."

"You played it when?"

He popped the stem and split the peel. "Before the rehearsal when they called five minutes."

"On the walkie? Like everyone could hear it?"

"Yeah." He listened to his earpiece. "There they go again. I'm going to go put on your song. Knock 'em dead."

I couldn't let myself wonder why Tina hadn't come for me when everyone was called to set. I had to focus on my killer entrance, delivering my lines and remembering my fight choreography.

The smoke machines were running when I went back into the pool hall. Tina was standing near Judd and looked like she had no intention of finding me anytime soon. I fought to put it out of my mind. Isaac Hayes' *That Lady* came on and I was immediately swept into the tune. I found a private-ish spot and worked out a pose for the doorway. Was a pose too much? Cliche? I saw some guys were rigging the door to pull it closed behind me. So, no pose in the doorway. I would catwalk-strut in, then take a strong stance after the door shut.

I focused on getting the acting in the scene right since most of the fight footage would be too chaotic in a wide shot to be useful. And both Pooch and I were going to need to cheat a lot of our transitions between sequences, which might give the whole thing a sloppy effect. But it was worth trying. You never knew when you'd catch magic. Since most of the industry had switched to shooting digital, it had even become fairly common to shoot the rehearsal in hopes of catching accidental magic.

I was confident that if I could get through this shot at least one time, the rest of the setups would be a lot easier. At the very least, they'd be shorter.

I went back outside and a guy in a headset explained he'd be cuing me to enter. He pointed his finger at me with an arcing motion to demonstrate the signal, then reminded me to clear the door so they could pull it shut. I closed my eyes, prayed to be my best, then started singing *That Lady* in my head until Judd yelled, "Action!" The headset guy and I stared at each other waiting for the cue. It seemed like a long time. Then, his eyes went wide and he pointed his finger at me.

I threw the door open, strutted to my mark and settled confidently as Ra looked up from shooting pool. Our eyes locked and half a smile curled up the left side of my mouth. It was easy to pretend we were old friends reuniting to help each other out. That said, I'd decided to add a history where Charlie and Easy had dated when they were younger. Figured it would add chemistry and raise the stakes of their reunion. They'd want to look good, impress each other, make the other remember what they were missing. But I didn't tell Ra. Other than Easy's opening compliment, there wasn't anything written into the scene that indicated they'd been lovers and I wanted to respect Ra's process and Clarence's script. I would just use it to fuel the scene for myself.

Ra straightened up and gave me a once over. "Damn girl, you holdin' up."

I let my smile widen. "Right back atcha, Easy." I sauntered over to the pool table and he handed me a cue.

He nodded to his men. "Take five. I'm alright." He stared at me intensely. "You still play?"

I grabbed the cue stick and he didn't let it go. I pulled at it again and he still didn't let it go. I wasn't sure what was happening. I looked up from under my curls and our eyes locked. For a minute, I thought he might kiss me. Then he smiled and let go of the cue. It seemed clear Ra had also decided our characters had history.

The door opened again and the two stunt guys came in followed by Pooch in a fur-collared full-length leather coat. He had to be dying waiting outside in the heat. Luckily, the scene opened with one of the stunt guys ceremoniously taking Pooch's hat and coat. We got through the dialogue with only a few mistakes, nothing worth stopping for, then went for the fight sequences. The stunt guys had told me not to worry too much about striking them, to focus instead on remembering the choreography and hitting my marks for camera. But it was impossible not to be afraid I'd make a mistake and really whack one of these guys.

My first sequence was mostly for show, the two stunt guys flexing a few skills and approaching me menacingly and me twirling the cue stick like a parade baton in response. The two guys came closer and took swipes at me. I dodged them, swung the pool cue around, "hit" the left guy in the knees then "stabbed" the right guy in the chest, knocking him into the jukebox.

We all reset and started the second sequence. The guy on the left came at me, chopping with both arms as I blocked each shot with the stick. The guy on the right came at me from behind and I "jabbed" him in the chest again. Then I swiped at the left guy's head and he folded backward to avoid my blow, then popped back up just in time for me to "pop" him in the face with the fat end of the stick – then I came back around like a baseball player swinging a bat at his falling head. That was one of the moves I'd come up with to give Clarence some cool shots he wasn't expecting.

We reset and did the last sequence, the one that ended with me knocking my guys out and Ra delivering his knockout punch to Pooch, sending him flying backward into the waiting arms of a stunt team.

Clarence laughed, "Just move out, guys. Keep going, just finish it up."

We waited a second for Pooch and the stunt team to clear camera. I took a breath then looked to Ra.

He smiled. "Yeah, you holdin' up real good. Thanks for that."

His guys came running back in and took in the carnage. The tall one had a line. "You okay, boss?"

I handed Ra my pool cue, then he took my hand and kissed it. Another improv. "Yeah, I'm just about perfect."

I chuckled. "Yeah." My hand lowered. "Glad to see we can count on each other. I may have somethin' for you. I just came by to see if you were still who you were."

"Hey, I'm always Easy, baby. And now I owe you one."

I walked toward the door and turned back to face him. "That you do." I pulled the door open and started to walk out. Brooklyn was standing outside and I hoped she wasn't in the shot.

"Cut! That was fantastic."

Everyone started clapping.

I laughed. "That was the craziest master I've ever done."

Clarence hugged me. "That was great. Wait until you see how good you're gonna look."

"Yeah, all I have to do is get it right a hundred more times."

He laughed. "Exactly. But it'll be a piece of cake now, just bite-sized pieces of the scene. I'd apologize for doing that master except it was awesome."

"I'm sure you got some good stuff for the gag reel."

"That too. But, seriously Charlotte, you did great."

I smiled. "Thanks. I needed that."

"Now, I really can't wait to see what you came up with for the training scene."

I laughed. I didn't want to tell him that we were only working on one thing at a time and I had no idea what the training scene would look like. I'd been studying videos and wanted to try the opening high kick from the *The Way of the Dragon* lesson in the Chinese boxing scene because it reminded me of *Soul Train* and I was pretty sure I could pull it off. That was all I had so far.

We shot the dialogue stuff first then did all of my fight sequence's with Ra and Pooch sometimes in the background. I was grateful to be in the background for Ra's coverage as the day wore on. My arms and shoulders were aching and my whole body was too tired to keep fighting at a hundred percent. For once, it was better to go first.

The medic walked with me as I headed for the trailer after I'd been wrapped. "You need anything?"

I chuckled. "I could use a massage and a jacuzzi."

"You're gonna wanna do ice first. I'll bring you a couple packs. I've got a great gel for you too. Just make sure you wash your hands after you put it on.

I'll grab you a few Ibuprofen too."

"Can you make it aspirin?"

"Got it." She walked quickly to her cart as I shut the door and peeled off my wardrobe, hanging everything as I went. I was pulling my own flouncy skirt on when someone knocked.

"Come in!"

Tina popped the door open. "Hey, um, Clarence wanted to make sure you knew we were all meeting up for drinks."

I'd been hearing about people hanging out together after work and had honestly been surprised I hadn't been included yet. The part of me that wasn't insanely tired was wired enough to be excited. "What time is it?"

"Almost three."

"Aw, hell no. I've been here for--" I stopped and counted. "Seventeen hours. And I still gotta ice myself. The sooner the better."

"Okay, but you're missin' all the nightlife. People gonna start thinkin' you don't like 'em." She laughed.

I walked over to the door and sat on the top step. "Hey Tina, I think I was late to set earlier today. My first scene. What happened?"

"Seriously? Nothin'. Just got you whenever they said."

"Whenever the walkie said?"

"The walkie, Judd, Clarence. I have many masters."

I smiled. "Right. Of course. Cool. See you tomorrow."

"Did you get your call sheet yet?"

"No, but I'm sure I'll have an email by the time I

get home."

She nodded. "Crew call's around three p.m. but I wanna say you don't come in until four or five. Go ice up. Have a good night."

Patrick didn't hear me come in. I activated the ice packs and strapped them to my shoulders with Ace bandages. A bag of frozen peas alternated on my thighs and a bag of frozen corn sat curled around my neck. I found a rerun of a competitive cake decorating show and replayed the day in my head. It would be hard to explain a day like this to Patrick. It was intoxicating to feel like a confident pro all day when all I was doing was nailing dialogue. To feel that way after an entire day of doing my own stunts was a whole other level of intoxication.

"What're they doing to you?" Patrick stood in the archway with a lazy face.

"I'm fine. I'm great actually. Long day but it was amazing."

"Okay then." His eyelids flopped shut and slowly half-opened again. "I love you. Goodnight."

I chuckled. "I love you."

Chapter 14

I'd slept in then spent a couple hours soaking in a hot bath full of Epsom salt while running my lines. My body actually felt pretty good but I knew day two was usually when the stiffness showed up.

Brooklyn, Aliyah and Aaron were already in chairs when I sat in front of Tulip's mirror. She was wearing a loose aqua tank dress with a necklace of bones, shells and crystals tied into leather strands.

"Cool necklace."

Tulip lit up. "You like it? Scares some people."

I laughed. "I don't scare easy."

Some people loathed getting their makeup done. The guys especially seemed to hate having any kind of applicator come near their eyes. And a lot of actors had trouble relinquishing control over their appearance. I usually loved it. The makeup artists normally started with some sort of cleanser or primer smoothed onto the face with gentle strokes, then a coat of base applied all over the face and neck with a smooth sponge. It felt nice. After nearly three decades of modeling and acting, I was used to having strangers put Q-tips, brushes, mascara wands, eyeliner pencils, liquid liners and even glue, tweezers and false eyelashes on my eyes, so it didn't usually bother me. Sometimes the blush was a cream dabbed on with fingertips or a sponge, sometimes it was a powder blended onto the cheekbone with a big, fluffy brush. Either way, it usually felt like a short, cheekbone-only spa treatment. Last were lips – lined, then filled in with a lipstick or gloss usually applied with a cotton swab. I didn't love the feeling of a swab on my lips but it didn't bother me.

Tulip was filling in my eyebrows when Brooklyn leaned forward in her chair and checked herself out in the mirror. "I'm so glad I stopped plucking my eyebrows. It makes people look older when they have thin eyebrows. Don't you think?"

Her makeup artist smiled. "Yours look great."

Aliyah stopped texting and watched the two of them in her mirror's reflection. Tulip smiled at me in our mirror. I found myself feeling suddenly self-conscious again. Why was I allowing self-doubt again? It didn't usually penetrate me. But were my eyebrows too thin? Being fair-haired, I only plucked about three hairs a month. My brows naturally had arches that tapered off into points. If my hair weren't so light, they'd be nearly perfect, right? There was nothing wrong with my eyebrows a little pencil couldn't fix and I just wasn't meant to have youthful bushiness in my brows. Maybe Brooklyn didn't mean anything by it. Even though she said it when Tulip was working on my brows. And loud enough for me to hear on the other side of the trailer.

Aaron looked to Brooklyn while his hair guy massaged product into his dirty-blonde shag. "Whatever you're doing is working, trust me on that."

Brooklyn got up and gave Aaron a kiss on the cheek before exiting.

Aliyah went back to texting. Aaron sucked in his

cheeks and checked out both his profiles in the mirror. Tulip held the disposable mascara wand to my upper lashes and wiggled it through to the tips. She was applying a second coat when she whispered. "Don't think about her."

I smiled, grateful not to feel crazy. "I'm good. I'm here to work."

"Exactly."

Though I wasn't a huge fan of breathing in clouds of hairspray or the sometimes painful hair-pulling or pins sticking into my scalp, I usually enjoyed having my hair done as well. Today's look would be the "Farrah," the layered hot-rolled look made famous by Farrah Fawcett. A melon-colored flower pinned behind my ear pulled back one side of curls. It would set off the flowers in the mostly green-leafy print Diane Von Furstenberg wrap dress I'd be wearing.

Aliyah got up from her chair as I was leaving and followed me out. "You look great. Seriously, own it."

I smiled. "Thanks."

"She's rocked over that whole blown-line thing."

"Brooklyn?"

"Yeah. I mean, I get it but like, it's your stuff, you know? Don't spread it around just cuz you had a bad moment on an otherwise great day. I mean, we're all in a Clarence Pool movie, right? Life's good." She looked my way. "You guys are old friends?"

"Yeah. Long time."

"Any pointers?"

I stopped and smiled at her. It was the kind of question I asked a lot when I was starting out. Heck, I still asked people for their life lessons. But I didn't have to think about it. "Be unforgettable. If the past is any indication of the future, this movie will survive the ages and be studied in universities. It'll become many people's favorite movie. You have to rise to the occasion of that kind of opportunity – the opportunity to contribute something to the history of film."

She laughed. "No pressure, right?"

Now, I laughed. "You're doing great. I can tell he likes you. He seems really happy you're here. This isn't about him, he's fine. It's about you not catching a rerun of this in five years and wanting to slap yourself 'cause you were too scared to try somethin' or because you let yourself become cuttable. Gettin' cut or missing an opportunity to really contribute somethin' amazing – or worse, actually having a bad acting moment caught on film and passed through to the final cut because the bigger name was great. It'll hurt at the premiere but you'll really get caught up in it if it's the movie of a lifetime, a classic or an un-killable cult favorite. This could be that. With Clarence, that's always a possibility and he's really the only director you can say that about right now, so this is it. Film is forever. Kill it, leave it all on the floor, save nothing, use everything."

"Dang. You should write a book. I've asked that question a lot, you know?"

I chuckled. "Actually, I do."

"Then you know you get a lot of great answers but some become your new t-shirt, you know? You just gave me like ten new t-shirt slogans."

I laughed. "You just made my day."

She hugged me. "You just made mine. I'll see you on set." She nearly skipped back to her trailer as I headed for mine.

I decided not to chance it and walked to set as soon as I was dressed. Ishmael was playing *If You Want Me to Stay* by Sly & the Family Stone as I walked into Charlie's family living room. Brooklyn was talking to Clarence near the monitors in video village. They laughed and she laid her hand on his arm. Tina was standing nearby with Judd who was talking to Madison.

Aliyah came up behind me. "Ready to make some history?"

"I'm ready to contribute to it."

She high-fived me. "Let's get it!"

I loved her enthusiasm. It reminded me that I could afford to be excited about all of this. "Hey, are you on time? I mean, did someone call you to set?"

"Yeah. Why? What's up?"

There was a downside to her endless curiosity. "Nothin'. I just wondered."

"I heard Madison killed her scene."

I laughed. "You heard already? Didn't she just finish?"

"Ishmael. He's got those monitors in the sound truck."

Judd said something to Tina then yelled, "Ready for rehearsal!"

Everyone gathered on set as Clarence walked over with Brooklyn. Tina passed, then caught my eye. "You're here. Okay, good." Then she walked away.

Aliyah turned to me and made her eyes wide. "Whoa, cuttin' it close. That's kinda messed up. You should say something to her."

"Yeah, I don't know. Not sure she's the problem."

She snapped her head. "I'd be ticked."

I followed Aliyah to the group gathered around Clarence. Judd quieted everyone as Clarence had a last minute discussion with his cinematographer then turned to the crowd. "We're gonna do the interiors looking out the windows first then turn around. We'll come back to this at the location set next week to get you guys approaching the house. Madison and Charlotte, I need you both by the couch somehow."

Madison and I followed him inside the faux manor home and tried some starting positions then walked through our lines.

Clarence yelled out, "Then we see Tanisha and Ladonna in the windows."

Brooklyn and Aliyah took their places and Clarence looked at a camera's monitor. "What happens if they're in the same window?"

Judd motioned for them to both move to Brooklyn's window. Clarence made a cut motion across his neck a couple times. "It's the wrong kind of funny. Go back. Okay, then Ashley goes upstairs and JayJ knocks at the door."

Madison and Aaron did as they were told then I opened the door.

"Make sure we see Tanisha clock JayJ from earlier. Then we do this." He waved his hand between me and Aaron so we ran our lines. When we finished, he directed, "Tanisha and Ladonna duck when JayJ tries to talk his way inside, hands her his card, then Charlie shines him on."

I smiled at Aaron, then focused and did my line, "Doesn't sound familiar, but I'll be sure to call you if I hear anything." I closed the door.

Clarence yelled to Madison on the staircase,

"That's your cue."

She looked at her mini-script. "Someone at the door?"

I turned to her. "Jehovah's Witness. I told him we were beyond saving."

She laughed. "That's for sure."

Clarence looked happy. "Ashley exits. Charlie fixes herself a sweet tea and the New York sisters sneak away."

Judd clapped thick hands. "Okay people, in five."

The crew ran around making last minute adjustments as Tulip freshened my lipstick and puff-powdered my shiny forehead through a tissue while Jill from hair shot hairspray onto her palm and smoothed it over my locks. Tulip checked me from the front, smiled, then moved on to Aaron.

Judd yelled, "First positions."

Aliyah hit her mark then raised her hands up and exclaimed, "I can't believe I'm in a Clarence Pool movie!"

It was probably bad form but it was what many of us were thinking so after a beat, we all laughed then clapped.

Patrick, asleep on the loveseat, woke as I came into the living room. "Hey."

I gave him a kiss. "Hey baby."

"How was it?

"It went great. I still felt like there were people who seem irritated with me or somethin', but I think I figured it out. I think I've been arriving on set late."

"What? Why?"

"Tina's supposed to come get me so I thought it might be her, and maybe it is, but I think it's Judd, the

First A.D. Which would really suck because he basically runs the whole set."

Patrick sat up and was suddenly alert. "Do you know him? Did he hit on you? Why would he want to make you late? Is it just you?"

I settled in beside him. "I mean, he's been flirty-friendly in that way guys in L.A. are but no, he never hit on me."

"But does he know you? Did y'all work together before?"

"No. I met him on set. He's got a good resume and he seems nice enough. I can't figure it out. Oh, and I think Brooklyn was mean to me."

"You're not sure? Mean how?"

"I think she was callin' me old by insulting my eyebrows."

He chuckled, then stopped himself. "Baby, you have beautiful eyebrows. She's just threatened."

"By what? She's got another brand new hit TV show and her part is bigger than mine by at least two scenes."

"If I had to guess? Your relationship with Clarence. Your part is all about you, she's just a hired gun chosen in part because of her name value. She's probably one of those names the studio pushed."

That made sense. At the very least, it felt good. "Maybe."

Patrick smiled. "Oh hey, remember my friend Dal? The chef at White Linen? He's being accused of stealing the King-Yay! recipe. They're saying he did the 504Ever robbery."

"Who's sayin'?"

"Everybody. Social media, everyone at the gym,

everybody."

"But no one's formally accused him of anything?"

"The guy who owns 504Ever called him out by name in a Facebook post. Somethin' like, 'Why is everyone accusing Dal of stealing recipes?'"

"Well, I wouldn't call that a formal accusation. It's more like a leading question."

"Yeah, but who are all these people accusing him? It's like propaganda."

I sat up. "Patrick, I saw your friend before, after my lunch at Galatoire's. He was on the street in his Galatoire's chef jacket getting yelled at by a boss or owner or whatever. The guy was saying Dal had stolen recipes from them. That's where I heard the whole black market thing for the first time."

Patrick thought for a moment. "What was all that stuff about recipes being like magician's tricks?"

"People lie. I read about this big survey on lying and the number one reason people gave for lying was to make themselves look better. Maybe he lied."

His face shifted. "He saved my cousin. I know it's not related, I'm just sayin' you might want to reserve your judgements of someone you don't know."

I put my hand on his. "I'm sorry. I thought I was answering your question about who the other accusers could be. I wasn't thinking about your family's relationship with him."

"Oh yeah, I forgot I asked that. I'm tired. I'm goin' to bed."

The evening could've ended a little more smoothly but after the dating hell of L.A., I felt so freaking lucky to come home to my over-tired best friend, lover and answered prayer.

Chapter 15

The trainers had split off to work with me, Aaron and Layla. Aaron was working on kicks, Layla on street fighting and Hiroto and I worked on my flashback training scene. Since I was still fairly limber, we started with finding a few stretches that might look good on camera. I decided we'd show Clarence the split up the wall, a backbend that moved into a front toe-touch and an idea I had for sitting on the floor with one leg extended – the camera on the floor at my foot. I would point my toe into the lens, flex my foot then lean into a closeup of me pulling my face toward my foot. I wasn't sure how it would look but it might be really cool. Maybe even unforgettable.

Then we moved into the Wing Chun training exercises. Wing Chun was a Chinese close range combat martial art. Unlike the more dramatically sweeping Japanese Naginatajutsu, Wing Chun movements were mostly economical and decisive. In the same way that yoga was about stretching and strengthening at the same time, Wing Chun was about defending and attacking in a singular motion. There were a lot of arm-slicing-the-air movements with hands like blades. Hiroto also taught me some fist movements and wrist twists. He showed me a few kicks and we chose the one we thought looked most impressive and was repeatable.

Lastly, he showed me the choreography they'd come up with for the training scene we were shooting next week. We integrated the things we'd found I was good at and cut anything that wasn't working. I asked Hiroto if he could send me a video of him doing the final choreography so I could work on it at home.

Layla and Aaron were chatting as I thanked Hiroto and headed for the door. Aaron nodded at me. "Working on a Saturday."

I smiled. "Yeah."

He put his hand on Layla's shoulder for a moment. "I'm telling you, they're going to end up using our doubles for most of this stuff and we're out here killing ourselves on a Saturday."

I wasn't sure where he was going with this. "I'm the only one in the shots I was workin' on. It's a training scene."

"Yeah, wait'll you see how much other stuff they shoot while you're at lunch."

I wasn't going to take his bait. "Okay."

He walked over to shake his trainer's hand and Layla smiled at me. "He was tryin' that crap on me 'fore you walked up. Snake in the grass maybe, tryin'a get us to go on record complainin'."

"Do you think?"

"I'm just sayin' I don't know the cat. Gotta assume the worst."

I chuckled. "I'd argue with you about givin' people the benefit of the doubt but you make sense. Either way, I don't like all that kinda talk. Doesn't seem like a winning attitude."

Layla laughed. "No it don't."

Kicho and Astrid came in as I pulled the door open for Layla. We exchanged hellos and goodbyes and Layla walked out with me. I smiled at her. "Thanks, by the way. I appreciate you bein' honest with me about your perspective on Aaron. If I hadn't spent so many years swimming with the sharks, I might've really needed to hear it. Either way, I appreciate you lookin' out for me."

She gave me a quick hug. "It's a man's world. We gotta stick together."

"Amen."

Patrick was still at the gym so I turned on the TV. Hurricane Irene was pounding the East coast. With the six year anniversary just around the corner, every channel I tried was comparing Irene to Katrina. I wanted to throw something at the screen. Comparing nearly anything to Katrina just showed ignorance about the event. Though Katrina was the name of a hurricane, it became the name for the levee failure and subsequent devastating floods. It had become the name for the nearly two thousand dead, the abandoned Americans holding signs on rooftops, the thousands of people surviving days of horror in the Superdome and Convention Center, the Americans who were called refugees and accused of looting for gathering food and medicine for their families and neighbors and all the rest of the awful chaos and loss the flooded city suffered.

The country poured forth a surge of support in the wake of the government's failures, but they also publicly debated whether the city was worth saving. Some even blamed the city's character and morals for the disaster, despite the Independent Levee

Investigation Team calling Katrina "The greatest man-made engineering catastrophe since Chernobyl" when it was proven that the US Army Corps of Engineers were to blame for the levee breach.

The city was unquestionably bouncing back since funding had finally arrived. There was construction and road repair everywhere. Tourism was growing again and the film industry was positively booming, attracting a whole new wave of residents. But the population of children, the building blocks of the city's future, was still significantly lower than before The Storm. Even in neighborhoods where population had increased, the number of children had plummeted. Our culture had survived yet another blow, but it had lost many of it's future torch-bearers. With the influx of people from New York and L.A. and the gentrification that had started to creep into neighborhoods that had been virtually the same for hundreds of years, it was hard not to worry for the city's prospects.

The laptop screen came to life as I flipped it open. I searched "recipe black market" and found a "Black Market Manhattan" cocktail recipe, a listing of "recipes" for making virtual items in some video game and a listing for a pizza joint named Black Market Pizza.

I searched for 504Ever and found the restaurant's site. The home page featured a link to the *Gambit* vote and a photo of owner Travis Bend holding a plate of King-Yay!s. The "about" page didn't offer much more. The café had opened a few months ago offering a "local fusion" menu. There were some review quotes from local magazines and papers, and a description of Travis stating only, "The son of a successful restaurateur."

I looked up Travis' Facebook page and found his father tagged as family. I couldn't access the father's page so I Googled the name, Oscar Bend. Nothing. So, I added "restaurant" and tried again. An article from a Texas business magazine popped up stating that Bend owned a chain of Texas barbecue restaurants called Smoky's. It didn't mention where Oscar was from or whether he had a son.

I went back to the 504Ever site and looked for the name of the chef. It wasn't listed as a contact so I went back to the reviews. One called Chef Licious' menu a "fresh take on old recipes." Chef Licious? Not optimistic, I entered it into the Facebook search bar. He had a public page but no private page under that name. The photos were mainly of various dishes he'd engineered, and a few of the restaurant's interior and Travis. Chef Licious' profile photo was a logo of a chef's hat over the word "Licious" shaped like a plate with a knife and fork crossed behind it. The logo looked a little like a skull and cross bones. Maybe I wasn't young and hip enough to appreciate the juxtaposition. To me, it looked like a friendly poison warning.

The "about" page listed only a link to Chef Licious' Twitter page. I wasn't on Twitter so I Googled the name instead. There were a few mentions in local media but none of them revealed his real name or where he was from. There wasn't even a photo anywhere.

I clicked to Patrick's page, went to his "friends" and searched for Dal. The Dal Durant profile popped up so I clicked it. Dal was a native, a 610 Stompers parade dancer and a chef who'd worked at Galatoire's and a couple other local haunts. My access was limited without being his Facebook friend, but I did see some photos of him hanging out and drinking with various women – many of them obviously tourists. He'd shared an article about how to beat automated photo traffic tickets and a not-very-funny cartoon joke about sex addiction. I closed the computer when I heard Patrick come home and greeted him with a kiss at the door.

He smiled. "I've got a surprise." He pulled keys from his pocket and shook them.

I squealed. "Yay! For the house? Can we move stuff now?"

"We can start. A guy from the gym's meeting me at my old house to pick up the couch and the bed. We can take the boxes from here over now and you can start on the house while we go get the furniture."

I jumped up and down and the chandelier shook in the bedroom. "You hear that?" I ran to look and the chandelier was swinging back and forth. "Look!"

Patrick came up behind me.

I pointed. "It's swinging!"

"It's an old house, Charlotte. You were jumping. Come on, get your shoes on. I'll drop you off."

The guy from the gym ended up bringing another friend with a pickup and they filled both trucks before heading my way. I was still figuring out the kitchen when the guys hauled a dresser past me into the bedroom. Like many shotgun houses, our kitchen sat between the living room and the bedroom with no hallways separating them. I wasn't sure how I felt about guests having to go through our bedroom to use the toilet but I was truly excited to have a stoop on a French Quarter parade route. I felt like we were moving closer to the soul of the city.

As the guys were finishing up, I walked a few blocks and picked up a couple six-packs at what would now be our corner store. The neighborhood was magical with its wrought iron balconies and ornately carved and painted eaves. We all sat on the stoop sipping cold beers as men wandered past to a nearby gay bar. I'd always pictured myself here living surrounded by street musicians and happy revelers.

We thanked the guys and spent another hour or so unpacking boxes before taking off for showers and delivery food at the Garden District house. With tired muscles and wet hair, we blessed the cheese-stuffed dates, pork belly sliders and fried grit sticks.

The pork belly was outstanding. "How well do you know your friend Dal?"

He finished chewing. "I don't know. I've known him most of my life but I wouldn't say we know each other well. Why?"

"My old manager, Marilyn, used to say that the way you do anything is the way you do everything."

Patrick shrugged. "I guess."

"And I've noticed in my life that all appetites are related. Sex, food, work, all of it."

"Okay."

"Dal has a lot of pictures of himself drinkin' with women on his Facebook page. A lot of them looked to be tourists."

Patrick seemed less and less comfortable. "Yeah. Okay."

"Well, it just seems like shootin' fish in a barrel to pick up tourists. How're they supposed to resist the allure of a local inviting them to drink? Maybe go to their cool, local place? Maybe cook them some local food?"

He laughed. "Okay."

"Well? Is Dal the type of guy who likes to come by things easy? Takes shortcuts? Believes in get-rich-quick schemes?"

"Because he likes to avoid rejection at bars?"

I thought about that for a minute. "Yeah."

He laughed again. "Maybe he's just lazy and not picky. Is that a sign of a thief?"

"I don't know. Not when you say it that way. But we know he's not lazy. He worked at Gal's and he's a 610 Stomper. But he also believes in getting out of traffic tickets."

Patrick stopped eating. "What're you doing, Charlotte? Why are you digging through his page?"

"I was lookin' up stuff about the 504Ever staff and ended up lookin' him up." I decided not to ask if Dal was a sex addict.

Patrick picked up his fork again then hesitated. "I love the way your mind works. I do. But I don't like how this feels."

"What does it feel like?"

"Like you're digging up dirt on my friend."

I stopped eating too. "I can see that. Maybe I am."

He kissed me. "And maybe he stole the recipes. But I've known him a long time and I've never seen him do anything sketchy. Plus--"

I smiled. "He saved your cousin. I know."

"Exactly."

Chapter 16

The French Quarter house was far from ready for receiving guests but we invited a few people over for the parade anyway. Southern Decadence was a gay festival held over Labor Day weekend with parties, concerts, costume contests and two parades – one for floats and one for walking krewes. In the Garden District we lived just a few blocks from the giant Mardi Gras parades. Here, we only had to open our front door to be on the route.

The weather had been crazy Friday and Saturday with tropical storm Lee blowing bands of rain and wind through, tearing rainbow banners and ripping balloons from their balcony moorings. Today, things had calmed with only occasional showers pushing through. Patrick set up some folding office chairs near the couch in the living room in case people wanted to hang out inside.

I smiled when I saw Ra and Hud walking up with Jamal, the guy who played Brooklyn's love interest. I made introductions to Patrick as Ra, Hud and I exchanged hugs. Wendy from wardrobe arrived shortly after along with her beau. During a few work lunches, she and I found we had a lot in common. Kicho joined us as well. She'd been trying various things I'd recommended in my blog and said she was excited to see a real New Orleans parade.

I'd invited the cast in a casual way, hoping Brooklyn and Aaron would have other plans. Frankly, I wasn't sure I wanted the added distraction of having to entertain the super-famous Layla, Madison and Graham either. I wanted to simply relax and enjoy the first parade in our new weekend home. I felt rich just thinking about having a pied-à-terre. Entertaining megastars I didn't know well might make our two homes feel like the worn rentals they were instead of a place in a manor home in the Garden District and a second home in the French Quarter. I'd always had a gift for finding ways to feel rich on a limited income. I'd given Sofia my old car when she first moved to L.A. I was buying a new (used) one anyway and the trade-in value was only $1200. It was worth a lot more to someone without a car in Los Angeles. I knew I'd feel like a millionaire if I could afford to give a car to a lifelong friend. Only rich people gave their friends cars, right? Seemed like money well used.

Kicho and Wendy were in the kitchen pouring cocktails into plastic go-cups we'd caught at Mardi Gras parades. Kicho smiled. "It's so crowded out there. I wasn't sure I'd make it in time."

"Yeah, it's gotten pretty big. Last year, over 125,000 people attended. It started in the Treme back in '72 with this party of about fifty or sixty people. There was this very diverse group of roommates throwin' a going-away party for a friend. They called their place in the Treme 'Belle Reve' after the Mississippi plantation Blanche DuBois' refers to in *A Streetcar Named Desire* so they threw this costume party with a theme of coming as your favorite

'Southern Decadent.' They picked the Sunday before Labor Day so they could have a day of recovery after. I guess everyone had such a good time that they ended up doin' the party again and added an informal march. Then it went from there."

Wendy laughed. "You always know all this stuff locals don't know. Heck, I used to be a tour guide and I don't know some of the stuff you know."

I smiled. "I'm overcompensating. I mean, I learned all that for my blog and I really do want to know everything about this place – knowing that I can barely scratch the surface of the history and culture and knowing none of it will ever make me a native. So, yeah, I'm overcompensating for not growing up here."

Kicho smiled. "I love your blog. I've been trying some of the things on your list. The Nectar Creme snoball at Snowizard was especially wonderful."

"You had it? Yay! I'm so glad you liked it."

Wendy sipped on her drink. "I could go for a snoball right now."

I laughed. "I know, right?"

Patrick yelled from the front door. "They're coming!"

I grabbed my camera and headed out to the stoop. Part Mardi Gras, part *The Adventures of Priscilla, Queen of the Desert*, part political rally and all good time, the parade was a spectacle of feathers, falsies, "bears" and buns.

The official colors were pink, black and silver often expressed through glitter and sequins. I was excited to see the Pussyfooters round the corner and head our way. I'd first seen the dance troupe in the

2010 Mardi Gras parades. Dressed in pink wigs and corsets with short skirts, fishnets and white combat boots, they all looked to be over thirty and came in every size and shape. They'd been my favorite parade dance krewe since the first time I saw them strutting and shimmying their way down St. Charles. I spotted Christine Miller, the tour guide who'd helped me find the flask at May Baily's, and waved. Her eyes widened with recognition and she waved back. It was kind of exciting knowing someone in the parade.

A petite woman wearing a steam-punk inspired top hat with a sleeveless white button-down tucked into a black miniskirt with rainbow suspenders stepped down from her stoop four doors down. She looked like a dancer but she moved like a drunk. She stumbled toward the Pussyfooters and a man in a pink sash blocked her with his arms. She tried to push her way in again and a man in a tiara helped move her back to her stoop. She seemed to be crying. Tiara guy sat with her and nodded a lot and she seemed to recover. I hoped she wasn't a drama queen or an alcoholic or a flirt using the 'broken bird' tactic. That could be a lot in a neighbor. I snapped a quick photo in case I needed it for a police report some day.

From my perch, I could see the 504Ever owner, Travis Bend, walking through the crowd wearing a hat topped with a glittery rainbow. I nudged Patrick and jutted my chin in Travis' direction.

Patrick quickly spotted him. "Oh yeah, the restaurant guy. Who's the guy with the dreads?"

Next to Travis was the chef I'd seen in the kitchen when I ate at 504Ever with Ra. His mass of ratty blonde dreads was pulled into a rainbow scarf and his sandy beard worthy of religious zealotry flowed freely.

"The day I went in, he was cookin' with two other guys. Guess he's the head chef, Chef Licious."

Patrick laughed. "Chef Licious? Come on. It's all so much work to be different. It's like a total misunderstanding of what makes people here cool."

"Reminds me of L.A., like those guys I told you about who were tryin' so hard to be some different Goth thing, only they did it in exactly the same way. What's that Sheryl Crow song about you're an original but then you turn around and there's a hundred more? Like that."

A brass band passed and I danced along to *Down By The Riverside*. Patrick exchanged spots with Ra as I snapped photos for the blog. Ra looked at my screen as I checked a shot. "Wow, great zoom."

"I know, right? My dad sent it. I'm still figuring out everything it does."

He caught a strand of beads from a parading admirer. "Hey, did you get invited to the last photo shoot?"

"No. I'm guessin' you didn't either since you didn't know if I was there."

He shook his head. "Naw, but I figured you would. I mean, you're one of the seven sisters, right?"

I chuckled. "You'd think. Aliyah said she was left out of the one they did with everyone in costume."

"Did you go to that one?"

"Nope."

Ra shook his head. "Damn."

"I know. But it's fair. It sucks, but it's fair. I don't put butts in seats. No one's going to *Seven Sisters* to see a Charlotte Reade movie. Heck, they're far more likely to be going to see you in a movie. You're freakin' huge in China."

Ra laughed as the last of the parade passed. "I haven't seen you at much of the nightlife either, but I've only gone a couple times."

"I didn't get invited at first. I wasn't on the email list for some reason."

He turned from the crowd dispersing behind him. "Do you have an enemy?"

I hadn't really thought about it that way. "Maybe."

"Did you ever figure out why you were coming late to set? Is it Tina?"

"I don't think so. Judd maybe, but why? I never met him before this."

"And it can't be Clarence, and that's pretty much the chain of command."

"Sometimes I feel like he wishes he could fire me."

Ra laughed then stopped. "Oh, you're serious. Don't do that. You'll make yourself crazy. You're killin' it. What about Brooklyn?"

"Why do you ask that?"

Ra got serious. "Does she have beef with you?"

"No, I don't think so, but she's one of those survivor types, the kind who come at you to rattle you. She carves her space out, you know? Marks her territory. But hey, she's been at this a long time. She's probably just battle-scarred."

"Yeah, well just look out for yourself. And don't forget she knows Aaron from when they did that movie back when she was new. I see them both talkin' to Judd so watch that too."

I didn't like the idea of having to be paranoid. "What about Jamal? He's playing her love interest, does he know anything."

"She doesn't make time for him. He just knows her from here."

Hud walked up the stairs to join us. "Fun parade. That was kinda crazy."

Ra patted Hud's arm with the back of his hand. "Tell Charlotte she's killin' it."

I'm pretty sure I blushed.

Hud smiled. "Everything looks great. You're going to be really proud when you see the pool hall scene you two do together."

I hated not feeling confident. It was even worse revealing my insecurities but I felt I had to know. "So Clarence is happy?"

"Yeah, of course. Is he not telling you that? No, he's very happy. He said the stunts came out better than he thought they would. We didn't even shoot the double."

That made me feel better. I hoped Clarence was happy with my acting as well, but I was done asking for validation.

Kicho, Wendy and her beau stayed and helped us clean up, though we kept assuring them it wasn't necessary, that we still had boxes to unpack and weren't expecting a spotless house. People were still wandering the street outside when we finally closed the door and looked around our new place. We hugged and I smiled up at Patrick's moss-green eyes. "That was fun. I feel like we christened the place."

He smiled. "I really liked Hud. We got to talk for a while and he's great."

"I told you I found some incredible people out there. If I introduce you to a friend from L.A., you can know three things – they're smart, they're kind and they're amazing at something. Like, the-best-in-the-world type of amazing."

"What are you best in the world at?"

"Me?" I thought about it. "Here, I'm not sure yet. But there, I was great at figuring out who should meet who and bringing people together so they could make something or do something amazing."

He nodded then stopped. "Maybe here it could be something you do for you."

I smiled and kissed him. Then we went to work on the house.

We finished unpacking the last boxes, then watched a movie before Patrick turned in. I stayed up and worked on my blog. As the photos uploaded, I realized I'd caught a shot of Travis Bend and Chef Licious making their way down the crowded sidewalk. How could I figure out the chef's real name? If I knew his email, I might be able to find some trail on the web. If he'd used any photos of himself on Facebook, I could've reverse-image-searched them. I had nothing. So, I looked up Brooklyn instead. I clicked on her IMDb page and then to the page for *To Name A Few*, the movie she'd done with Aaron. I clicked to the complete listing of crew and scanned. Boom. Judd Fellows. Production Assistant. So, they'd all started out together. Except Aaron, he was already a star by then.

I opened the video of Hiroto doing my Wing Chun training sequence and worked on my moves until even the bar-hoppers were heading to bed.

Chapter 17

Aunt Ava was turning eighty-five. In New Orleans, they would've said she "made eighty-five," but now she lived in a gated community on the other side of the lake. Ava had always loved a party and her favorite kind were the ones in her honor. Her husband had been the perfect host until his passing years ago. I'd always admired their marriage. They had all the devotion and habitual love Maw Maw and Paw Paw had displayed for over fifty years, but they never seemed to end their honeymoon. It was downright inspirational. I hated that Ava had to let him go. And it scared me. I was finally letting myself believe that Patrick wasn't a player just pretending to be the most wonderful man I'd ever met. I was letting myself need him in my life, and that terrified me.

Patrick always made a fuss over Ava and she loved it. She was wearing a plastic shiny-gold crown inset with faux jewels over her reddish curls and a lovely white eyelet dress. Mom and my brother, Tate, were talking to cousin May on the lanai. I hugged my niece, Julia, and let her lead me outside.

Julia's hair had a dyed-blue streak running down either side of her face. With my job, I'd never gotten to have fun with my hair like that. I never even changed the cut of my hair without thinking about the potential cost of new photos and possible work-loss. Heck, I never even painted my fingernails in case I had a commercial audition and had to show my hands to the camera for product handling.

Julia's voice was excited. "Guess what we've been talking about."

I chuckled. "I couldn't even begin to."

"Wells Plantation. The family farm. The one with the symbol. Cool, right?"

"Sure." I hugged everyone hello and joined in. "Did we figure out anything?"

Tate shifted his weight. "Where is it exactly?"

"Ava said St. Francisville but I think she may have been mistaken. I looked it up on a map and it's not very far north for a place that was supposed to be 'up north.' Plus, it's in the foot part of the boot. Why wouldn't they just go to Mississippi instead of crossing the entire state to get to Texas?"

Mom grabbed a handful of nuts from a bowl on the table and replaced the paper doily cover. "Well, shoot."

"I thought about it, though. I thought about if she'd gotten it mixed up with another Saint-somethin'. But there wasn't really another saint town that seemed to have standing plantations or be old enough as a town."

Tate interrupted. "Sometimes the town name is younger than the property because the town wasn't incorporated until long after people settled there."

I shrugged. "True. But anyway, I looked up other Francis towns and came up empty so I tried 'villes. I looked into Farmersville and Cheneyville but I'm pretty sure the Wells Plantation was in Cloutierville."

Tate repeated. "Cloutierville."

Ava wandered onto the lanai carrying a cocktail and motioned to us. "We're doing a champagne toast in a few minutes."

My cousin Tate laughed in the doorway. "That means come inside so I don't have to look for you in half an hour when this thing finally comes off."

He was probably right but we went inside and picked at hors d'oeuvres. Ava tasted the artichoke soup and decided it needed more butter.

I sidled up to her. "Could the Wells Plantation have been in Cloutierville?"

Ava got another spoon from the drawer and took another taste. "What did I say?"

"St. Francisville."

She waved her hand dismissively. "Oh, that's where my darlin' husband's people were from. Generations."

I smiled. "So it could've been there?"

"Cloutierville? Yes, of course. I think it's written on that family tree in the attic, but that sounds right."

Julia jumped in. "You should take someone from that antique shop to see the flask at the brothel. Maybe they could tell something by looking at it."

I finished off a cucumber canapé. "That's not a bad idea."

She seemed excited I'd agreed. "That guy who showed us all that cool stuff might do it."

Mom came up behind us to secretly ditch a deviled egg. Her whisper was too loud. "She said they were her grandmother's recipe. Bragged a bunch. If those are her grandmother's recipe," she got quieter, "they are to be avoided."

I laughed. Mom always had a way of making an

insult sound like kindness. A true southern belle.

She pointed to a plate of canapés topped with candied-bacon. "That's slap-ya-mama good."

Ava put her spoon in the sink and rinsed her hands. "Aren't they wonderful? Everything salty should have a little sugar in it and everything sweet should have a pinch of salt. Then it tastes like life. I think Millie made those."

Mom smiled. "Well whoever made them is to be commended. A-plus."

I reached for the recommended canapé.

Lillibette rinsed a plate and put it in the sink. "How's your movie goin'?"

"Honestly? It's a little rough. I mean, it's amazing and I love the character and I feel like the luckiest every day, but it's been rough."

Mom grabbed a stem of grapes from the cheese plate and plucked a few. "She works insane hours."

I smiled. "I do. But the crew has to do it every day. I work like an average of three days a week I'd say."

Mom waved her finger while she finished chewing. "But she trains for her stunts on her days off."

"That's true, but I have a lot to learn in a really short time. But that's not it. I can do the long hours and the physical stuff's going pretty well. It's the personalities."

Ava folded a tea towel and hung it over the oven door handle. "You don't like the other people?"

I felt suddenly ungrateful. "I do. They're mostly great. There's just a few people that remind me of the reasons I decided to leave L.A."

Lillibette laughed as she headed into the pantry. "You didn't leave L.A., you just never left here."

It was true.

Julia joined us. "Can't you just tell Clarence?"

I shrugged. "You never wanna be the problem. With all that pressure and millions of dollars at stake, the last thing Clarence needs is a fragile ego that needs protecting. No. If you wanna play with the big boys, you gotta be able to take the big hits."

Lillibette had clearly missed all but my last sentence and injected, "Saints are lookin' good this year."

I high-fived her. "Who dat!"

Julia wasn't satisfied. "But he's your friend. Can't you just tell him?"

"What? That I think people are picking on me?"

Mom pumped a canapé in the air for emphasis. "Saboteurs."

I chuckled. "Julia, if I want screen time, I've gotta earn it. That's the bottom line. I'm just focusing on the work."

Lillibette laughed. "I would want revenge."

May passed through. "True. I don't even know what for but I can vouch for her vengefulness."

Lillibette nodded. "I would. I'd at least wanna call them out."

I smiled. "It's not like I've never had thoughts of sayin' something to them but I don't even really know if I'm just bein' paranoid. I mean, if it's really the people I think it is then there's kind of a grand conspiracy to make me look bad."

Lillibette coughed. "Fired."

I shot her a look.

She shrugged. "What? That's what you're sayin'. They're tryin' to get you fired. Stand your ground."

Mom licked her fingers then wiped them on the towel hanging on the oven door. "She's not wrong."

"Yeah, but Mom, I have absolutely no power on this set. I have no Oscars, no star on the Walk of Fame, no covers of *People Magazine* and no box office draw. I don't put butts in seats. The studio didn't want me. If Clarence wasn't Clarence, I'd probably never even have gotten an audition. This is what lucky looks like."

Mom ran a hand over my hair. "I just hate that this is what lucky feels like. I was hoping it would be different here."

I smiled. "It is. I get to come home and complain to Patrick or stay up talking about cool stuff I got to do. It's totally different."

She smiled. "Yes it is."

My brother came back into the kitchen holding a dirty plate. I took it from him and rinsed it. "Hey Tate, did you ever find Birdie's maiden name? Mom, did you know it?"

Mom popped another canapé and shook her head no.

Tate ignored the cucumber bites and went for the spinach dip. "There's nothing. Dad said her papers say 'W.' Birdie W. Stewart. It wasn't uncommon at the time to only use your married name."

"Yeah, you said. Dad didn't have her birth certificate?"

"Nope. Why would he? Do you have mom's?"

"I don't know. Maybe when she died? I have no idea. Just seems strange."

Tate shook his head. "Some things just get lost, Charlotte."

"A maiden name?"

He laughed. "You still have your ex-husband's name."

Mom's face got disapproving. "Hey."

I wasn't sure why I was defending myself. Patrick didn't seem to mind and my union's rules made it difficult to change names. There was already a Charlotte Stewart registered as an actor so I'd have had to choose another name. "You know that's because of my job."

Mom offered, "You could take our family name, be Charlotte Tate."

"And publicly reject Dad? I don't think so."

She nodded. "I wasn't thinking. Charlotte Reade's a lovely name."

Tate nodded too. "He did say the pipe was Birdie's dad's and that it was given to her dad by her mom when they fell in love. Then he died while Birdie was really young and she left home young."

"Where was home?"

Tate looked upward, recalling. "I think they were living in Alexandria by then. I asked if Birdie's mother was the daughter of a wealthy plantation owner. He said Birdie told that story but he never took it as true."

"So all we need to do is find someone with a name that's like Birdie and starts with a W who may or may not own a plantation or be trash."

Tate replayed the sentence in his head then nodded. "Yes." Then he laughed.

Chapter 18

Patrick agreed that it was time I talk to Tina so I went to work with a mission. I wished I could remember the guy at the gate's name as we greeted each other. Each time I got a new part, I met dozens and dozens of people. This movie had a cast and crew of over 300. It was also important to remember who did what job. And for each actor's name I memorized, there was an accompanying character name. Best estimates are that the average person meets about 10,000 people in a lifetime. The average lifespan is 78.7 years which comes to about 128 people a year. Between work, auditions, parties, premieres, meetings and regular life, that kind of math didn't apply in our profession.

Tina tugged on her ever-present cap as she passed.

"Hey. Do you have a minute?" I led her into my trailer and closed the door. "Do you have any idea why I've been late to set?"

"I come when--"

"I know, I'm not asking about you. I'm sayin' is there any reason you can think of why I've been late to set? 'Cause I have. A bunch of times. And one is way too many."

She looked at me hard, deciding. "I feel like Judd

sometimes isn't on top of it with you. He's got a lot on his plate."

"Sure, sure, of course. Can you do me a huge favor? Can you make sure I'm always on time?"

"Sure, but like I was sayin', I come for you as soon as he tells me."

It was my turn to decide. "I think someone's tryin' to get me in trouble or fired or something. I'm not even sayin' it's Judd, I'm just sayin' it's costing me. Not good for the movie either. And Clarence, I know he's frustrated."

Her voice became conspiratorial. "Who do you think it is?"

"Honestly, it doesn't matter. And I don't really know so there's no point in going there, it just needs to stop. Clarence fought for me to get this part and I'm making him look bad. I can't have that." I was trying to stay strong but tears were backing up. "I just can't."

She smiled warmly. "I got you. Don't worry about it, okay?"

I laughed. "I'll try but worrying is kinda my thing."

"I hear you. But I got you. Seriously." She gave me a hug and walked me to the makeup trailer.

I settled into Tulip's chair and smiled at her in the mirror. "Patrick's visiting for lunch today. Maybe you can meet him."

Brooklyn laughed from the other end of the trailer. "I would never invite my man to a set. Disaster. Especially this one. Forget all the fights it could start, it just makes you look bad in general. 'Bring your boyfriend to work day' isn't a thing. I would never."

Tulip ignored her. "I look forward to it. Sounds like a great guy."

I smiled. He was. I was settling into feeling Patrick was everything he seemed to be and that this might all be real. He seemed to have no trouble falling in love with me and believing all was well. He was still divorcing when we met but he seemed so much less jaded than I was. I'd fought so hard to keep my heart a welcoming place but his ease made my residual neurosis obvious.

I left the trailer still wondering if I was stupid for inviting Patrick. I hated when I got stuck on something I wasn't even sure was true. I'd felt like that a lot since filming had started. There were the times I was left out of photo shoots and felt like the kid in high school who wasn't allowed to sit at the "cool kids" table. All those stares of irritation when I'd arrive to set late, like they all thought I was a prima donna. I still heard Brooklyn's voice when I plucked my two or three errant eyebrow hairs every few weeks.

Brooklyn's voice seeped between the makeup and wardrobe trailers. "I get it. You're stuck now. I'm just sayin' I wish you never hired her. It's like amateur hour. Girl's too old to be this green, so she must think she's worth waitin' on."

Wendy grabbed my arm and I jumped.

"Sorry, didn't mean to scare you. I was just saying hi."

I tried to calm myself. "Hey."

"You okay? I seriously didn't mean--"

I laughed. "No, I'm fine. We're fine. I'm just on

edge."

She smiled. "Big scene today."

"Yeah. Just me. I'll definitely be gettin' my coverage today."

"I heard. Sounds like everyone's been battling for screen time. I heard Brooklyn's all bent today because she's shooting second unit."

"She's not working with Clarence today?"

"Nope. Hud's got it."

My head was spinning. Was Patrick right? Was Brooklyn jealous of me? Threatened by me? She was a household name in plenty of demographics and I was still "the girl from..." whatever movie or TV show I'd done that was a hit at that time. "What's wrong with Hud? He's an awesome director."

She popped a piece of gum and offered me a piece. "He's not Clarence. She feels snubbed."

The ten minute call came over Wendy's wire. Tina appeared immediately. "We need to get you in wardrobe."

I smiled at Tina then waved to Wendy. "I'll see you later."

"Knock 'em dead."

Tina stopped and listened to her earpiece. I couldn't read her expression. "Clarence wants to see you in his trailer."

My heart raced. "Seriously?"

She kept her eyes down. "He probably just wants to give you a pep talk before your big scene, work some things out. He does that sometimes."

I really wanted to believe her. "Yeah?"

"Yeah, of course. Especially with the stars."

I stood nervously as Tina knocked on the trailer

door. "It's Tina with Charlotte."

It was quiet for a while. I began to wonder if this was all an elaborate plot to make me late to the set again. Then we heard a door close and a sink run.

Tina knocked again. "Hey! It's Tina with Charlotte."

"It's open."

Tina popped the metal latch and opened the door for me as I climbed the textured steel stairs.

Clarence smiled and sat on a chair facing the couch. "Hey, have a seat. I just wanted to get some things straight."

My heart thrummed as I sat into the couch.

"I haven't been happy about some things, and the lateness thing was really getting to me so I'm glad to see you on time lately."

I interrupted, my chest aching. "There was a problem with--"

"Honestly Charlotte, I don't care. I coulda had a lot of people in this role. You know that. Coulda made the studio happy and hired a name."

I felt everything slipping away. "I know and I'm grateful."

"I feel like you're not passionate the way you used to be. I'm getting pressure I didn't see coming. Diva complaints."

"Diva?" I laughed.

He didn't.

"Can I ask you somethin'?"

He nodded. "Yeah, sure."

I took a breath. "Are you happy with the work?"

"The dailies? Yeah, they're great."

"Okay, because I come to work everyday with

one goal. I know the studio didn't want me and that there were lots of questions about me. My goal at all times is to make sure that after people see the movie, no one will ever question you again. That's it." I felt suddenly calm.

Clarence was still for a while. "This is not how I thought this was gonna go."

I smiled. "I'm all about this. I'm not out hangin' with y'all at night 'cause I'm working my routines. I don't know what the diva stuff is about but I'm all about this. I'm focused on the work. I want you to be proud you picked me. I want it to be somethin' you can brag about."

He laughed. "We both know how much I'd love that."

I laughed too.

"Charlotte, look, I wrote this scene for you because I know you're gonna kill it. You've come so close so many times and it just never works out for you to catch fire." He smiled and I felt the years between us. "I wrote this part so everyone could see what I see, so they could see what you're capable of. This is the scene where it's all about you. We get to see the student in you becoming a master. We're gonna give you the time you need to get it right."

A tear escaped down my cheek. I patted it away gently so as not to mess up my makeup. "Thank you."

He laughed and hugged me as we stood. "Actors never wipe away a perfect tear."

I pulled away and smiled. "Yeah, well... I get to be a real person with you. Besides, after that funeral scene, you already know I can cry on cue."

He laughed. "For hours! It was like a magic trick.

You and Madison were like dueling teardrops. And she sheds award-winning tears but you went tear-for-tear with her. It was a boo-hoo battle! A tear-off! Clash of the cryers!"

"War of the weepers!" I laughed with the extra loudness of relief. Our friendship would survive this and he still believed in me.

Someone knocked at the door. I heard Tina's voice. "They're ready for you."

Clarence gave me another hug. "Alright Charlie, let's see whatcha got."

"I'm gonna try to do you proud."

Tina followed me into my trailer and helped me dress quickly. "You good?"

"Yeah. Rattled, but good."

The "dojo" was set up for my flashback scene of training in Japan. I felt pretty in the coral maxi dress with slits all the way up my legs. I was barefoot and wore no accessories save the wide, coral scarf pulling my straightened, teased and flipped *That Girl* hairdo from my face.

The guitar plucking and soft drumbeat of Ann Peebles' *I Can't Stand the Rain* came over the speakers. I'd have to remember to thank Ishmael.

Clarence spotted me and his face lit up. "You look amazing. This is great."

"Look." I kicked one of the slits open exposing my thigh almost to my hip.

He threw his hands into the air. "Genius!"

I laughed. I might even have blushed a little. "I haven't tried the routine in wardrobe so there might be some problems I didn't work out yet but we came up with some good stuff. I think you're gonna like it."

His arm encircled my waist and he tugged at me teasingly, reassuringly. "You're gonna kill it."

I hoped he was right. I started with the stretches I thought might look good on camera. Clarence liked the backbend that moved into a front toe-touch and the split up the wall, but he flipped when I told him the idea for the camera on the floor at my foot.

After we shot the master of everything, the crew relit for the floor shot. I felt like I might be contributing something to the history of film. I pointed my toe into the camera, flexed my foot then leaned into the close-up of me pulling my face toward my toes.

Clarence yelled, "Cut!" then shot me a thumbs up. "I love it. Let's go again."

Though I was hungry, I didn't want to eat too much at lunch knowing I'd have to go right back to the training scene. I was happy to hear Patrick had caught the last few takes in Ishmael's trailer. I would tell him later about feeling my job slip away and digging within myself to remain calm and find my words.

It was great watching Patrick put faces to so many of the names I'd mentioned and letting my work-friends finally meet the man I'd talked on about. I felt my worlds colliding – my L.A. movie-making life and my New Orleans happiness-driven life. I wanted it to blend perfectly in a have-my-cake-and-eat-it-too way, but I knew about cake.

Patrick always got along easily with people but it was hard for some of them to understand his devotion to preserving the French Quarter. And "non-profit" wasn't usually a popular concept in showbiz. Bruce and Seven ganged up to explain that Patrick should throw the doors open wide for filming in the Quarter instead of giving filmmakers a hard time about parking trailers, etc. Bruce even offered to put Patrick in the movie if he'd "make 'The Big Easy' a little easier."

Patrick was used to people wanting a little wheel-greasing from him, but I knew he always judged the people who tried it. Patrick had already said he didn't want to hang out on set, but he promised to stay for a couple of takes after lunch. I did my best to get back into the right headspace and ignore where he stood or when he left.

We shot coverage of the Wing Chun training exercises with the slicing-the-air precise hand movements, the wrist-rolling fist movements, the knee kicks and extended kicks and the attack sequences. Clarence loved all of it. He had me do a few of the kicks into the camera lens to match the earlier stretching shot. We did a lot of coverage on the hand and fist sequences. I had to admit they were pretty cool. My body moved in tight pivots as my hands shifted through the sequence like I was "Tutting."

I hoped it all looked good but I focused more on my intention – to earn the respect of my Sifu, my master. It was an easy enough intention to hang onto since my entire being wanted to prove Clarence's instincts about me right.

We ran the attack sequences until I was aching, then finally ran out of angles to shoot.

Though I hadn't done any truly spectacular stunts, a bunch of people clapped when we wrapped for the day. Clarence gave me a giant hug. I felt suddenly amazing, like maybe I'd done something memorable. "That was awesome. That was snatch-the-pebble-from-my-hand good."

I beamed. "Really?"

"You're two for two with these martial arts scenes. I'm lovin' all the stunt work and the stylized stuff. Wait until you see what it looks like. You have no idea how long your legs look in the kicks. It's incredible. And your hands..." He tried to mimic some of my hand slices and fist rolls. "I think I'm gonna keep the music. We'll see, but I like it. I could see you connecting with the sweet gloom of it." He was talking more excitedly now. "So, I'm thinkin' we escalate in the final fight scene with the Hapkido stuff. Hiroto and master Kano say you're doing great. They've got a coupla crazy things they wanna try with you. I can't wait for you to blow me away!" He gave me another squeeze and walked away. Once again and more than ever, failure was not an option.

Though I didn't like my crazy hours interfering with Patrick's sleep, I was happy to find him groggy on the couch.

"Hey." He blinked his eyes against the light. "How'd it go?"

"Another night for gel packs and frozen peas."

He reached up and took my hand. "Aw, baby." He sat up. "Here, sit."

I grabbed the frozen bags and sat next to him on the loveseat. "I think Brooklyn tried to get me fired. Wendy said Brooklyn worked second unit today and she was mad about being directed by Hud."

"I told you she's threatened by your relationship

with Clarence."

"But she and Clarence have been all over each other like they go way back or like they're flirting or somethin'. Meantime, he's been second-guessing hiring me."

Patrick chuckled. "No he hasn't."

I took a breath. "Yes, he has. He told me so today."

Patrick seemed suddenly angry. "When?"

"Before my scene."

"Before your big scene?" He was wide awake now.

"Yeah, but I handled it really well. You woulda been proud of me. I let him know I was all about the work and proving him right about hiring me. Then he said some really nice things about wanting the world to finally see what I'm capable of and he let me know he wanted me to shine, so it was pretty good overall."

Patrick was quiet a minute. "I accidentally went to the wrong set when I got there today. I saw maybe three takes of Brooklyn and Jamal's scene before I could get outta there."

"How was it?"

"I've seen Chuck E. Cheese puppets deliver lines with more life."

"Harsh." I laughed. "Come on, we love her new show."

"I'm just sayin' she's got every reason to feel threatened by you. You could outshine her in this."

I let that race through my mind for a moment. I'd never really had such a supportive partner. Patrick took my side, defended my position and built me up. It was hard to believe I'd survived over twenty years in the industry without that to keep me afloat. I couldn't help but wonder what I might have achieved if I'd had that kind of support all along. What else might I have become with someone calming my fears and cheering me forward? Fear and depression took time and energy, and could interfere with opportunities. Maybe there were still dreams I could dare to dream.

I tucked Patrick into bed, turned on a video of Hapkido moves and iced my shoulders, back and hip. I thought about the day I'd had and smiled. Then I remembered the time I was competing on beam in high school and was doing a split-leap/split-leap move where you only got the difficulty points if the second leap was higher than the first. My first leap had been perfect. The best and highest leap I'd ever done. But I'd only get the points if the second leap was even higher than the highest I'd ever gone. I gave it all that was in me and I'm pretty sure I had it.

Then my foot came down onto the edge of the shellacked wooden beam and slid off the side. The slick beam ripped at the skin of my thigh creating a foot-long raspberry that burned like a thousand tiny, lit matches. I'd hit my coccyx when I slammed onto the one-inch pad on the basketball court floor. Sparks shot up my spine and through my eyes as my breath rushed out.

I'd tried to shake it off. I stood with my hands on the beam finding my bearings. Pain shot through my blood-dappled thigh. I pumped myself back onto the beam and stood. Everything was wiggly and I felt my blood pressure weakening. I skipped straight to the dismount and posed, arms arched back with a beaming smile slapped on my face. The judges gave me a point for showing up and another for my dismount. It was the lowest score I'd ever gotten.

What if I couldn't "escalate?" I wasn't a stunt person. I'd only ribboned three times as a gymnast and that was thirty years ago. I told myself it was fine if they used a stunt double for the high kicks and some of the more major tumbling moves. But I knew myself. Film was forever, and I was going to kill myself trying to make sure I was in every frame afforded my character. I started the video again.

Chapter 19

I was glad I wouldn't be there for Brooklyn's last day. As an explosives expert, her part of the finale fight scene was to plant and detonate various bombs and other pyrotechnics. She'd be gone by the time I worked again. Because of Graham's schedule, we'd already shot the final reunion-reveal-showdown scene between the sisters and their father and brother. I was worried the reveal of Jake Covington faking his own death and being the "murderer" might be cheesy, but Graham reminded us all why he was still the coolest cat in showbiz. Aaron was sufficiently creepy when it came to light that JayJ had hit on his own half-sisters. As usual, all of the women playing sisters were fairly fantastic.

Layla, Aliyah and Kicho had all improvised moments where they said some great line with their arm around my waist or standing very close to me. I realized they were trying to make sure I got coverage in the final scene, and I loved them for it.

I'd already done my training for the day. I would run the counts to the video tonight after Patrick went to bed. I pulled into a parking spot in front of the ARC's front office door. Margie was organizing teenagers, explaining which beads went into which bins and what to do with the toys and stuffed animals. I'd first sorted Mardi Gras beads with Margie Perez after seeing her sing at French Quarter Fest with Tom and the gang. After Tom and I split, volunteering at ARC became the best way to spend a day with her.

"Hey!" Margie gave me a welcoming hug.

"Y'all look busy today."

She looked around. "Yeah. You know the old joke about why New Orleans is sinking?"

"Because of all the beads in the attics."

She chuckled. "Well, the Times-Pic did a piece about that and told people places they could donate their beads. We were top of the list and got the most mentions so I was optimistic we'd get a few bags, but the thing went viral. The joke, I guess. Anyway, everyone was passing it around--"

"Yeah, I did too."

She chuckled. "Exactly. So, it's been amazing. We just unloaded twenty-eight boxes from a pickup truck. They were from a church that collected them all in one Sunday."

"And they boxed them?"

"Yeah, so at least they can sit in a neat pile until we get to them. I just unleashed those kids on the giant box in the back room. You wanna work with them?"

"Sure." I followed her to the cardboard box big enough to hold my two-seater sports car.

"It's getting low, so can you climb inside and hand them stuff, help 'em remember the categories and everything?"

Sounded like fun to me as far as volunteer work went. "I'm in."

In order to graduate high school in New Orleans, students had to complete 300 hours of community service. When people wondered how this city rebuilt itself after The Storm – from sewerage and mail to streetcars and grocery stores – creating community-oriented volunteer-minded citizens should top the list of answers. I could safely assume these kids were used to hard work and following direction. But I noticed they didn't say "ma'am" to me and I couldn't remember them addressing Margie that way either.

We were working at a fairly good clip. The two ponytailed girls and one wiry guy were good listeners and rarely needed to be told the same thing twice. But I noticed it took them a while to identify the different krewe beads, which seemed strange. Most New Orleanians could tell the Bacchus barrels from the Orpheus harps with their eyes closed. The brunette-ponytailed girl held up a brown plastic blob on her outstretched palm. "What's this?"

I straitened my back and laughed. "That's a plastic pile of poop."

The kids exchanged confused looks.

I went back to detangling piles of beads. "Probably from Barkus. Maybe Tucks."

"What's this?"

I turned and saw the fleshy sack in the wiry boy's hand. Were they messing with me? "A boob."

He stared at the toy breast in his hand. "Seriously?"

I stood upright and took in their three collectively confused faces. "Wait, where're y'all from?"

The sandy-ponytail girl answered. "Michigan."

My jaw dropped a little and I blinked a few times, then laughed. "So, you've never been to a Mardi Gras parade?"

They shook their heads.

"Oh my gosh." I laughed some more. "I'm tryin' to imagine what you're thinking of us throwin' plastic poop and fake boobs off of floats. Oh Lordy."

The guy smiled weakly. "Well, yeah."

I leaned in for another pile of beads and handed them to the ponytail girls. "Okay, so these are all from different krewes. That's the bins you're sorting them into. So, like, Endymion is a superkrewe and their motto is 'Throw 'til it hurts' and they're known for a lot of things, but these plastic Caesar guys? That's a signature throw." I grabbed another clump. "These are from Muses which is a female superkrewe that has a giant lit-up stiletto float and a giant bubble bath float. Shoes are their thing and if you're really lucky or work hard enough with signs and costumes and whatever, you might catch a glittery hand-decorated shoe. These beads and bracelets with the shoes? All Muses." I pointed. "That bin there."

The brunette giggled. "So, why poop?"

I laughed. "Probably Barkus, which is the dog parade. Y'all would love it. All the dogs are in costumes. Most of their owners too. And the floats are like decorated shopping carts or wagons or whatever. Or it could be Tucks because their signature float is a giant toilet and they sometimes throw rolls of toilet paper."

They all laughed. Up came the boob. "And this?"

"Honestly, I'm a bit surprised by that one. If you've never been to Mardi Gras, I'm sure all you've ever seen are drunk women flashing for beads in a movie or whatever."

They nodded.

I handed another pile of beads over. "It's always beer, beads and boobs in the movies. And it's that way on Canal Street if you want that, 'specially around Bourbon. But if you go Uptown, it's babies and barbecues. Every krewe has mandatory beads each member has to buy, like the signature beads and medallions, but what people throw is pretty much dependent on their personal taste and expendable income."

Brunette grabbed another pile from me. "They pay for the stuff that gets thrown to all the tourists and everyone? Is it expensive?"

"They pay for everything. The cops for the entire route, the bands and dance troupes, the stilt walkers and riding clubs, all of it. The metal stanchions for the crowd on Canal and parts of St. Charles, the clean-up, the floats, everything. It can be from hundreds to thousands of dollars per krewe member. My neighbor spends between five and seven thousand a year for Muses."

The guy looked at the beads in his hands. "Holy-- Why?"

I laughed. "Because it's weeks of the greatest, biggest free party in the world and we're proud to host it, and because it's a tradition, and because any excuse for a party, and because money can't buy happiness but it can pay for Mardi Gras, and because people value a good time more than money here and because if you'd ever been you wouldn't have to ask. It's awesome. It's not for everyone but it's at least as fun as you think it is dancing in the streets, singing with neighbors and strangers, watching kids jump rope with beads they tied together, all of it."

Sandy ponytail took another bead clump and threw it into the Thoth bin. "Sounds amazing."

I smiled. "You know what's amazing is you guys comin' down here and helpin' out when you didn't even get to go to the parades."

They laughed and we kept sorting as they asked questions about Egyptian symbols, go-cups and Mardi Gras balls.

I stayed after the kids left and visited with Margie while weighing, tying and stacking sacks of sorted beads. I shook a bag of beads and topped it off before lifting it onto the scale. "Mia Borders and Big Sam's Funky Nation are playing Harvest the Music. You goin'?"

"I'll probably stop by after I get outta here. How's the movie? Must be great working with all those people from L.A. again."

I tied the sack and plopped it onto the stack. "I probably haven't been social enough. My friend Hud, one of the producers, he might come to the Square. But I've hardly spent any time with Clarence as just friends. We work crazy hours and I train any day I'm not workin', so goin' out for after-work drinks at four a.m. is a bit extreme for me."

She laughed. "We're not in college anymore."

"Nope. Or L.A."

She shook her head. "Nope." Margie had lived in L.A. for years as well. It was something that bonded us.

"I had all these ideas in my head that I was gonna show Clarence all the reasons I'm in love with this city, take him to cool places to meet cool people. Hud's gone to a few things with me. Ra too. But it feels like instead of getting to show Clarence why I love it here, I've just shown him how different we've become. We could go to three movies in a night. Now I go to music and festivals instead, and I don't even know what movies are opening this week."

She handed me another sack. "And football season's starting soon."

"See, football means almost nothing in L.A."

"No sense of priorities."

We laughed. I weighed the next sack and tied it off. "Honestly though, I would probably still have made the time to go out if it weren't for Patrick. Clarence is used to me bein' the last to leave every party, but that was because I mostly didn't have anyone to go home to. There seemed no point in going home to an empty house and I convinced myself I might miss somethin' if I went home when most people did. Now, I'd rather be home doing Patrick's laundry than doing that thing where everyone but me is gettin' drunk-as-heck and I'm tryin' to hang in there with their declining humor."

Margie chuckled. "It doesn't sound like you and Clarence have become different, it sounds like you changed and he didn't. That's not the same thing."

I thought about that. Had I left Clarence feeling abandoned? He'd written Charlie for the last-to-leave L.A. woman he knew and loved, not the New Orleans happy homemaker he'd found here.

Mia Borders was onstage when I arrived at Lafayette Square. A bouquet of springy curls fell over her sunglasses and bounced as she passionately sang and played guitar. A group of women in front of me seemed to know every word to every song, both

207

covers and originals. Borders had a rich voice and a good mix of soul-folk songs. With her red guitar strapped across her chest, her cool vibe and her talent, she was a sort-of female Lenny Kravitz. We were so spoiled for music here.

During the break, I checked out the food booths. Like so many events in the city, Harvest the Music wasn't just a great collection of local cuisine, artists and musicians, it was also a way to give back. All the food and beverage money went to the Second Harvest Food Bank. I'd volunteered there once and sorted canned and dry goods with a group of about thirty local high school students. Though the group was diverse, they had one unique thing in common – all of them told me they'd been on the receiving end of those boxes of food after The Storm. I could imagine that would color their experience of doing that work, and erase some divisions between them.

When I got to the front of the line for the shrimp and grits, I spotted Patrick's friend Dal putting a lid on a large, steaming pot. It was far too hot for that kind of work. It was hard to imagine life here before air conditioning and ice. I waved to Dal and he came up to the counter. "Hey, Patrick's girlfriend, right?"

"Charlotte. And you're Dal?"

"Yeah, hey. Can I get you somethin'?"

"Shrimp and grits. Hot today to be cooking."

He chuckled. "Yeah."

"Is this a new place? Didn't you work somewhere else last time I saw you?"

He kept his gaze away. "Yeah, didn't work out. People talk too much."

It seemed like he was saying he'd been fired

because of the theft rumors. I decided to ask about something less personal and potentially humiliating. "Hey, can I ask you an odd question?"

"Long as I can refuse to answer."

I laughed. "Of course. Do you know how the 504Ever owner and the chef knew each other?"

"They didn't. The story goes that Travis Bend ate at Gal's, loved his meal and asked to meet the chef. Chef Rex sung the praises of his sous chef and next thing you know – Travis hired him away to give him his own menu. You'd think he'd vouch for me with all this recipe mess, but he's stickin' with Travis."

Now it would be practically rude not to ask, "People still think you took the recipes?"

"People forget, not everything looks like what it is. Even sugar looks like salt."

I felt a tap on my shoulder and turned to find Christine Miller, the tour guide I was always spotting in the pink crowd of parading Pussyfooter dancers. "Hey!"

"I thought that was you." She motioned with her chin. "Your food."

I took the warm styrofoam bowl and handed over six tickets. "Thanks. And thanks for talkin'. I'm sorry we got interrupted." I really was. Who knew when I'd have another bite at this information apple?

Dal waved. "Say hey to Patrick."

"I will. I'm hoping he'll come after work. Especially 'cause I walked here. It'd be nice to get a ride home to a cool shower. Thanks again."

Christine motioned to the tall Bettie-Page-alike beside her. "Caroline is a Pussyfooter too. And Sabine."

Sabine was built like Wonder Woman, all curves and power-poses. In L.A., I was almost always the tallest woman in any room. In New Orleans, I was almost never the tallest. Caroline was my height and Sabine was even taller. I felt like I'd found my tribe.

Sabine smiled. "Christine says you're the one who writes *LA to NOLA*?"

I tried to hide my shock. "My blog? Yeah." I remembered I had shared my post on Christine's *Brothels, Bordellos and Ladies of the Night* tour on her Facebook page and she'd linked it to her website.

Sabine got excited. "I'm a huge fan. I subscribed about a year ago and I tell my friends about it."

"Really? Wow. That's great. Thank you. You made my day." There were times when I wondered if there was a point to all the effort I put into each post. It was amazing meeting a subscriber who didn't know me and loved the blog. Especially a local. "Group up. I'ma put y'all in the blog." They struck a curvy pose and blew kisses as I shot a few photos.

I followed them back into the crowd and would've joined their group of friends if I hadn't spotted Patrick looking for me. I excused myself and headed his way through the men in summer suits coming straight from the nearby courthouse, the sloppy-cool college crowd, the tie-dye wearing senior-set and the moms playing with babies in noise-reducing earmuffs. I liked being near the front so I could get good photos but I knew Patrick worried it was rude to be so tall in the front. I met him off to the side, kissed him and offered my plastic spork. We blessed the food quickly then split it as Big Sam's Funky Nation took the stage.

The band was as funky as the name promised. And the built-and-beautiful Big Sam slid, bounced and bump-and-grinded his way through songs, solos and audience call-backs. There were even songs that seemed to have skits – one act plays of funkiness between guys who'd clearly been playing together for some time.

Calling their unique sound "Noladelic Powerfunk," it was definitely not your Paw Paw's jazz. The amazing bass player strummed, plucked and thumped his way through beats that were part groovy heartbeat, part percussion and part Commodore's *Brick House*. All I could say after was, "Wow." I was certainly going to have a lot to blog about. It helped knowing Sabine would be looking forward to the post.

Patrick and I found the car on a side street. I suddenly remembered. "I saw your friend Dal. That's who I got the shrimp and grits from."

"He was working a booth?"

"Cookin', but he served me."

"Guess the new job's working out."

I shook my head. "Different new job. Sounded like everyone still thinks he stole the recipes and it got him fired."

"Who thinks so? His new job?"

"I guess his old job. And that guy I saw him with outside of Galatoire's. I was kinda nervous to ask him anything about it."

Patrick looked concerned. "Ask him what?"

"I don't know. About the robbery. About how that Travis guy and the chef met each other. Stuff like that. I know he saved your cousin, but you trust him, right?"

Patrick chuckled. "You're being 'framed' at work. It happens."

I thought about that. Then I heard Dal saying, "Even sugar looks like salt."

Patrick's voice snapped me back. "Do it like acting. What's that thing you say? Don't judge – justify. Travis is a trust fund son of Texas barbecue chain guy lookin' to make it in our local cuisine scene. His chef invented some crazy hipster beignet and that's their whole thing."

"Start with a guilty premise? You're still sayin' they did it to themselves?"

"I'm just sayin' I trust a guy who saved my cousin over those guys." Patrick was more of a gut-guy than an evidence-guy.

I laughed. "Book 'em, Danno."

Chapter 20

Brooklyn wasn't on the schedule, but she showed up carrying a box of gifts. As she lifted the tiny cardboard pet carrier, I immediately recognized the Pet Rock packaging from my childhood. I'd always thought the guy who invented that was a genius. He'd figured out a way to sell us rocks at five bucks a pop back when five dollars could fill a gas tank. Stupid as it was, I had to admit I loved mine as a kid.

Brooklyn handed one to Layla who squealed. "I always wanted one of these. Aw man, my daddy said go out in the yard and go get you one. Thanks Brooklyn. Good lookin' out." As she opened the box, she squealed again then lifted it out to show us all. "Look!" The groovy graffiti-like logo for *7 Sisters* was painted on top. Dang. It was the perfect gift.

Aliyah stepped in and took a seat, interrupting the moment. She was young and didn't recognize the rock or the box Brooklyn handed her. "You all heard about Aaron and Astrid, right? Been flyin' under the radar this whole time, but good and busted now."

Tulip handed me a clear plastic mask-on-a-handle to cover my face with as she dusted hairspray over my giant mane of curls. "Yeah, that's what I heard."

Brooklyn, clearly deflated, handed me a Pet Rock.

I pulled the top tabs open and took out the smooth

stone. "Thanks. This is a really cool gift. I had one of these as a kid but this is even better because of the logo. It's pretty much the perfect gift. So thanks."

She smiled. "Thank you. I'm glad you like it." She put Tulip's box on the counter in front of us and waved as she left.

I held the box up. "Thanks again."

Tulip and Aliyah exchanged a look after the door closed. Aliyah smiled a bit. They seemed to be conspiring somehow.

Astrid came in, put her Pet Rock on the counter and settled into a chair. "That was weird. Brooklyn just gave me this then kissed me on the mouth."

We all laughed and Layla said, "What?"

"Yeah, she kissed me right on the mouth."

I was fascinated. "Like she had a crush on you?"

Astrid pulled a ponytail holder out of her hair and ran her fingers through her brunette locks. "No. I don't think so."

"Like a threat?"

She turned to me. "More like a confrontation."

Aliyah reached over and put her hand on Astrid's thin arm. "She's wrapped. Don't worry about her. She'll be gone by the time you're outta that chair. She's only got so many of those rocks to hand out."

Tulip laughed.

Layla got up, took off her smock and grabbed her rock. "Yeah, y'all laugh. I wanted one of these since way back when. I'm leavin' happy, best believe."

I laughed. "I know, right?"

Aliyah shook her head. "It's gonna take more than a painted rock to get me past all the havoc she wreaked. Naw. She tried to get me fired. And of course, I can't say nothin' to Clarence or I look catty and like I can't handle my business."

That was true enough. But I was surprised. "She tried to get you fired? How? How do you know?"

"I got friends everywhere. She doesn't know who she's messin' with. But she's gonna do what she always does and eventually it'll bite her back."

I looked at myself in the mirror. My eyes were smoky and my lips were glossy red. With my huge halo of strawberry blonde curls, I looked like Roseanne Vela on the cover of a 70's *Vogue* – only older. I felt like the warrior goddess of Studio 54. I realized I was at least as cool as the woman I hoped I'd be when I was a kid looking at those *Vogues* and dreaming of some future me. "I don't know. In my experience, karma is far crueler than I could ever be."

Aliyah laughed. "Yeah, but she's not as fun as instant gratification."

I laughed too. "Maybe not. I don't know. I'm a long-haul kinda girl."

Tulip flounced my hair and picked up her phone to photograph me from all angles. "I get impatient with my microwave."

In the old days, all the departments would take Polaroids of us. They'd punch a hole in each and hang them from a big metal ring they'd wear on their belt. With digital photography replacing Polaroids, now they'd have to print them first so a lot of people just kept everything on their phones. Somehow, it seemed like a step back.

Tulip gave me a careful hug and smiled. "You look amazing. Knock 'em dead, Charlie."

Holding an umbrella against the sun, I waited

with Kicho near the vans lining up to take us all to set. Brooklyn was talking to Clarence. Tina stood with her back to his, talking on her phone in video mode. I was pretty sure that was against the rules but no one seemed to notice.

Judd, Layla and Madison joined them, then Aaron, Ra and Aliyah. Guys had it so good in hair and makeup, usually a half-hour tops. Women sat in those chairs for hours.

Aliyah took Tina's phone and they nodded at each other. Then Aliyah started talking loudly at Brooklyn.

Astrid and Hud joined in as Kicho and I walked up to the group.

Aliyah had everyone's attention. "Because it's messed up. It's not sisterly of you. You got it to spare. You should be lifting women up, not comin' at all of us for our bread and butter. Everybody here worked hard to get here. You ain't special."

Brooklyn's smile was frozen. "I'm sorry that you feel that way. You seem to be very angry."

Everyone stood like statues taking it all in as Aliyah wound up for another round. "It's not like I'm just some angry person. You angered me when you came for my job. And for Layla's and Kicho's and Charlotte's and Astrid's."

Brooklyn picked up her box of boxes. "You sound crazy right about now."

"Like a fox. Like Foxy Brown." She held Tina's phone up. "You want me to play this?"

Brooklyn chuckled. "What is it?"

Aliyah held her finger to the phone. "You tellin' Clarence to cut Astrid's lines today."

Clarence looked at Astrid, Kicho and me.

Astrid was crying.

Aliyah stood strong. "You're wrong for that! You're not even in the dang scene and you're still tryin'a cut people's lines. Traitor!"

I couldn't believe what I was watching. It was like every fantasy I'd ever had of telling someone off after they'd clearly and thoroughly wronged me. Karma was crueler than I'd ever be, but I now understood the value of a showdown. I felt an immediate sense of satisfaction, faster than guilt and compassion could show up. From an acting-preparation perspective, it was actually the perfect way to start our day. Now, I'd be able to find the joy in fighting my enemies and leaving the streets of the French Quarter littered with their bodies.

Brooklyn kissed Clarence on the cheek and walked away. We all waited for Clarence to show us a proper reaction to what we'd witnessed. He waited until Brooklyn was safely away, then grabbed Aliyah and hugged her. He held her out at arm's length by her shoulders. "Bring that today." He dropped his hands and we collectively relaxed. Then he clapped his hands once, startling many of us. "Oh man, I might want to reshoot your confrontation with your brother if you can bring that." And just like that, Clarence made it clear we would keep it about the work. As much fun as he made the set, as much as he focused on his passion as a filmmaker, he was a consummate pro. He'd go down in history as an industry-shifting auteur but he was a gifted leader of enormous egos, tempestuous personalities and sensitive artists – as well as hundreds of crew members.

Judd waved his arm toward the vans. "Come on, guys. Show's over. Let's get to work."

I saw Tulip give Aliyah a wink as she headed to the back of the group. Tina passed by and I grabbed her hand. "Hey."

She looked up at me from under her Saints cap. "Hey. You good?"

I smiled. "I'm great. I feel weird about feeling great, but I feel great."

She gave me a hug then tipped her cap at me. "Life's short. Eat dessert first."

I smiled. "Excellent advice."

When we got to Dutch Alley, the crew was bustling while lookie-loos gathered around on the sidewalk. Sly & The Family Stone's *Thank You (Falettinme Be Mice Elf Agin)* set the tone for our big fight scene. I grabbed Clarence. "No one ever shoots here. It's kinda cool this is what you chose. You say 70's French Quarter scene, most people think mule-drawn carriages and wrought iron balconies. Definitely not a secluded Spanish-style alleyway."

He waved his arm around the low-lying buildings. "Turns out they redid all this in the 70's so it looked pretty much like this then." He smiled at me. "You good?"

I smiled back. "Yeah." Then I laughed. "I'm great! I'm ready to shoot this thing."

Clarence laughed. "Let's get it."

Stevie Wonder's *You Haven't Done Nothin'* pumped through the speakers in the alley. It was the song we'd played for the final scene with the father. I let the song help me focus on avenging my father's murder. Hud bop-walked past biting his lip. "Oh, it's so good."

I dance-walked behind him into the alley until I got to Aliyah. We hugged. I laughed. "Wow. Don't tick you off, right?"

She laughed and the giant afro-poms on either side of her head shook. Then she stopped laughing. "No, but seriously though – don't." Then she laughed again. "I'm just kiddin' you." Then stopped again. "But don't."

It was time for my curls to shake as I laughed. "I won't." I stopped. "Seriously, I won't." Then we both laughed. I smiled. "Seriously though, thanks for that. That was amazing. I'm not used to people standing up for me."

"Went too far comin' after people's livelihood. She made it too easy. That's how I live with me. I only led the woman to water. She didn't have to drink it. Didn't mean to drag Astrid through it but it wasn't the first time Brooklyn had come for her. She had a right to know. I just poured a little pepper on it."

"You look amazing, by the way. I meant to say it last week when we did the reveal scene."

"Have you seen you? Those crochet bell bottoms are the jam."

I beamed. "Thanks. I made them. You just made my day again."

She spun me around to see my backside. "You made those? I'd be wearing a ball of yarn if they asked me to make something like that."

"I already had 'em. I brought a photo to my fitting and the pants made it all the way through all the meetings. I'm kinda excited about it, like I'm contributing something maybe memorable to the movie."

Aliyah looked at me sideways. "Those are all-the-way sexy. People will remember."

I looked down at the pants I'd invented with my hands and imagination. The top was a tightly-woven boy-cut bikini with a dainty drawstring. The long legs were an open weave that got wider on the way down to the six hearts crocheted across each hem. They were pretty cool. "You think?"

"I know. Those pants are gonna steal my coverage. And after all I done for you."

I laughed. "Thanks. I do feel pretty good in 'em."

"You're a freakin' queen. Own it." She snapped her fingers in the air and spun away.

This was it. My last day after months of filming. Soon, everyone would go back to L.A. and I'd go back to looking for work. But for now – I was a freakin' queen in unforgettable pants with an enviable explosion of curls and a few Hapkido moves to show off.

Hapkido was a Korean martial art employing throwing, grappling and joint locks as well as kicks, punches and other percussive strikes. I liked it because it used leverage instead of brawn so it was a good fit for my strength level.

A few of the stunt guys set up on the roof, ready to jump down into the scene and attack me, Kicho, Layla and Ra – the over-forty set. It was fairly common to see men over forty in fight scenes but I thought it was pretty exciting that grown women were the stars of this fight. On horseback, Madison would ride through the scene at some point and take out a few guys approaching from the flea market, then chase one guy through the Lindy Hoppers dancing to a jazz band under a pavilion. None of that was supposed to happen until after lunch.

We all had moments to shine. Astrid had a great fencing battle with some showy flips, mostly courtesy of her double. Kicho's chainsaw stuff was terrifying, even with a fake blade and wires holding most of the weight. Aliyah's part wasn't as showy but she had one close-up where she blew poisonous dust through a straw into the camera. That was probably going to look very cool.

Ra never needed a double. He did a split-leap more than five feet off the ground, "kicking" men's faces on either side of him. He was like a real life superhero. Layla had a fun moment where she pulled a switchblade from her fantastically immense afro and snapped it open with a twist of the wrist.

It was hard to believe I was actually a part of all of this. I'd always loved stunts, always been blown away that there were people willing to risk life and limb for my entertainment. I'd always done my own stunts, but this was another level. Clarence had told me once that of all the things he found interesting about me, the one he actually envied me was that I got to fight Sammo Hung, best known in America for his choreography work with Jackie Chan. I really hoped to wow Clarence today but all around me, amazing people were doing amazing things.

Though my spine was padded, there was no way to hide knee, elbow or lower spine pads so we'd be using a mat for some of my stunts. That almost guaranteed they'd have to use a double to get all the angles they needed. Then it hit me – the mat was

Kelly green. They could remove it digitally. Adrenaline shot through me as I realized I might actually get to do the whole scene myself. If I got through this whole movie with all these fight scenes in different disciplines without a double, I'd feel so proud of myself. I'd feel like a real stunt person. It was within my reach today.

First, we did the move where I threw a guy over my hip, spinning him sideways to the ground. In long sleeves and pants, he got to wear full pads and was skilled at taking the tumble over and over. I was always scared of hurting people but I fully committed to the elbow to his gut and the chop to his throat.

I was so happy I'd be fighting Hiroto for my biggest stunts. We did a few fancy kicks then I dropped into a low, spinning kick, swinging my leg out and dropping Hiroto on his back. I hit him with a groin "kick" and a throat "chop," then popped up. Hiroto kipped up and we squared off again. I "stomped" his foot then "head-butted" him. Hiroto staggered backward and I extended my right leg sideways from the hip, straight into his face. He did a flip backward and fell to the ground. It went perfectly.

I suddenly felt like that girl on the balance beam again, realizing I'd just done better than I thought I could and now I had to do something even more challenging. Hiroto stopped staggering and came back at me with the exact same sidekick. This time, I scissored my legs and dove feet first between his legs. I grabbed his planted foot and pulled his leg under me, slamming him to the ground. I "punched" his groin with my elbow, then my fist and jumped up as he curled into a ball. I stood over him, my curls dancing across my face. "Tell Daddy hey." Then I smashed my wedge heel into his face.

Clarence's voice cut through the fantasy. "And spot Madison and run after her down the alley."

I looked around quickly, spotted a sign on a wall across from me, then ran offscreen.

"And cut!"

Everyone started clapping. Hiroto and I would have to do most of it again and again, but we'd made it through. We'd all gotten the avenging scene and our biggest fight moments behind us. And I wasn't a shivering bloody mess who had to walk away defeated. I actually felt something like victory.

Lunch was bittersweet. We had "last-itis," where everyone was aware that they were doing everything for the last time. But we were all pretty darn proud of ourselves too. Many of us were silently bummed to go back to not having work, but we all felt a huge sense of accomplishment and excitement to see the finished product. People exchanged contact information and promised to stay in touch but most wouldn't. We all knew and accepted that. We'd all shared this amazing, exhausting, unique experience that would forever bond us, but it was no guarantee of ongoing friendship. It was like summer camp. Ra was already wrapped but he was one of the few people I knew I'd see again. Though I owed Aliyah a lot, our future friendship was a toss-up since she lived in L.A.

We only had a few hours to get the last scenes. They were already shooting the band, the crowd and the dancing Lindy Hoppers when we got back from touch-ups. Madison mounted her horse and went over the stunt with the coordinator. She'd be riding through the crowd for a shot from a crane above us and another at her eye level. Things went so much faster when they used two cameras at once. Then the double would come in and do the whole thing again with a camera at the crowd's eye level as she and the horse narrowly missed stunt people planted in the mix. There would also be some insert shots of the horse's hooves among the crowd's feet and, of course, a bunch of reaction shots from the crowd, the band and the dancers.

Normally, most of the actors would've hung out in their trailers enjoying the air conditioning and prep time, but everyone was crowded around monitors or hanging out in whispering groups enjoying their last moments of camaraderie. After an hour or so, Madison hugged Clarence as Judd announced, "That's a picture wrap on Madison." We all clapped and took turns telling her goodbye as the crew set up for the rest of us. I couldn't say she and I had grown particularly close, but we would forever be "sisters." It was kind of weird and kind of wonderful. I'd been impressed by her work for most of my adult life, even before I'd thought about becoming an actor. My career was normal to me, but I wasn't so jaded that I couldn't get excited to have worked with Madison Frye and Layla and Graham freakin' Paisley.

Judd settled everybody back down and we took turns running through the crowded alley. I was assigned a dancer to bump into. I introduced myself to her, shaking her hand. "Are you one of the stunt people?"

She shook her 40's era hairdo. "No ma'am. I'm a dancer."

I smiled. "Is there someone who can catch you if you fall?" I spotted one of the guys I'd seen doing a stunt earlier. "Are you doing anything on this one?"

He looked startled. "Not anything particular."

"Can you keep an eye on her? I have to push her and I want someone behind her who knows what they're doing in case I actually knock her over."

"Got her." He laughed. "Hey, tell Daddy hey." Then a bunch of people laughed.

Judd called out. "First team."

I went to my mark and ran the route in my head until I heard, "Action." I managed to do it three times without ever hurting the dancer and then I was done. Clarence grabbed me for a hug as Judd announced, "That's a picture wrap on Charlotte." Everyone clapped. Actors had to be the only people who received applause for getting laid off.

Clarence beamed. "You killed that. The scissor thing? I think that's my favorite stunt in the whole movie."

"Really?" I felt like a giddy girl. "You liked it?"

He cocked his head. "You're not listening. I loved it. I'm ecstatic."

I felt suddenly overwhelmed. "Really?"

He laughed. "Charlotte. I'm the king of the fight scene and I'm telling you, it's my favorite fight moment in the whole movie."

I felt a little bit embarrassed that a tear escaped down my cheek.

He rubbed it off and smiled. "Show off."

When I finally got home, Patrick let me ramble

on about the day. I told him about the fight sequences and Clarence saying my scissor stunt was his favorite. I told him about lunch being fun and sad. I told him about Aliyah, Tulip and Tina setting up Brooklyn and publicly shaming her for sabotaging all of the women in the cast. And about the stunt guy who said my "tag line" to me like it might be something memorable. I even got into how it felt to wear pants I'd crocheted, but I could see I'd outlasted his enthusiasm.

We said goodnight and I called Sofia.

She answered breathlessly. "Hey. I just got Nia to bed. I was afraid the phone was going to wake her."

"Oh, sorry. I can call another time. I just finished work and I'm too wired to settle in at all but I can call tomorrow."

"Yeah, okay. When do you go back to work?"

"No, I'm finished. I'm done. I'm wrapped."

She gasped. "Oh my gosh. You're done? How was it?"

"It's too much. I'll call you another time, but it was amazing. And I did a good job. Oh, and Brooklyn got put in her place in front of everyone."

She sighed. "Ugh."

"What? I thought you'd love that."

"Nia's up again." Her voice became soft. "You need to tinkle?"

I heard the tiny music of Nia's voice in the background. I smiled. "Tell her I said hi."

"Yeah, I'm gonna go. Call me tomorrow or something."

I wasn't anywhere close to sleepy. I opened my computer and clicked onto a folder labeled "symbol."

I opened the photo Julia had taken of the Wells Plantation symbol stamped into a wax seal on the bill of sale for Lottie. Why did Dad's grandfather have a pipe with the same symbol? And why were Birdie's parents trash? Birdie W. What if the W was for Wells? Could that have been her maiden name? That might help explain the pipe. Could Birdie's mother really have been a wealthy plantation owner's daughter? Lily's sister? I felt my thoughts getting a bit scattered. I'd had a long and very distracting day. The pipe was supposed to be a gift from Birdie's mom. Maybe her mother was a slave. That might explain why Birdie thought they were trash. What if Birdie's mother was a slave from the Wells Plantation and Birdie made up the story of wealthy plantation owner's daughter to hide the truth?

Down the hall, I heard the chandelier shaking. I dropped the laptop on the loveseat and ran down the long corridor. The chandelier shook fairly violently. Patrick was fast asleep beneath it.

Chapter 21

I felt a little weird about checking up on Dal's story but Patrick had me thinking. What if Dal was being set up somehow? With our city's murder and violent crime rates, it wasn't likely that the police were prioritizing arresting the recipe bandit. Why bother accusing him when Travis Bend didn't even seem in any hurry to press charges? If it wasn't about arresting Dal, what would the owner get out of trashing his reputation?

Brooklyn must've known it was unlikely she'd get any of us fired but she accused us all of stuff anyway. She hoped to gain advantage? She was jealous? Insecure? Angry? Honestly, I figured she was just a survivor in an industry designed to keep her out.

What if that was it? What if it was about trying to survive in an industry designed to keep things like King-Yay!'s out?

Chef Rex came to greet me, gave me a huge smile and kissed my hand. "So good to see you. Really enjoyed your article. Next time we'll have to get a picture together. Maybe in front of the Galatoire's sign."

"I'd love that."

"Your friends are in the movie business? I haven't seen any of Pool's movies but the guys in the kitchen were pretty stirred up about the people at your table.

I'm curious to hear what I can help you with."

I thought about making up some elaborate ruse about researching a role or interviewing for the blog but decided to skate on the idea that people generally liked talking about themselves. "You had a sous chef here that ended up gettin' hired by Travis Bend?"

He motioned for us to sit at a table near the door. "Travis Bend? A lot of our sous chefs get hired away. I try to take it as a point of pride but I'm not runnin' a culinary academy here. It gets to me sometimes. Breaks of runnin' a superior kitchen."

"Of course. I can see how that would be frustrating though. But there was a sous chef that went with Travis Bend?"

He rubbed his knee. "Bend. Where do I know that name from?"

"The owner of 504Ever. The King-Yay! guy?"

Chef Rex laughed. "Sure. Yeah." He laughed some more then settled. "Luke. That was the kid's name. Pretty good. Good knife skills."

Luke. I could kinda see how a Luke might become a Licious. "Did you sing his praises to Travis Bend?"

"Sing his praises? I doubt it. I'm a man familiar with my faults and I can tell you I don't often share credit. I may not stir every pot but that kitchen is mine. I take the praise and the blame for most everything that comes out of it."

"So you can't think of any reason you would've sung Luke's praises to Travis?

He chuckled. "Kid was a bit of a loose cannon. Never really fit in."

"The dreadlocks, I'm guessing."

"Dreadlocks? He didn't have dreadlocks then." He laughed again and shook his head. "What kinda chef has dreadlocks? It's not like the kid's Jamaican. Whatever happened to dressin' for the job you want? Had a kid come in for a busboy job the other day in a wife beater and a baseball cap. No job interview should involve underarm hair."

I laughed. "Agreed. Do you happen to have a photo of Luke? I'd be curious to see him without the dreads."

"Can't imagine we would. Maybe in some group shot but I can't think why."

"Did he ever go by Licious?"

Chef Rex laughed again. "Licious? No. He was a clean shaven, short-haired kinda preppie sort. Some of the guys called him Beckett sometimes."

"Beckett?"

"His last name. You know how men do that. I've always just been Rex though."

"Chef Rex."

He laughed. "Yeah, okay. That too."

"Yeah, I've always been Charlotte. Although people might start callin' me Charlie."

"Gotta watch that." He laughed. "Look, the kid was good. He had good knife skills. But I'm not one for sales-pitchin' my help away. I don't think I've ever even met that Bend character. He seems more trouble than he's worth, you ask me. King Cake beignets? How can you ice a hot beignet?"

My eyes went wide. "Right? The colored sugar would slide off. You'd have to let it cool."

"And no one wants a cooled beignet."

I nodded vehemently. "Have you tried one?"

He laughed and stood from the table. "Won't catch me dead. No ma'am. Nope."

"You could be missin' out."

He kissed my hand as I stood. "A chance I'm willin' to take."

I laughed. "I tried one. Rubbery. You're not missin' anything." We laughed together. "Thank you for everything. I'm so glad you liked the blog post. That wasn't a lunch we had, it was an experience. I really tried hard to capture it all."

He pointed at me as he walked away. "You nailed it."

All the way back to the house I kept thinking about the name Beckett. I'd assumed Beckett was the first name of Travis Bend's friend in college. It wasn't uncommon for southerners to name their boys for their mother's family so last names were often used as first names for boys. My brother and my cousin were both named Tate to carry on their mother's maiden names. But what if Beckett was the friend's last name? My mind kept wandering to questions about why they'd lie about not knowing each other. They'd even made up some elaborate story about Chef Rex singing praises. But I kept reminding myself that those questions were pointless until I saw the photo in Jason's unit again and asked about Beckett's name.

Jason didn't come to the door at first. I fixed the black-and-gold bow on the Saints wreath hanging on our door a foot away. I knocked again and waited.

Jason was holding a frying pan full of onions. "Hey. Come on in. I was just throwin' some supper together but you caught me at a good spot."

"Are you sure? I can come back."

He turned off the burner and put the pan down. "We're good. What's up?"

I smiled, feeling a bit exposed. "Could I see that photo again? The one with Travis Bend in it?"

He headed for the built-in shelves. "Sure. What's up?"

"I don't know. Maybe nothing." I pointed to Beckett's face. "Beckett, right? Was that his first name?"

Jason looked stumped for a moment. "Huh. That's what we always called him but now that I think about it, I don't know."

"Do you mind if I take this with me so I can scan it? I'll bring it right back."

"Sure but--" He grabbed his cell phone and snapped a photo. "I can just send it to your email. Good?"

"Great. Thanks!"

Patrick wasn't home yet. I headed straight for my computer and downloaded the photo. Then I looked up the picture I'd snapped of Travis and Licious walking past the crying neighbor at Decadence. I sized the photos so I could see the faces side by side. I curled my finger on the screen, blocking out Licious' rainbow scarf of dreadlocks. Another email from Jason popped up so I opened it. "First name Lou?"

I wrote back. "Luke?" Then waited. I refreshed the page then opened the new email.

"Luke Beckett. That's it."

I shot back, "Thanks!" and leaned back. Why did Licious and Travis lie about knowing each other? And wasn't Licious supposed to be a local? Why lie about being local? I'd heard native New Orleanians receive priority treatment for permits and stuff, but enough to lie about it? And wouldn't you eventually get caught in a city where everyone knows each other from school?

Maybe they thought it would make them seem more legit – somehow make them more competitive in a crowded industry. But it wasn't like Beckett pretended to be related to John Besh or the Brennans or some other local name with weight to it. And non-locals broke through all the time. If the food was good, people would eat it no matter who cooked it. Emeril was proof of that.

So why lie? I thought about all the reasons characters lie in movies. The number one reason people lied was to make themselves sound better. Maybe that was all there was to it.

There was always money. Money was a big motivator for most people. Money might even be worth lying for to some people. Patrick seemed certain the recipe theft was some sort of promotional stunt. If they were the kind of guys who were willing to fake a break-in for free advertising, they might be willing to lie about other things for money. And as Marilyn said, the way you do anything is the way you do everything. Maybe these guys were in the habit of lying to get what they wanted.

Jason had said Beckett was a bad influence. Maybe Beckett instigated the whole thing. Those dreads had to be fake. He couldn't possibly have grown them that quickly. It was hard to imagine why anyone would want fake blonde dreads, especially a chef. That said, they rendered him nearly unrecognizable.

But hadn't the dad separated the guys? Maybe even offered to bribe Beckett to leave Loyola? What if Beckett took the money and they lied about him leaving? The dad lived far away. It' be fairly easy to keep that secret without family checking up on them after graduation. Patrick had said that Travis was a trust fund kid. Did Jason say it too? A trust fund might need a signature. Or maybe he wasn't literally a trust fund kid, maybe Travis just enjoyed living off his parent's wealth. Either way, he might need his dad's money or signature to buy something or to start a business.

The dad would never have given Travis the money if he'd known it was for a business venture with the bad-influence kid from Loyola. That might be a good reason to fake an identity. Then it would make sense that Beckett would come up with fake dreads "Licious" and avoid photos of his face on social media.

I dialed Patrick. "Hey. How do you find out who paid for a property or like who owns a business?"

"You ask someone who works in my office and has access to the records."

I laughed. "Excellent. Can you look up who owns 504Ever."

"The Texas barbecue king."

I was jarred. "How do you know? You couldn't have looked it up that fast."

"I looked it up back when the robbery happened. That's why I thought it was a publicity stunt."

"That's why?"

"Yeah. Guy's used to things comin' easy. Not

likely to work hard."

I laughed. "You work hard and you had a pretty easy childhood."

"Yeah, but I would never open a restaurant to sell bad donuts. That's way more work than I'd be up for."

I laughed again. He had a funny way of looking at things but he wasn't wrong. "You'll be happy to know that I finally think you're right."

"Good to know. About what?"

"I think the owner did it. With the chef. They knew each other in college and the dad would've never helped his son get the business if he'd known the chef was Travis' bad-influence college friend so we know they lied about pretty much everything. I can't think of one reason to believe them about Dal. And if it's not Dal, why point the finger at him?"

"To keep people off topic."

"Exactly. They've got everyone standing in line for one of their who-dunnit donuts thinking about motives and villains, and all they had to do was break a window."

Patrick interjected. "An insured window."

"With a deductible, but yeah, probably insured. And they didn't start accusing Dal until all the press and social media had quieted."

"And the whole *Gambit* voting thing."

I slapped my thigh. "You're right!"

"Solved. I'll tell Dal."

"I don't know. I still don't have anything tying them to the actual break-in."

"The break-in that got them a ton of publicity?

"Except the video of the guy climbing over the counter. Not exactly somethin' you'd think an owner would do. I just wish I were certain."

"They did it. Case closed."

"Circumstantial case closed."

He chuckled. "Close enough."

"I have a photo of Travis and Licious together in college if you want to give it to Dal."

He laughed. "Of course you do."

"What? Why are you laughing?"

"Because you can't just know what you know. I should've known you'd never admit I was right without proof."

"It's a good thing. It also means I'll never truly doubt you without proof either."

"I'll take it. Go put on your party dress. I'll be home soon and we'll go to your thing."

I pulled up the photo of the "King-Yaygler" again, though I knew it by memory after all the press and social media. The image had become so familiar, I was fully expecting some people to choose his get-up for their Halloween costume this year. The thief wasn't wearing gloves but didn't seem worried about leaving fingerprints as he climbed over the counter. Made sense if he was an employee whose fingerprints would be there anyway. An Easter bonnet with food items. Possibly a chef. What was that light-colored glitter shape on the toe of the boot? Another food? But everything else was just random. Unless he was a professional clown.

I opened the photo from Decadence again. Travis and Licious were dressed in street clothes with festive flourishes. Travis wore a hat topped with a glittery rainbow. Licious had his ratty blonde dreads wrapped into a rainbow scarf. His clothes were mostly obscured by someone with a kite on his head walking in front of him. I followed the rainbow-ribboned kite tail down and saw that Licious was wearing glittery boots. They were navy with splotches of color coming down the front.

I zoomed in and it became clear the top shape was a glittery red crawfish. The next shape seemed to be an okra and the one below that was a red apple? No, a tomato. A locally grown food made more sense. And on the toe was a green apple? No, a pear. Except pears weren't local. Mirliton. That was probably it. Like in the fried balls from 504Ever. Maybe mirliton was always the missing ingredient.

Wait!

I clicked the surveillance photo again and looked at the burglar's shoe sticking out from under the striped clown pants. Boom. It really was Licious. And I had proof. I smiled, closed the computer and got ready for a night out.

The wrap party was at the Mid-City Rock-n-Bowl and lot of the crew was bowling when we arrived. A colorfully-costumed D.J. spun 70's records while a disco light spun over the dance floor. I already knew Clarence wouldn't be there. As much as he would've enjoyed bathing in compliments and gratitude all night, he hated goodbyes.

Wrap parties were about a lot of things. After twenty-hour days, overtime, golden time, forced calls, meal penalties and all the other wallet-fattening ways to test our stamina, wrap parties were a way to blow off steam. They were an opportunity to say goodbye or finally hit on a coworker. They were a venue to show off other talents like dancing and bowling. And they were a place to lock and load memories as people reminisced and shared jokes we "had to be there" to understand.

Hud and Bruce introduced our blooper reel from the stage next to the dance floor. We all gathered under the disco ball to watch as Hud thanked everyone for their contributions and hard work. "Unfortunately, not everyone could stay for tonight's festivities but none of us would be here without Clarence."

I cheered along with others.

Hud raised his *7 Sisters* emblazoned go-cup. "To Clarence."

We all raised our cups and cheered. Many people clicked their cups and drank again. I smiled at Patrick and hoped he didn't feel too left out.

The blooper reel spared Brooklyn her blowing-a-line-dozens-of-times moment but she was one of the people who "had a scheduling issue" and wasn't able to attend. I had to admit I was glad. I liked the way things ended. And I still respected her work on her new huge-hit show and watched it every week. I wanted to keep the balance Aliyah had struck.

Patrick loved Aliyah. He called her, "The queen of removing vagueness." Within minutes of finding her at the party, he'd thanked her for sticking up for me. "You're welcome here anytime. We have a spare place you can stay in next time you're in town. You and Charlotte could have a sleepover."

My first blooper was the day I had the really long dialogue scene with Madison and Astrid inside the Garden District manor home set. I was wearing a minidress with wide-belled sleeves and accidentally knocked over a lamp. I instinctively lunged for it, catching it before it crashed to the ground. Then I held it up like a trophy and Clarence came over to congratulate me as the prop woman gingerly grabbed the lamp from me.

I did have a lot of good memories. This had been the longest and most involved job of my career. It was certainly the most grueling, but undoubtedly the best. Disco dancing with Layla, Aliyah, Kicho, Madison, Astrid, Hud, Ra, Tina, Tulip, Emmett and Hiroto, I felt blessed. Looking at Patrick, I knew I was.

Chapter 22

A lot of acting was about waiting, especially in the film industry. They say that it takes ten years to become an overnight success. That's a lot of waiting. There's waiting to get auditions, to hear if you got the callback and to hear if you got the job. There's hours of waiting when you work, and then months of waiting when you don't. And there's the waiting for the movie you filmed to become the movie everyone will see, the movie you may've been cut from, the movie that might launch you. Acting was not for the impatient. Today would be my first day of waiting for the movie to become itself and be seen by the world.

With no idea when the waiting would end, I was glad we'd gotten tickets to the Saints game in the Superdome. It was nearly ninety degrees outside so I picked one of my short-sleeved black and gold Saints shirts and put on my lucky earrings, an enamel Sir Saint in one ear and a complimentary Saints helmet in the other.

Patrick was carrying an iPad when he walked into the room. His face looked hurt somehow.

"What's wrong?"

He was still looking at the screen. "You know how I was so excited that Steve Gleason is doing today's coin toss since it's the five year anniversary to-the-day of when he blocked the punt?"

"At the Dome reopening after The Storm. Why? What's up?"

Patrick looked at me. "He just announced he has ALS."

"ALS? Like Lou Gehrig's disease? What are you talking about?"

"He has ALS. He's known for a while."

I felt sick. Steve Gleason was one of the city's biggest heroes. After decades of losses, the Saints lost their Dome to Katrina. Thousands of people lived horrible existences inside the Superdome waiting for relief and rescue. The place became a symbol for the levee failures that resulted in epic flooding and for the suffering of the American citizens abandoned during political infighting.

The city made a big deal about the Superdome reopening. There was a giant banner unfurled over the entrance reading, "Our Home. Our Team. Be a Saint." U2 and Green Day played *The Saints Are Coming* to an emotional crowd along with local favorites Rebirth and New Birth Brass Bands and a young Trombone Shorty. It was the first time the Superdome had ever sold out.

People were in a good mood and excited to see the new coach, Sean Payton, and the new too-short, formerly-seriously-injured quarterback, Drew Brees. But it was Steve Gleason who would go down in history that day. Anyone who was there when he blocked that punt early in the game against the arch-rival Atlanta Falcons swore it was the loudest the Dome's ever been.

"Isn't his wife due next month?"

Patrick was buried in the iPad again. "Yeah."

"What does it mean?"

Patrick looked up again. "He'll wither away and then die. Young. Or he'll be Stephen Hawking."

We were quiet most of the way walking to the Superdome. The whole city was wearing their black and gold and people were always in a happy place on game day.

Dal was waiting at the bottom of the steps and waved when he saw us. "Hey! You found me. Like a needle in a haystack with all this black and gold everywhere."

I felt a little badly that I'd suspected him of the 504Ever break-in. Heck, I'd wondered if he'd stolen recipes from Galatoire's too. I pulled the photos out of my bag. "Here."

Dal took them and stared at the Loyola photo on top.

I pointed. "That's Travis Bend." I moved my finger. "And this is Luke Beckett, AKA Chef Licious." I moved my finger again. "And this is my neighbor who says Travis' dad didn't want Beckett anywhere near his son." I nodded to Patrick. "And Patrick is sure that the dad paid for the restaurant. Seems like it demonstrates a pattern of deception. Licious was created to hide Beckett's identity so they could get Travis' dad to pay for 504Ever. We know Beckett wasn't local so Licious can't be local, so they were fine deceiving all of us and their customers as well. Then, I noticed this." I motioned for him to flip to the next photo, the one of the surveillance footage, and pointed to the shoe.

Dal looked puzzled. "What is that, a Muses shoe?"

"It's glitter, right? Now look at this."

He flipped to the next photo and I pointed to Licious' boot. Dal looked at both photos then up at me. "It's the same shoe."

Patrick laughed. "Cheap or lazy. Didn't wanna throw out his glitter boots."

Dal chuckled. "Arrogant."

I smiled. "Probably just figured no one would notice."

Dal stared at the photos.

I had to ask. "What're you gonna do with it? At the very least you should be able to back 'em up offa you."

Patrick smirked. "I'd do what they did. Use it to smear them in social media."

That sounded a little harsh. "You could use it to clear your name."

Dal nodded. "The press might be interested too."

Patrick remained firm. "You could clear up the burglary with the police."

Dal nodded again. "I guess I could do real damage if I got creative."

I could imagine Dal might feel spiteful. Every time I saw him, he had a new, less-great job. This was a small city and word traveled quickly. "Do you have any friends on the force? I know one guy. Officer Landry. I could ask him who you should talk to. I printed that photo so you'd have it, but Patrick emailed you a copy in case you need it."

Patrick grinned. "With his dad's contact information if you decide you wanna go that way."

Dal pushed the photos into a pocket then extended his hand. "Thanks."

"Sure, yeah. Glad I could help. Do you know what you're gonna do?"

He looked up the steps. "Watch the Saints kick the Texans all up and down that field, that's what I'm gonna do."

Patrick and I yelled together. "Who dat!?!"

Our seats were up high but we had a great view of the field. The young lady on my right hadn't been to a game since she was eight. For her, the Superdome was the place her dad used to take her when she was little. She was eating peanuts, dropping the shells on the floor, "for old times sake." The guy on Patrick's left had stayed inside the Dome after The Storm.

Patrick seemed misty. "You know how I got the tickets for the game five years ago? This woman told me she stole her no-good husband's hundred-dollar-each tickets. She said she knew she couldn't sell them, but she'd be happy to sell me her go-cup for two hundred bucks. So she holds up the go-cup and it's got the two tickets in it. She says, 'You can have the tickets for free.'"

I was tickled. "Got it."

"It was a mall parking lot two days before the game, and I didn't know her from Adam, but I just had to go. I knew it mattered. In my life, I've never been at a more important sporting event. And you know that's sayin' a lot. Now I keep my ticket with my birth certificate, passport and Obama inauguration ticket."

"Wow."

He laughed, remembering. "It was SO loud. First was the countdown to the banner drop. I don't remember a lot of Falcons fans there, but that made

244

sense because there were no hotel rooms left. I had friends on the field for U2 but they didn't have tickets to the game. There was no way to really see the crowd until you were at the top of the ramp looking down at everyone converging. It was just... vast."

"That's how I felt at the Victory Parade after the Super Bowl. Like I was surrounded for miles by love and joy and optimism and enthusiasm. And black and gold. It was amazing."

"Right. So most of the crowd was just happy to be there rechristening their Dome. We were used to losing. The Saints finished the 2005 season three-and-thirteen, making them the second worst team in the league. We were wearin' paper bags over our heads to cheer on our 'Aints,' but we loved them and we were used to losing."

I laughed. "People here don't need to win to celebrate, that's for sure."

"So they hire Payton and Brees and they win two games in a row in 2006. But both were away games. It was the first time the Saints had ever opened the season with two consecutive wins so people were feelin' good, but we were playing the Falcons and expecting to get our tails kicked. Then ninety seconds into the game, Steve Gleason blocks the punt and the place just explodes. I've never heard anything louder. I've stood next to Niagara Falls and it wasn't as loud. It was crazy. And it went on like that for the whole game. Sustained. I had a headache for two days after but I didn't care. So, it becomes a touchdown, and it's the first one in the Dome since The Storm and we end up eventually winning by a mile. After, everyone's chanting in the halls, yelling Who Dats. I ended up walking home on Bourbon and it was all locals. I'd never seen that. It was... I couldn't imagine not being there." His face was soft. He looked around the Dome and I could see he was reliving it all.

I smiled. "Dang. I have no choice but to imagine."

Going to the Superdome was like going to church in some ways. We usually went on Sundays. The community would gather to celebrate something we agreed on. We had rituals for standing, sitting, singing (and dancing), and we prayed for our Saints. We also had a tradition around our coin toss. Each game after the toss, a different player would walk out into the field, pound his hand down through the air and start three rounds of Who Dat chants, "Who dat!?! Who dat!?! Who dat say dey gonna beat them Saints?"

Everyone stood, clapping and screaming as Gleason limped onto the field with his hand on Brees' shoulder. Many people hadn't heard his news yet but it was fitting that he chose the fifth anniversary in the house of rebirth to reveal what he hoped to find victory over next. His amazing play became a symbol of the city's ability to win against the odds, to pull a play out of thin air and ignite a new history. Maybe Gleason could do it again for himself. He'd married a local girl so the one thing we did know was that he'd be here for whatever was ahead.

The game was amazing. The guys wore their throwback uniforms, opting for the ones they wore five years ago over the newer, shinier (better looking) uniforms they'd gotten this year. We danced to *Second Line* after every field goal and *Halftime (Stand Up and Get Crunk)* after every touchdown.

Considering we got forty points (to the Texans thirty-three), there was a lot of dancing. Newly acquired Jimmy Graham, a basketball player from University of Miami, crawled toward the end zone, John Riggins-style, dragging three men with him. And new Saint, Mark Ingram, had his first career touchdown. I tried to capture the noise level on my video camera and while I was filming, Jabari Greer grabbed an interception. The change in already-insane noise nearly blew out my camera's microphone.

Afterward, people chanted Who Dats in the halls and Bourbon Street was flooded with fans in black and gold. It was all amazing, but I couldn't help envying that Patrick got to be there five years ago. Having attended the Victory Parade, I knew how deep "you had to be there" could run around here.

There were revelers sitting on our stoop as we arrived at the French Quarter place. They started to disperse but we assured them they were free to stay as we headed into the living room. In L.A., everything had been about exclusivity. There were bouncers with lists, velvet ropes, businesses without signs, all kinds of barriers between the "us's" and the "them's." I mostly went to places where I knew the velvet rope would open as I arrived. I was willing to go places where I had to check in on a list or somehow prove my worth, but I avoided going anywhere I suspected I wasn't wanted.

New Orleans valued inclusivity. In the Galapagos years ago, I'd seen a sea lion, an iguana, a flightless cormorant and a penguin standing next to each other on a sea cliff. At a game, party, boil, parade or festival, you might see a toddler, a college hipster, an attorney in a seersucker suit and a tie-dye-wearing senior citizen dancing, singing, eating or cheering together. The social life of a waiter and a business owner could often be the same here, whereas waiters could only get into those fancy parties by working them in L.A.

Of course, I was glad I'd gotten to walk all those red carpets and see behind all those ropes. I met fascinating people in expensive camera-ready clothing. We had things in common that were rare, like having a break-up publicized or meeting Presidents and popes. But I remembered dancing with a venture capitalist at a premiere after-party once and cameras started to appear. There were about ten of us women dancing with him and he laughed. "You know why they're taking our picture, don't you?"

I smiled. "Because you look like a mac-daddy with a harem?"

He laughed. He still wasn't used to women trying to curry his favor. He whispered loudly over the music. "It's because we're actually dancing in L.A. They want to record the moment."

I remember laughing but being sad that it was kinda true. I loved dancing. It made me feel alive and connected and joyful. But he was right. In L.A., it could be another thing for people to judge and find lacking, so people mostly just didn't.

It was hard to come down after the game, especially with all the partying on our street. I worked on a puzzle and Patrick played with his iPad as we watched an episode of *Harry's Law* we'd recorded. We'd survived a really long movie shoot together and I was settling into believing Patrick might really be the best man I'd ever met. As much as he loved movies, he had no love for the lifestyle. I was so used to people wanting to be close to me to walk down those red carpets and get on the other side of those velvet ropes that I was still adjusting to none of that really appealing to Patrick.

After he went to bed, I texted Sophie, "You awake?" but she never texted back. Even on the west coast, it was pretty late.

I opened my computer and downloaded my camera to start the blog post on the anniversary football game. As the images whirred past, my mind returned to Birdie's maiden name. Birdie W. Birdie Wells? Wait, that would mean her father was Wells, not her mother. Her father was the son of a wealthy plantation owner? But, that wasn't the story. What if Birdie really was the daughter of a slave? A slave from the Wells Plantation? What a small world that would be. What a random connection between my own parents. Maybe that was the missing ingredient in my genetic gumbo. My mother's family could've owned my father's grandfather? It all seemed a bit far-fetched but it could explain the pipe, and a slave from the Wells place might have the last name Wells which did begin with a W.

I instinctively listened for the chandelier to rattle, but of course we were at the French Quarter place. If there were family ghosts here, they were someone else's family.

I could accept that the Wells symbol being on a flask at May Baily's might be totally random and unrelated to anything other than commerce, but Dad's family pipe definitely came from Mom's family plantation. That happened. My parents were connected somehow long before my brother and I came along to seal their bond. One of Dad's grandparents being a slave would certainly answer the riddle of how he came to have the pipe. Awfully fancy pipe for a slave, I thought, but I had to admit I actually had no idea what a slave's pipe might look like.

I looked into the smoky glass of the long antique mirror sitting atop the fireplace mantle. Long strawberry blonde curls framed my rounded features. I had my mother's long legs and my father's wide-bridged nose. All the rest was unidentifiable genetic soup and a little mascara.

I'd put myself in the shoes of my ancestors before, imagined wearing hoop skirts and drawstring underwear down to my knees. And I'd thought about things I might have inherited from those who came before me, the courage of those who'd crossed the ocean before there even was an America, the pioneers who'd helped settle this country and Lily, the woman who'd left her family fortune for love. But I'd never really looked at myself and seen them.

I turned my face in the light searching for... I wasn't sure what. I'd always felt like I was just myself with pieces of my mother and father built in, but now I felt connected to some longer story. I felt destined somehow, like my parents were meant to find each other. As a child of divorce, it comforted me. As a puzzle solver, it intrigued me. I'd built the edges and sorted the pieces into piles but I had no idea what the final picture would look like. There were too many missing pieces. Pieces of me.

Genealogy had always been of some interest. I liked the stories. But this was the first time it really hit me that they were the stories of me, of how I came to be. I'd always been fine with vague, short, oft-repeated legends of chandeliers and overseers but now I needed to know what connected my parents.

Maybe that was the family secret that Mama Heck supposedly guarded. I'd always heard it was a gift, but maybe the chandelier had been payment for keeping the secret. Maybe the initials carved into the chandelier were the secret. "LW DW" or "SW OW" or some combination thereof. Lily Wells and her sister? But why would initials be a secret? Why was Birdie's maiden name a secret? Why so many secrets?

APPENDIX

These people and places mentioned in the book are real and open for business as of this publishing. For more information on anything mentioned in this book, use the search tool in LAtoNOLA (latonola.com), the blog upon which many of the book's recollections are based.

610 Stompers
https://610stompers.com

Abita Strawberry Lager
https://abita.com/brews/strawberry-lager#

American Academy of Dramatic Arts in New York
https://www.aada.edu

ARC Bead Sorting
http://www.arcgno.org/news/
arcofgreaterneworleansneedsmardigrasbeads

Armstrong Park
http://www.pufap.org/index.html

Audubon Zoo
http://audubonnatureinstitute.org/zoo

Bryan Batt
http://www.bryanbatt.com

Suzy Bergner
https://www.instagram.com/suzybbad/

Big Sam's Funky Nation
http://www.bigsamsfunkynation.com

Mia Borders
http://miaborders.com

Broussard's Restaurant
http://www.broussards.com

Chris Owens
http://www.chrisowensclub.net/pages/home.html

Dancing Man 504
https://www.facebook.com/Dancing-Man-504-239176338346/

Jeff "The Dude" Dowd
https://twitter.com/jeffthedudedowd?lang=en

Dutch Alley
http://www.dutchalleyartistsco-op.com

French Quarter Fest
http://fqfi.org

GW Fins
https://gwfins.com

Galatoire's
http://www.galatoires.com

Gambit Weekly
https://www.bestofneworleans.com

Garden District Book Shop
http://www.gardendistrictbookshop.com

Steve Gleason
http://www.teamgleason.org

Harvest the Music – has ended its run.

M.S. Rau
https://www.rauantiques.com

May Baily's Place
http://www.dauphineorleans.com/nightlife

Mel's Drive-In
http://melsdrive-in.com

Christine Miller – Two Chicks Walking Tours
http://www.twochickswalkingtours.com

Palace Cafe
http://www.palacecafe.com

Margie Perez
https://www.facebook.com/MargiePerezSings

The Pussyfooters
http://www.pussyfooters.org

Raising Cane's
https://www.raisingcanes.com

Rock-n-Bowl
http://www.rocknbowl.com

The New Orleans Saints
http://www.neworleanssaints.com

Satchmo Fest
http://fqfi.org/satchmo

Second Harvest Food Bank
http://no-hunger.org

Shamarr Allen & the Underdawgs
http://www.shamarrallen.com

Snowizard
http://www.snowizardsnoballshop.com/index-main.php

The Soul Rebels
http://thesoulrebels.com

Southern Decadence
http://www.southerndecadence.net

Superdome
http://www.mbsuperdome.com

Trashy Diva
http://www.trashydiva.com

Treme Brass Band
https://www.facebook.com/TremeBrassBand/

White Linen Night
http://www.neworleansonline.com/neworleans/festivals/
artfestivals/whitelinen.html

ABOUT THE AUTHOR

Best known for her role as Leonardo DiCaprio's sister in Quentin Tarantino's *Django Unchained*, Laura Cayouette has acted in 45 films including *Now You See Me*, *Kill Bill* and *Enemy of the State*. Television appearances include *True Detective*, *Friends* and a recurring role on *Queen Sugar*.

Laura earned a Master's Degree in creative writing and English literature at the University of South Alabama where she was awarded Distinguished Alumni 2014. She currently resides in New Orleans.

Website: lauracayouette.com
Twitter: @KnowSmallParts
Facebook: http://bit.ly/1VxJIvr